JET XV

†

Sahara

Russell Blake

First edition.

Books@RussellBlake.com

ISBN: 978-1705571019

Published by

Reprobatio Limited

CHAPTER 1

The convicts in Werl Prison milled in the common areas as the faint sound of chanting from outside the walls drifted like smoke on the autumn breeze. A protest had been underway most of the afternoon, hitting its peak in the hours before sunset. Now that dinnertime had come and gone, some of the stridency had faded from the voices, but the protest leaders seemed tireless in playing to the assembled television cameras, and more activists had arrived with the coming of night to replace any laggards who'd headed home for sleep.

The media circus had begun as a staged event to highlight the number of immigrants that were part of the prison population – the theme being that unrestricted immigration policies had resulted in a dramatic increase in crime, not to mention the cost to jail the lawbreakers in conditions comparable to those of a four-star hotel in their home countries. Other marches that had been simultaneously planned for two other prisons were also underway, part of a nationalist wave sweeping across Germany. The new surge of populism alarmed the current government, which had been largely responsible for the influx of northern African immigrants stoking the public's ire, and the establishment was well represented by a phalanx of riot police carrying Plexiglas shields and batons.

Inside the high brick prison walls, the scene was more orderly. Guards surveyed the hundreds of inmates from strategically located stations around the central courtyard or from watchtowers, those at the latter locations armed with sniper rifles. Due to overcrowding, the prison population was allowed to congregate in the open areas until ten p.m. before retiring to the cells, which were strained to the

1

bursting point from the recent increase in convicts.

Near one of the cell block entrances loitered a group of seven men, all swarthy and obviously of Arab blood, their beards announcing them as some of the strict Muslims imprisoned along with rank-and-file German criminals. Tariq, a tall, gaunt man with olive skin and a lush black beard, leaned into his companion and muttered in Arabic, "It is almost time. I only need ten minutes. You know what to do."

His companion surreptitiously glanced at a cheap plastic watch before flicking his eyes to the guards. "Good luck, my brother. We shall make it so."

Tariq detached himself from the group. After sidling through the open doorway, he stopped at the nearest cell and ducked inside. He crossed to the stainless steel sink, felt beneath it, and retrieved a makeshift blade honed to a razor edge in the machine shop from a piece of scrap metal. A splash of water, and he drew the blade down across his cheek, removing an inch of scruff before rinsing the hair down the drain and continuing the process of shaving away his manly pride.

When he was done, Tariq walked to one of the bunks and kneaded the unusually bulky pillow. He grunted and looked around and then removed a pair of dark green slacks and a matching shirt and jacket. He stripped off his prison togs and quickly donned the uniform, breathing heavily as he struggled into the jacket. A pair of worn boots several sizes too large completed his outfit, and within seconds he was at the open cell door, the blade in hand, head cocked while he listened.

A shout greeted him from the courtyard, and then another, and then whistles joined the melee as more voices yelled in anger and alarm. Tariq waited until the half dozen cries had become scores, and then sliced his forehead with the blade. When the warm trickle ran to his eyebrows, he returned the blade to its hiding place beneath the sink as blood streamed down his newly shaven face. He allowed a suitable amount of crimson to darken the collar of his shirt before clamping the cut closed with his fingers and moving from the cell. As more voices hollered from the courtyard, he gave the nearby yard entrance a wide berth and continued down the corridor to the next doorway. A glance outside revealed a riot in process, with the guards attempting to restore order with their batons and whistles as inmates swung at each other with bare fists.

Tariq edged into the courtyard and along the cell block wall until he was near one of the guard posts, where a short German guard with the physique of an anvil called to him. "How bad are you hurt?"

"Bad enough."

"Get to the infirmary. We'll have this lot under control in no time."

"Will do."

Tariq brushed past him and strode to where two guards were watching from behind bulletproof glass by the administrative entryway. When he reached the heavy steel door, one of the men tripped the lock release, and the metal slab swung open. Tariq stepped through, and the hydraulics reclosed the door with the heavy thunk of a bank vault, and then he was marching along the pristine hallway, brushing past other uniformed guards, who gave him room, his bloodstained shirt and face telegraphing his destination.

He knew from studying blueprints that the infirmary was halfway to the main prison entrance, down a flight of stairs on the basement level. He'd correctly determined that an injured guard during a prison riot wouldn't be subjected to the usual rigid scrutiny that anyone roaming the halls would under normal circumstances, and his confidence grew as he reached the stairwell and another guard moved aside to allow him to pass.

"Need any help?" the man asked.

"*Nein*. It's a scratch," Tariq answered in fluent German.

"Good luck. Doesn't look like a scratch to me. You've lost a lot of blood."

"Thanks."

At the basement level, Tariq stopped at the second doorway and tried the handle, which twisted in his grasp. He stepped into a dark room and felt for the light switch. The overhead fluorescent bulbs flickered to life, bathing the area in cold white. He locked the door behind him and strode to where a tall metal cabinet stood by one of the massive fan housings that lined the wall.

During the summer months, the huge blades would have been spinning at high RPM, forcing air up into the building; but now, in late autumn, the weather was cool and the ventilators were shut down. Tariq knew that there were six similar vaults scattered around the compound, but had chosen this one due to its proximity to the infirmary, as well as its accessibility by the maintenance crew that two of his men were part of.

Inside the cabinet he found a power screwdriver, a hammer, a penlight, and a chisel right where expected. He pocketed the chisel and slid the hammer into the waistband of his pants, and then went to work with the screwdriver on the nearest housing, the tool's whine loud in the confined space, but a necessary evil that was part of his calculated risk. When he had a section of the housing free, he lifted it clear and peered inside the shaft, which was black as the grave. He replaced the screwdriver in the cabinet and extinguished the lights and, after switching on the flashlight, climbed into the shaft and began a crawl that would take him a hundred and forty-six meters to an exhaust vent on an outside wall.

Tariq wasn't worried about the housing being discovered. By the time anyone sounded the alarm about a prisoner escape, he would be long gone, and it would take hours of studying security cam footage to understand how he'd evaded all the safeguards designed to keep inmates imprisoned, much less from what area he'd escaped. The courtyard scuffle he'd arranged would occupy at least a half hour of the guards' time, and when a head count ultimately turned up a missing man, it would take yet more precious time to identify and search for him.

It wasn't a perfect plan, but it was adequate, and his escape was now a foregone conclusion as long as he didn't make any stupid mistakes. Tariq crawled with dogged determination, ignoring the pain in his knees and elbows caused by rivets embedded in the hard surface. When he reached the exhaust vent, he eyed the iron braces that formed a protective grid in the dim glow of the penlight, which he then flicked off and pocketed.

The chisel made short work of the braces where they connected to the concrete, softened over decades to the point where it took only a few blows with the hammer to slice through the walls and tear the screws free. The designers of the prison had never contemplated the ventilation grids as barriers to keep inmates in or intruders out, so they weren't the heavy, military-grade hardware with which most of the rest of the prison had been built.

Three minutes after starting on the grid, he kicked it free and could stare out into the night air, the sound of the protest from the far side of the compound faint but audible.

Tariq lowered himself feet first until he was hanging from the cavity, and then released his hold and fell into the darkness. He dropped four meters and landed hard, wincing from a lance of pain in his right leg as he rolled and then forced himself to his feet. He tested his weight to confirm nothing was broken, and then took off at a measured clip for the perimeter fence, which was more an afterthought to keep graffiti artists away from the walls than a serious impediment to escape. At the fence he used the claw end of the hammer to scrape away enough of the soil at the base to squeeze beneath it, and then he was on the far side, jogging toward the road, where a car would be waiting to spirit him away.

He reached the strip of pavement and cursed under his breath when he didn't see any likely cars – all appeared empty, their windows lightly misted with condensation. He glared at his surroundings, his mind racing, and ducked into the shadows of a doorway as headlights bounced along the road toward him. A vehicle approached, and his breath caught as it slowed and coasted to a stop ten meters away. Tariq peered from the doorway and saw that it was his ride, and exhaled in relief before looking around to confirm nobody was watching, and sprinted for the car.

A woman sat behind the wheel with a grim expression, which surprised him only momentarily – nobody had consulted him on who would pick him up, and it made sense to use someone who would be unlikely to arouse suspicion if stopped. He opened the passenger door and dropped heavily into the seat as the woman put the transmission into gear. He'd barely pulled the door closed when she took off, the motor buzzing like a leaf blower from beneath the tiny hood.

"We have another car waiting two kilometers away. This one is for the traffic cameras," she said in Arabic, her accent musical in spite of the circumstances. "Stolen four hours ago." Her eyes flitted to the dried blood on his face. "Do you need medical attention?"

"No. It's already clotted. Just get me to the other car and I'll be fine."

"There's a bottle of water and some orange juice in the glove compartment."

Tariq nodded at the thoughtfulness of his followers at foreseeing that he might need fortification after his sprint to freedom. "Good. Any problems? You're late."

"They closed down some of the approaches because of the protest. Couldn't be helped."

A handheld radio crackled, and a baritone German voice emanated from the speaker. The woman's expression didn't change when the transmission ended, and she barely slowed as they reached an intersection. "We'll hear on the police band as soon as they put out the word on you. So far, nothing. Just a lot of traffic about the protest and crowd control."

Tariq allowed himself a rare smile and rubbed his smooth chin. "Everything is working perfectly."

"So far," the woman agreed.

"Let's hope it continues. We only need a few hours of fortune favoring us and we'll be home free."

CHAPTER 2

Al Ghurayfah, Libya

Salmon and crimson had painted the western sky as the sun sank like a burning ember into the pall of haze hanging over the high ridge that stretched to infinity along the southern reaches of the desert. Only a few of the homes in the small town had lights burning in their windows; the majority plunged into darkness with the passing of day, electricity an impossible luxury in an outpost at the edge of a sandy hell, the heat stifling even as night fell.

A battered Toyota truck bounced along a rutted dirt street and pulled to a stop in front of a single-story mud-brick home. Two men carrying Kalashnikov assault rifles climbed from the ancient vehicle and approached the front door. It opened after a few moments, and after scanning the empty road, they entered.

"My friends!" said the man who'd let them in. "Come. Sit with me and celebrate the escape of our friend and spiritual leader. It is a joyous occasion we've been awaiting for too long."

"Before I forget, this is for you, Mounir," one of the new arrivals muttered, and handed him a USB thumb drive. "He instructed us to give it to you once he was free. Said you would know what to do with it."

Mounir smiled, revealing yellowed teeth. "Let me take a quick look at it, and then we shall enjoy some hot tea and discuss what is to come." He called out down the hall. "Salma! We have visitors. Make a pot of tea, and be quick about it!"

"Yes, Mounir," a woman's voice answered.

"This way," Mounir said to the newcomers, indicating a room at the end of the hall. "I'll just be a few minutes."

The guests sat on the floor, where a number of carpets lay to soften the hard stone, and set their rifles aside while Mounir padded to another room to examine the contents of the thumb drive. He was gone for five minutes, and when he returned, his eyes were bright with excitement. He offered a reptilian grin and sat across from them, his expression animated.

"He is a genius. There can be no doubt. His plan will bring the infidels and their devil master to their knees. It is all that we have been waiting for, and more."

"What can you tell us about it?"

Mounir thought for a moment. "Our enemies will be dealt a death blow that will strike fear through the hearts of all who support Israel. Soon we will take control of Libya, which will be just the beginning. Once we do, no one will be safe from our wrath — nothing that they do, no preparations or safeguards, will help them. It will completely change the balance of power, and all of the cursed bitch's allies will desert her when it becomes obvious that she is going to pay the ultimate price."

"But how?"

"A biological agent developed in a former satellite of the Soviet Union. Weaponized by the Chinese after the wall came down, and more lethal than anything seen before. Enough of it to destroy those who willingly help our enemy, because they can never be sure when the next attack will be mounted or from what direction it will come."

The men's eyes widened. "He has secured this agent?"

Mounir frowned and yelled toward the kitchen, "Damn it, woman. I said prepare tea and a plate of food for our guests. Where are you?"

"I'm sorry. I'll be right there," Salma said. A metal pan rattled on a counter, and Mounir shook his head.

"You see what I put up with? Allah tests us all in His own way."

The men laughed, and a slim woman wearing a floor-length robe and a hijab and niqab that covered her face and hair entered carrying a tray with an antique tea set on it and two baskets of rolls and dates. She knelt with practiced skill and placed the tray before Mounir, and then straightened and backed away with her eyes averted. Nobody said anything until she'd retreated into the kitchen, and then Mounir made a show of pouring his guests tea and offering them the meager bounty of his larder.

Salma listened as the men joked in the living area, and when she was sure they were distracted by one of her husband's rambling stories, slipped from the kitchen and skirted the exterior of the house until she arrived at the window of the room that served as his office. She slid it open and climbed through into the darkened chamber, and moved quickly to where a computer's green power light glowed in the corner.

Salma tapped a few keys, and the screen blinked to life. The USB drive the visitors had brought was still in the socket, and she scanned the contents of the directory before removing a thumb drive of her own from within the recesses of her robe and inserting it into an adjacent socket. She quickly skimmed the main document and then tapped more commands, copying the original to hers in under a minute while she continued to read. The drive blinked off and she retrieved it, listening intently to confirm that the men were still deep in discussion and oblivious to her actions.

When she didn't hear anything to alarm her, she returned to the window and climbed out into the arid night. The information she'd copied was too sensitive to delay by trying to keep up appearances, and she needed to leave immediately, while she could. With Mounir being as unpredictable as he was, she couldn't assume that they wouldn't be uprooted with the morning light to travel to some even more remote berg, where she'd never have the opportunity to escape him.

No, the years of waiting, choking down nausea and bile as the filthy swine had taken her whenever he felt like it, pretending to love a man who smelled like a goat and had the grace of a boar, had finally come to an end, and she would be free once again.

Assuming she could make it to safety in a country ravaged by war and destruction.

She'd been preparing for this day for some time, and had taken extra precautions when she'd overheard him on a phone call discussing the escape of one of his fellow scum from prison. Mounir's attitude had changed after that call; she'd sensed a quickening in his feverish plotting, and the meetings with other terrorists became more frequent, until this nocturnal visitation had closed the circle and given her what she needed.

Salma retraced her steps to the kitchen and jotted out a suicide note that she'd recited in her sleep for many nights while dreaming of finally leaving, never to return. She explained that she was despondent at being unable to conceive a child, was depressed at the misery that was her life, and had decided to end it all by throwing herself into one of the deep ravines in the nearby foothills rather than suffering further humiliation. She signed it with a flourish and allowed herself a trace of a smile, and then set it on the tile counter and slipped out the door again, a kitchen knife in hand in case anyone tried to accost her.

Salma moved silently to the street and then took off at a run. She'd secreted a backpack with clothes, money, and a satellite phone in the hills outside town. She would fake her death, leaving her torn veil near one of the more treacherous ravines, and end the trail there. Whether or not Mounir believed that she'd killed herself, his ego would never allow him to admit that his wife might have left him, and he would be likely to go along with the story she'd laid out rather than concede to the world that she'd despised him.

If things worked out the way she'd planned, she would have bought herself enough time to escape for good, and her first act of freedom would be to send a text to a number she'd memorized years before but had never dared write down, and then head north to where she could get clear of the cursed desert nation before its filthy denizens were the death of her.

CHAPTER 3

Tel Aviv, Israel

Moonlight illuminated the street as Jet crept forward. She stayed to the shadows, her black clothes and knit ski cap rendering her close to invisible, so that her movement along the sidewalk was almost imperceptible in the gloom. Her footsteps were nearly silent, her rubber soles placed with precision as she made her way toward a tenement that loomed over her like a sentry, its windows dark, the façade covered with graffiti. Beneath the cap, her face was obscured with black base so it didn't reflect any light, and her gloved hand clutched a suppressed pistol.

She paused at the base of the building and looked up at the roof three stories above. Rather than making for the entrance, Jet circled to a tree and pulled herself into the branches, and when she was eight feet from the base of the façade's iron fire escape, slipped her weapon into her belt and waited, listening.

An airliner on takeoff from the nearby airport shattered the night, and Jet used the cover of its engines to mask any sound she'd make on the fire escape. She took a deep breath, gauged the distance a final time, and threw herself into space, arms outstretched.

Her hands locked on the edge of the platform, and she heaved herself up with a barely audible grunt, her daily syllabus of hundreds of pull-ups and push-ups serving her well. The noise of the plane faded, but not before she'd mounted the steps and was peering over the roof lip.

A figure huddled on the far side, where the menacing snout of a sniper rifle protruded from beneath a black tarp that concealed shooter and weapon. Jet hoisted herself the rest of the way onto the roof and crossed to where the gunman was positioned in eight fluid steps, her pistol in hand.

"Bang. You're dead," she said, weapon pointed at the figure.

A curse in Hebrew greeted her announcement, and the sniper tossed the tarp aside and scowled up at Jet. "How the hell–"

"You left yourself wide open. If this were a real operation, you'd be history."

"I booby-trapped the stairs. Motion detectors on the ground floor. I did everything by the book."

"Maybe you need a new book. You didn't secure your perimeter." She explained how she'd used the tree to reach the fire escape, and the young man's eyes widened.

"Yeah, but how often will that happen in real life?" he blurted.

She frowned and looked him over. "To you? Only once. Then you'll decompose into something useful." Her voice hardened. "Your job, if you're going to survive, is to expect the unexpected. To develop hyper-alertness and take nothing for granted. Any pro would have expected you to have taken countermeasures, so they'd have been useless against anyone but a rank amateur or a beat cop."

"You knew I was up here," he argued.

"Just like if something goes wrong on an assignment, those hunting you can be assumed to know where you're going to take your shot from." She sighed. "I'm not here to argue with you. I'm supposed to give you the tools to save your life. If you want to ignore them, that's fine, but I'll fail you because you'll be a danger to yourself and everyone else on your team. My job is to keep egotistical jerks who think they already know everything from going into the field and botching their assignment. So figure this out and realize you screwed up, or I'll bounce you from the program and you can go back to cleaning latrines."

A small handheld radio vibrated in her pocket, and she fished it out, her eyes never leaving her student. "What?"

"I need to see you. Stat." The voice was that of Colonel Berensen, the commanding officer of the Mossad training facility.

She depressed the transmit button. "We're in the middle of an exercise–"

"Sorry. It can't wait."

"10-4." Jet slipped the handheld back into her pocket and regarded the sniper. "I'll be back. In the meantime, study your surroundings and figure out how I'm going to get up here next time."

She spun and made for the roof access door, her forehead wrinkled. Berensen had never called her in from her training duties; this was a first in the month that she'd been serving as an instructor after retiring from active duty following her last mission. That had been the deal she'd made with the director after announcing she was done – she'd earn her keep by training new generations of operatives so that her skill set would be passed on rather than lost to posterity.

Back on the street, she picked up her pace to a jog until she reached the golf cart she used to navigate the huge facility – a former air base that had been converted to a Mossad and Special Forces/IDF facility, although the two groups never saw each other. For security reasons, Mossad operatives were kept segregated from everyone else on the base, including each other, once they were deployed in the field, as had been the case in her training days. Mossad valued secrecy above all other qualities and did everything possible to avoid potential operatives from being able to identify each other – the fewer bonds between them, the better; you couldn't divulge to an enemy under interrogation what you didn't know.

The cart whirred away from the three-block urban neighborhood that had been constructed from scratch at one end of a former runway, and she made for the administrative building, where the colonel and his support staff kept long hours. As she neared, she could see faint light from the windows. She guided her cart into an open slot beside four others and switched it off, and then entered the building and made for Berensen's office.

Jet rapped on the doorjamb, and Berensen looked up from his computer screen, his expression clouded. "Sorry to interrupt. Couldn't be helped," he said, and pointed to a chair. "Have a seat."

"What's this all about?" she asked, sitting.

"You have a call. I'll put it on speaker and duck out."

Jet's eyes narrowed as the man stabbed a box on the desk to life and exited the office, closing the door after him. Jet leaned forward and was unsurprised when the director's distinctive voice boomed from the speaker.

"Thanks for coming on such short notice," he began, but Jet cut him off.

"We don't have anything to discuss. I'm keeping my part of the bargain."

"Yes, yes. I know. But I've had a situation come up that I want to run by you."

"No more fieldwork. I was clear, wasn't I? That was our deal," Jet said, an edge to her voice.

"I haven't forgotten. But this is…different."

"It always is. I'm out of play. Period. Now if you don't mind, I have to get back to my students…"

"We have an operative in deep cover. In Libya. She's under considerable duress, and we need an experienced field op to help with the rendezvous and extraction. Your name came up."

"Too bad. No means no. I'm not interested."

The director hesitated, and she could hear him blowing smoke before responding. "Your old flame. Father of that lovely daughter of yours. David – wasn't that his name?"

"What does that have to do with anything?" Jet snapped.

"You probably don't know this, but he had a half sister. Which would make her your daughter's aunt, wouldn't it?"

Jet took a deep breath, wary of one of the director's tricks. "David didn't have any siblings. He was an only child."

"I'm sure that's what he told you. But it isn't true. He had a half sister who was six years younger. And like David, she answered the call when we reached out to her."

"Why are you telling me this?"

"The operative in Libya is his sister. And we believe she's in trouble."

"You must have dozens of agents who could do this."

"We want a woman. With the situation on the ground in Libya at the moment, we feel that's the best chance of success."

"It's a war zone since the Americans took out Qaddafi, isn't it?"

"That would be the tame description. It's anarchy. Warlords running many of the metropolitan areas. Competing criminal gangs acting as judges and executioners. The government, such as it is, is nothing but a bad joke that everyone ignores. There are black markets in everything from weapons to organs to humans – we know of dozens of active slave markets operating in the region. The media doesn't cover it, but it's one of the worst humanitarian disaster areas on the planet, and all because Qaddafi was overthrown. Before that, Libya was the most prosperous country in Africa."

"I was there maybe eight years ago. As you know. It didn't seem that much worse off than its neighbors."

"Yes. That was before. Even a year after Qaddafi was overthrown, things were functional, at least by Libyan standards, but now it's reverted to the Stone Age. But with your familiarity of the place, and being as you're a woman, you would be far more likely to blend in than if we sent someone in completely cold." The director hesitated. "We don't have a long list of operatives with Libyan experience."

"I'm not surprised." Jet thought for a moment. "Why would I agree to do this after we made our deal?"

"It's your daughter's aunt. Her father's sister. From what I understand, he meant something to you. I thought I'd run it by you first to see whether you're interested. If not, we'll move to plan B…"

"How do I know you're not lying? Making this up? It wouldn't be the first time you invented something to get your way."

"The familial resemblance is obvious. If you're willing to take the job, I'll send over her file. She's unmistakably David's sister. You'll know it immediately. And of course we have all the documentation from her birth through now, so it's not in doubt."

"Why didn't he tell me about her?"

"He didn't know she was with us. All he knew was that his father had been a rolling stone, so to speak. They weren't close – I don't think they spoke five times in their lives. And from what I gather, the father spent all of fifteen minutes with his daughter, so it wasn't like David and she could have had much in common to share."

Jet considered the director's story. It was plausible. David had been compartmentalized in all things, and if he'd had a half-sibling he barely knew, he'd have had no reason to share that uninteresting factoid with Jet. That his sister might have also been recruited didn't surprise Jet in the least – the Mossad sought specific traits, some of which ran in the blood, like strength of character and determination. Why not attempt to recruit the sister of one of their best, especially if she'd come from a difficult upbringing where she'd been forced to be a loner?

Jet sighed, already knowing her answer. "What's the scenario? Don't leave anything out. Your little omissions almost got me killed last time, so full disclosure or no go, understand?"

"Absolutely." It was the director's turn to pause. "It all started with a prison break last week in Germany…"

CHAPTER 4

Tripoli, Libya

The formerly bustling port of Tripoli was almost unrecognizable since the revolution, and now more closely resembled a scene from one of the squalid backwaters in sub-Saharan Africa than the former jewel in the African crown. Aged tramp freighters tugged at mooring lines like fighting dogs, their seams leaking rust into the murky water, waiting their turn to dock and offload their cargo and return to their home ports. Crowds of sweating laborers milled around the waterfront, calling out offers to anyone who would listen, most rail thin from malnutrition, their skin dark as charcoal in the glare of the sun, many without shoes and wearing little more than rags.

A two-hundred-seventy-meter cargo vessel that was a decade past its safe operating life sat at the farthest jetty, where a crane was off-loading crates emblazoned with Chinese script while a throng of bored workers watched with dull eyes. The ship's name, *Tian Xiu Li*, was emblazoned across its black bow in mustard lettering that looked as though it had been applied by a shaky hand, and its crew of Asian seamen watched the unloading process from the relative safety and comfort of the deck, well away from the dangers that roamed the waterfront in the form of armed militias and pistol-packing intermediaries out for a cut of whatever they could squeeze from unsuspecting sailors.

A functionary in a perspiration-stained official tunic stood in the shade of one of the cranes with a clipboard and a stub of pencil, noting the crates as they were stacked in a holding area by one of the warehouses that lined the harbor. Beside him was a tall man with chiseled features and a gray beard, his clothing of a better cut than most and his direct gaze that of a man accustomed to having his orders followed.

"What brings you down here today, Idris?" the customs official asked.

"Just making sure that my cargo makes it off the boat in one piece," the bearded man answered.

"Haven't seen you here in person in quite some time. Must be something pretty valuable to force you out of your air-conditioned office, eh?"

Idris shrugged and looked away. "Not really. It was a slow day, so I thought I'd come down and see how the other half lives."

They both laughed, and the functionary moved to one of the stacks of crates. "Any idea what's in these?"

"Go ahead and open them. Just boxes of cheap garments. The usual, Hakim. Nothing worth your time, I assure you."

The customs officer eyed Idris skeptically. "A bunch of Nike and Puma knockoffs brought you to the docks? Why do I have a hard time believing that?"

"No doubt because you're too cynical in your old age, my friend. But go ahead and open a few. I really don't mind."

Hakim continued past that stack and stopped to watch a larger crate being lowered to where a decrepit forklift was waiting to haul it into the warehouse.

Idris removed a packet of cigarettes from his breast pocket and shook one free. "Smoke?"

Hakim took the proffered cigarette and eyed it. "I heard these might be bad for you."

"Nonsense," Idris replied with a grin. "The only things you have to worry about are women and sticking your nose where it doesn't belong. Avoid those and you'll live forever."

Idris held Hakim's stare as he lit his cigarette for him, and then one for himself. The pair watched the large crate come to rest on the concrete, and Hakim tapped ash from the tip of his smoke.

"I'm thinking I might want to have a look in that one." He studied his clipboard. "Not sure I see it on the manifest."

"Could be an oversight. Who knows what goes on in the Chinese mind?"

"Still. Now I'm curious."

Idris sighed and nodded. "You have an unfailing nose for these sorts of things, my friend. Come into the shade and let's discuss how best to ensure that nobody has to stay in this heat a moment longer than necessary."

"It is unbearable, isn't it?"

"Life is suffering, is it not? Come. Let's discuss how to make our lives a little easier for the time being."

Ten minutes later, Hakim strolled from the dock, a spring in his step and two months' salary in cash in his pocket. Idris watched him depart and nodded to the forklift operator, who made quick work of moving the container into the warehouse, followed by three more with the same markings. When he was done, Idris pulled the metal door closed and dialed a number on his cell phone.

Later that afternoon a pair of SUVs rolled to a stop by the warehouse, and a trio of hard-looking men accompanied Idris into the building while their drivers and bodyguards waited by the vehicles, submachine guns at the ready.

At the first of the crates, Idris removed part of the wooden siding to reveal a row of green metal canisters packed in Styrofoam sheaths. He pulled one free, revealing faded Chinese script on the side and an internationally recognized symbol – a biohazard logo.

"Just what the doctor ordered," he said.

One of the men took the canister and examined it closely, and then nodded to the others. "Pay our friend here and get these into the trucks."

The youngest of the trio removed a phone from his pocket, tapped a series of keys, swiped twice, and then held it out to Idris. "Enter the account digits there."

Idris complied, and moments later the device pinged twice. The young man nodded. "It's done."

"Pleasure doing business with you," Idris said, his grin back in place. "Let me know if you need anything else."

"We may. We'll be in touch."

"Excellent news. I'm always available."

The transfer of the canisters took fifteen minutes, and when the vehicles drove away, Idris squinted through cigarette smoke as their brake lights receded along the waterfront. He had no interest in what the miscreants who'd taken the canisters planned to do with them, nor any guilt over possibly involving himself in some horror. He was a businessman, an import/export entrepreneur who'd seized the opportunity presented by the collapse of the state and stepped in to provide a valuable service, nothing more. He could arrange for virtually anything to pass in either direction through the port – contraband, drugs, weapons, human beings – it was all cargo that carried a price.

The canisters had been transshipped to a little-used port in China, where they'd been packed along with the rest of the items he'd imported to Libya, and had made their way to Tripoli without any of the annoying possible inspections many of the more mainstream hubs conducted.

What their ultimate owners did with them wasn't his affair, any more than the countries that produced the vast majority of weapons used for mass murder cared what their products were used for or where. If he hadn't facilitated the transaction, another like him would have, and he was pragmatic about the ways of the world after watching his country disintegrate into anarchy after another government had toppled the leader when he'd dared to propose trading the country's oil in gold-backed currency rather than the dollar. That sin, coupled with refusing to allow the country to have a privately owned central bank – controlled by the dynasty that controlled the Bank for International Settlements in Basel, and through it virtually all central banks in the world – had signed Qaddafi's death warrant, and the U.S. had obligingly had him murdered, and plunged the nation into chaos.

Idris dropped the cigarette on the dank concrete and crushed it with the toe of his expensive loafer. Before a provisional government had even been installed in Tripoli following the "rebels" overthrowing the regime, an agreement to create a privately owned central bank had been signed by the country's "representatives," and hundreds of tons of the nation's gold stores had gone missing. All discussion of trading oil for gold-backed dinars stopped with Qaddafi's execution, the message delivered to anyone else stupid enough to dare reject the petrodollar for oil trade. First Saddam Hussein, whose sin had been the same proposal to pull out of OPEC and trade Iraq's oil for gold-backed currency, and then Qaddafi. Only Syria's Assad and Iran were left as regimes that rejected the petrodollar and wanted something of tangible value for their oil, and both had been targeted by the bankers' mercenary armies for their audacity.

It was the way things worked. Idris was a small cog in a complicated machine, skimming a few million here and there while the real players destroyed nations for profit. If his customers wanted some forbidden substance for some nefarious purpose, that was their business. He wished them nothing but well, and indeed hoped that they returned for more transactions. They'd paid promptly and caused no trouble, and had arranged for their shipment in China, so all Idris had been required to do was pay off a few port authorities and the captain of the ship – and, of course, his good friend Hakim, who for all his pretense was in the same business as Idris, only at a lower level on the food chain.

"*Mashi*. It is done," he murmured, and took care to double lock the warehouse door before turning to one of his facility's armed guards and nodding. "Night," he said. The man's eyes glowed white in the darkness as he cautiously nodded back; a hired gun working dangerous duty in one of the most perilous ports on the planet, doing what he had to do to put food on his family's table at a rate that equated to fifteen dollars a week, for which he was expected to kill, or give his life defending his post.

Idris made his way to his waiting car. His driver had spent the better part of ten hours behind the wheel in case his master required something, which was par for the course. Idris hummed a pop song as he walked along the waterfront, debating his choices for dinner companionship from the myriad youthful romantic possibilities created by Libya's financial ruin, a man without a care in the world who'd just had another in a long string of profitable days.

CHAPTER 5

Tel Aviv, Israel

Jet looked in on Hannah, with Matt by her side in the hall, and then entered her darkened bedroom to smooth the sleeping girl's hair. After several moments watching her daughter slumber, she crept back to the doorway and took Matt's hand.

"Did she feel hot to you? Running a fever?"

"Not at all," Matt whispered. "She was fine all day. Don't worry if she's got a little scratchy throat. Kids get sick. It's normal. They're little Petri dishes, running around with each other in school. It's bound to happen."

Jet didn't look convinced. "I don't know…"

"Seriously. She's fine." Matt pulled her into the hallway and closed the door. "But what about you? Let's talk about that."

"I'm conflicted, Matt. I mean, I swore I wouldn't do any more ops. The director knows that. But this is a special case…"

"Aren't they all? I mean, every single time it's 'this time is different,' isn't it? You can't keep doing this."

"I know. I thought it was over. But it's David's sister…"

Matt frowned. "So he says. But where's the proof? How do you actually know that's true? I wouldn't put anything past them."

"They're sending someone over with the file. Her entire history. Apparently there's a strong familial resemblance. I'll know."

Matt sighed. "Let's assume she is. I mean…Libya? That's got to be one of the most dangerous places on Earth right now."

"No question."

He eyed her, his expression serious. "You're seriously thinking about going?"

23

She smiled faintly. "It's been pretty boring around here lately."

He didn't return her smile. "Yeah. Training and having a normal life with me and your daughter. Who'd want that when they could risk everything for some quasi-cause?"

"I wouldn't even be considering it if she weren't David's sister, Matt. You have to know that. Besides, it sounds like a straightforward extraction. The only reason they approached me is because I've been on the ground there before."

"And because they knew they could guilt you into agreeing."

"I haven't agreed to anything."

"Yet." Matt released Jet's hand and walked to the dining room. Jet followed. "I know you," he continued. "You've already made up your mind. This is how you act when you're trying to convince me you haven't."

"I want to see the file first, but yes, I'm leaning that way."

"And how long did they say this little adventure would take?"

"Not long. Though we didn't discuss logistics in depth."

He sat at the dining room table and eyed the chandelier overhead, which they both knew was bugged. "You made a deal with them. They agreed. You weren't going to do any more missions. No more risking your life."

"True. But—"

The doorbell interrupted them. Jet's mouth hardened into a thin line, and she marched down the hall to the entrance and swung it open.

The director was standing there clad in a typically rumpled gray suit, his skin yellowed from nicotine, his gray hair thinner than she remembered, a manila folder in his hand. He cleared his throat, and a waft of stale cigarette stink drifted into the hall.

"I brought the document we discussed," he said. "Signed by the prime minister."

He held out an envelope, and she opened it and scanned the single page. When she met his eyes again, her expression was unreadable. "Seems pretty clear. No more active duty. My obligations discharged by continuing as a trainer. No caveats or exceptions."

"Correct. If you decide to take on this operation, it's not obligatory in any way. It would be completely voluntary, no coercion, no threats. As of the signing of that letter, you're officially retired, and nobody can force you to do anything ever again."

Jet looked him over. "I presume you brought the file?"

He nodded. "Are you going to invite me in?"

"My kid's asleep, and my…I have company. How about I review this and get back to you tomorrow?"

"I'll be up late tonight. There's some urgency to this."

"There always is."

He removed a thicker envelope from his breast pocket and passed it to her. "It's all in there. Anything operational I've left out, but all the background is in those pages. If you decide you want to help, then I'll send you the operational side. But I should warn you that the situation is in flux. It's…dynamic."

"Does it cover why she was in so deep and for so long?"

"Yes."

Jet shook her head. "I can't imagine spending years in a scenario like that…"

The director nodded wearily again. "It's definitely not for everyone. She's sacrificed a lot. Which is why I thought you might…that her predicament might resonate with you. She's out on a limb, completely on her own, in hostile territory, and she needs to come in. Says she has the mother lode. Her words, not mine. So we have to do everything we can to help."

"A simple rendezvous and extraction, I believe you said."

He looked away. "I might have been overly optimistic about the *simple* part."

"Do you have assets in place to help with the extraction?"

"We're working on it."

"Not a great answer."

His shoulders lifted slightly, and he studied one of his palms. "An honest one. We would need you to be prepared to leave immediately."

"I'm not going into a hot zone with nothing but high hopes.

Never again. Your last couple of rush jobs almost got me killed. That won't fly anymore."

"You'll be instrumental in the planning process. You have my word."

"I'll need to understand exactly what I'm up against."

"At this point, it's an extraction, nothing more."

"I'll look over the background and call later." She cocked an eyebrow. "Is there anything else?"

"No. I appreciate your considering taking this on. I know there's been some bad blood…"

"No bad blood. You've just sent me into the lion's den more times than I can count, and left out key parts of the story that could have gotten me killed. Nothing personal, I know. All part of the job."

"It's not always easy making the right judgment call on how much to disclose."

"I understand. Which is why I quit. I don't want to die because you made an error in judgment."

"Fair enough. Look it over and let me know."

"Will do."

She shut the door and returned to the dining room, where Matt was sipping a glass of juice. "I read that Tel Aviv is the most expensive city in the world. Based on what this cost, I believe it." He met her gaze. "Well?"

"This is a letter from the prime minister absolving me of all past offenses, and excusing me from ever having to do anything for anyone, other than train recruits," she said, placing the letter in front of him on the table. "And this is the dossier on David's sister."

She opened the envelope and withdrew a half dozen pages. On the first were four black-and-white photographs. Jet studied them for several beats and nodded. "You can see the resemblance in the eyes and nose. And her chin. She's his sister, all right." She continued scanning the documents, which consisted of a miniature birth certificate, school records, military service, and other background information that established her bona fides and her background. When Jet was done, she pushed the pile of documents to Matt, who looked them over with a practiced eye before sitting back.

"So now what?"

Jet reached across the table to take his hand. "I'm afraid we both know."

"When?"

"Probably first thing in the morning. Maybe sooner. I won't know until I see the ops sheets."

"Would it change anything if I said I hate this?"

"It would make me love you even more if you let me do what I need to do, even though you hate it."

"I'd like to pretend I'm a better man than I am, but this bugs the crap out of me. You were supposed to be done with this. For good."

"I know. Take care of Hannah for me. Libya isn't that far away. I shouldn't be gone too long."

He squeezed her hand and managed a sad smile. "Does it matter if I don't believe a word of that?"

"Neither do I. But I'll play along. It's Hannah's aunt, Matt. That makes her family whether I like it or not."

"Hannah needs a mommy more than an aunt she never knew existed."

"And I'm planning on returning, Matt. I promise you I will. I know when I've pushed my luck."

"The cat with ninety lives gets real. That's a hopeful sign."

She rose and tugged his hand. "Let me call the director, and then maybe you can help me pack or something."

That elicited a grin. "I like the sound of *or something.*"

"I figured you might."

CHAPTER 6

Tripoli, Libya

Moonlight silvered the surface of the water inside the harbor breakwater, where dozens of cargo ships lay at anchor, their running lights blinking through a creeping mist. A foghorn from the port soughed through the stillness of the night, blending with the occasional clank of anchor chain and the boom of watertight doors slamming aboard the vessels.

Waves crashed against the breakwater from the remnants of a Mediterranean storm, sending plumes of white foam high into the dark sky. The battering had been constant over the centuries, and the heavy boulders were worn smooth from nature's incessant polishing. The putter of an occasional fishing skiff making its way to the mouth of the harbor carried across the water, joining the roar of trucks and cars from onshore to create an uneasy dissonance.

A flat-bottomed native craft with a wheezing outboard motor plied its way along the water to where the hulking forms of what remained of the Libyan navy were docked at four jetties, the ships barely afloat, with one so badly corroded from lack of maintenance that it had capsized and lay half submerged on its side. The little boat slowed as it neared the docks, and the pilot cut the engine as it approached the closest pier, allowing momentum to carry it the rest of the way. A deckhand on the bow tossed a line around a piling and pulled the small craft to the side of the dock, where another man on the stern lashed a rope to a rusting cleat and tied the hull close to the weathered surface.

A guard walked toward the new arrival, his machine gun leveled at the boat. The captain exchanged a few words with the man and handed him a wad of currency, and he retreated into the shadows without a sound.

When the deckhands were sure that they were no longer being observed, the captain whispered instructions, and one of the crew climbed onto the pier carrying a bundle in a burlap sack. He glanced around and then took off at a run toward the main building that housed the unity government's naval force, along with a collection of deniable "advisors" from the U.S. and several other NATO member countries, who had been stationed there following the fall of Qaddafi.

The deckhand approached the building, set the bundle down in front of one of the three entrances, and activated a timer. When the LED display blinked red three times, he turned and retraced his steps to the boat, sprinting the final thirty meters, sandals flapping like the broken wings of an injured bird. He leapt aboard the skiff and the others cast off, and then the motor revved and the craft skimmed away from the base before disappearing into the night.

The bundle at the door exploded three minutes later with a muffled boom. Lights blinked on in the barracks as the two thousand men stationed inside jolted awake, prepared for an attack by any of the competing forces who constantly vied for control over the port city. Within moments armed figures began pouring from the entrance, the door of which had been blown off its hinges by the bomb, and more took up defensive positions at the windows, their rifles trained on the darkness beyond the reach of the building's lights.

More gunmen spilled from the barracks, but the first dropped their rifles and clawed at their throats before collapsing, racked by seizures. Bloody froth foamed from their mouths and noses, and they gasped and wheezed as their respiratory systems shut down. By the time the men realized that they'd been subjected to a chemical attack, over a hundred were down, and their commanding officers were screaming instructions from inside the building, where still more were dropping to the floor, the nerve agent having dispersed inside as well as out by the blast.

An hour later, a third of the men who'd been in the building were dead or dying, and the rest had taken up positions well away from the blast site. The spectacle of their comrades twisted in tortured agony, rigor mortis stiffening their limbs, was seared into their brains as crews in hazmat suits arrived from the nearby military garrison. Emergency vehicles clogged the streets leading to the naval base, and roadblocks were hastily erected for crowd control as the curious arrived like vultures to rotting carrion.

Across the harbor, the skiff tied off to a dock by the old city, and the captain killed the engine and led his men across the former Shari Al Fatih Boulevard – renamed Tripoli Street, at least in common usage, after the revolution – to one of the mosques that dotted the area. Inside, they sat with a stoic man who spoke in a hoarse whisper.

"The first reports are promising. The blow was a mighty one. Hundreds of casualties and the forces in complete disarray. It will be just a matter of time before their farce of a government is brought to its knees, and then we can install proper leadership that will honor the Prophet's teachings. No longer will foreigners dictate our future." He paused and lowered his voice even further. "This is only the beginning. You have done well. Very soon we will be ready for the next phase."

"We are honored to be a part of the fight," the captain said.

"We will all be tested in the coming days, but I have faith that you will perform. This was only the first salvo. I will call upon you for even greater responsibility in the near future. For now, go to your homes and pray. Thank Allah for your success, and kiss your children. It is their future we are building."

"Thank you. We are nothing but insects in the scheme of things."

"We all play our roles. Now go and rest, because soon you will embark on the next leg of this journey, and when you do, you'll require all the energy you can muster."

CHAPTER 7

Al Ghurayfah, Libya

Mounir sat in his living area staring despondently at his wife's suicide note and the niqab that a local urchin had found in the mountains to the south. With him were his two closest confidants, Brahim and Mohamed, who had come to grieve with their friend and master when they'd heard the news of the tragedy.

"I can't believe it," Mounir muttered. "She gave no indication. I mean, she'd been depressed over not being able to bear children, but she didn't…she didn't seem unhappy in any other way."

"The mind of a woman is a mystery," Brahim intoned, nodding sagely.

"Indeed it is. You gave her a good life," Mohamed agreed. "There is nothing for which you should blame yourself."

"I know," Mounir said. "It's just…I can't believe it. It came out of nowhere."

"She's probably been considering it for a long time."

"Or maybe she had a hormone imbalance," Mohamed suggested. "You know how women can get."

Mounir shook his head. "That this happens right when Tariq has escaped and our plan is finally being put into action…I don't know. It feels…off."

"Any time someone is taken from us suddenly, it is a shock. That's to be expected," Brahim said.

Mounir frowned at him. "Since when are you such an expert on women and loss?"

Brahim's expression didn't change. "I know little of most things, but of loss, too much."

31

Mounir sat in silence, rocking slightly, lost in thought. His friends exchanged a worried look, but didn't speak. He was obviously having a difficult time processing the death of his wife, and given the volatility of his personality, it was safest not to irritate him with more platitudes. They could sense the anger seething below the surface, and didn't want to serve as targets if he exploded in rage.

Mounir finally sat forward, and when he spoke, his voice held no trace of grief. "The boy who brought us her headdress – I want you to find him and ask where exactly he found it. Have him take you to the spot. He's called Jamal, and his family's home is by the mosque square. They repair shoes."

"Now?" Mohamed asked, glancing at the wall clock.

"Yes."

"It will be dark in a few hours, Mounir."

"Then take lanterns and flashlights. Nobody's seen a body. So we can't be sure that she's actually dead."

Brahim's eyes widened in comprehension. "You think she faked this? Why?"

"I don't know. But she decided to end her life on the day that I received the specifics of the plan, and that makes me suspicious. Almost immediately after, in fact. The timing is too close for me to assume anything. I have to know for sure."

"You suspect *Salma* of…betraying us? Why?"

"I…I don't know what to think. She never seemed happy. Not genuinely so. I remember when we met, I wondered how I had gotten so lucky – she was so beautiful. Perhaps…perhaps she never loved me at all. Perhaps this has always been about something…else."

Brahim frowned. "You've been married for what, three years? That is a long time, my friend. I mean, anything is possible; yours was not an arranged marriage. Why would she have married you if not because she wanted to?"

"I have always been a target of our enemies, even if I have been a relatively inconsequential player until now. My duty is not to guess; it is to know. So go. Find this boy Jamal. Have him take you to the ravine, and don't return until you've found Salma's remains."

"That terrain is treacherous during the day. Dangerously so at night."

Mounir's eyes narrowed and his face flushed. "It is not a request. If we have been betrayed, time is of the essence. Now go."

Mohamed and Brahim did as asked, and on the dusty trek to the square, spoke in low tones. "He's seeing ghosts. He hasn't slept in two days. He isn't making sense," Brahim said.

"Yes, but his words are to be obeyed. Do we have a choice?"

"No. But we'll be up all night ourselves." He sighed. "We can stop by my house to get lamps. We'll need them."

"After we find the boy."

Jamal was playing with two other children the same age in the shade of his parents' shop. Brahim and Mohamed introduced themselves to his father and told them of Mounir's request. Mounir was well known in the town and considered a serious man of deep faith, and the father approved Jamal taking them to the spot where he'd found the scrap of clothing.

"Just be home before dark," he warned his son, who was small for his seven years.

"I will, Papa," Jamal assured him, and set off with the men on foot. After stopping for lanterns, they continued through the town to a trail that the local boys used to access the hills when hunting rabbits and birds.

The ascent took over an hour, and by the time Jamal had stopped to point out a scraggly tree by the edge of a gulley, the light was bleeding from the sky. "It was there. I was hunting, hoping to get a bird, and it was moving with the wind."

"How did you know it was Salma's?" Brahim asked.

"I didn't. It was only after I got back to town that I heard the news of her death. So I brought it to him. That's all I know."

"There was nothing else?" Mohamed asked.

Jamal's brow creased. "Like…what?"

"I don't know. Anything. Any trace of where she'd…fallen?"

Jamal shook his head. "I didn't look. Like I said, I didn't know about…that she'd…died…until after I came back." He hesitated and regarded the men. "I promised my father I'd come home before dark."

"Of course," Mohamed said. "You can go. Thank you for leading us here, and be careful going back down the trail."

Jamal left, and Brahim eyed the steep face of the ravine. "So where do we start?"

Mohamed sighed. "At the beginning, I suppose. Let's see if we can spot where she threw herself off."

Brahim stared up at the darkening sky. "You see that?"

"No. What?"

"Exactly. No vultures. You'd think if there was a body down here, there would be buzzards, even a day or two later, wouldn't you?"

"I don't know. Inconclusive," Mohamed said, but his voice betrayed his doubt.

"Come on. You take the right side, I'll take the left. If we're lucky, she left some tracks."

Forty-five minutes later, the sun was dropping behind the hills, and they hadn't found anything. After studying the ridge for hundreds of meters in each direction, they could spot no sign of a body below or any indication of where someone had jumped. Yet while the rock face was steep, it wasn't sheer, and unless Salma could fly, she would have struck the craggy cliff.

Brahim switched on his lamp and Mohamed did the same, and they continued along the ridge until they came across a trail that led down to the bottom. "Might as well go down and check the bed. Not a lot of places she could be."

"Maybe Mounir's not so paranoid after all?"

"No point jumping to conclusions."

Mohamed grinned. "Funny choice of words."

The men picked their way down the side of the ravine to the dry, gravelly bottom and worked back toward where Jamal had found the headdress. The moon was high in the sky by the time they had hiked a kilometer without coming across anything, and when they stopped to rest, both men's expressions were dour.

"I think we can say with assurance that there's no body down here," Mohamed said.

"And no sign of one on the way down, either."

"So where is she?"

Brahim sighed. "We're assuming that Mounir is right and that she did all this because of Tariq. But what if she just got tired of putting up with Mounir every day and decided to make a break for it? What if this is all coincidence?"

"That she just happened to leave at the exact moment he got the final details of the plan?" Mohamed asked, and spit to the side. "I understand what you're saying, but if she didn't kill herself, I think we have to assume Mounir is right. In which case, we have a huge problem."

After two more hours of searching, they had traversed the entire ravine and were so cold their teeth were chattering as the high desert temperature dropped toward freezing. They climbed another trail to the top, breathing heavily from the exertion, their lanterns dimming as the batteries ran down. By the time they made it back to Mounir's, they were exhausted, coated with a film of trail dust, and grimly determined.

Mounir greeted them at the door, his expression matching theirs.

"You didn't find her, did you?" he demanded.

"No."

Mounir checked the dirt street outside and stepped from the door. "Come in."

When they were seated on his rug pile, he glared at them, his eyes bright with fury. "I went through everything on the computer. One of the logs shows that the contents of the USB drive with the plans on it were copied the night Salma disappeared. So it's worse than I suspected. She was spying on us and waiting for her chance to betray us."

"Then we have to assume that she's sent it to whomever she's working for."

"Maybe. But how? There's no internet or wireless service. Only cell. And the reception is too weak for data – it's been a constant problem since they installed the towers. So, no, that's probably why she broke and ran. She needed to get somewhere she could relay the information. Which means she has to be heading for Tripoli. There's no other way."

"A single woman on the road north? The problem may take care of itself," Brahim said.

"Perhaps. But I want to mobilize our network. Find her. She can't have gotten far on foot. She probably assumes we believe she's dead, so she'll be cautious, which means moving slower." Mounir frowned, and his face turned ugly. "Find her and bring her to me. There's a special circle in hell reserved for traitors and spies, but before I send her there, I plan to demonstrate that this world holds something worse. Find her. Whatever you have to do. She knows everything, and she must be stopped."

CHAPTER 8

Tel Aviv, Israel

Jet sat in a SUV with windows tinted so dark they were nearly opaque, reading the case file on Salma's undercover work as the wife of a known Libyan terrorist who was believed to be responsible for a host of atrocities both in-country as well as throughout the Middle East – and a known associate of Tariq, one of the most vicious and intelligent masterminds of the Wahhabi sects that had found a foothold in Europe since the Libyan and Syrian crises had flooded Spain, Italy, France, and Germany with refugees, some of whom were zealots of the most extreme sort.

She studied a prison photograph of Tariq, his cruel features and smoldering eyes typical of the extremist breed. Jet was more than familiar with the Wahhabi interpretation of Islam, which was the most violent and brutal of the many possible, and which encouraged Jihad against nonbelievers – including, of course, Israel. An export of radical clerics in Saudi Arabia, Wahhabism was at the root of all Muslim terrorism worldwide, exported by the Saudis in an effort to prevent the metastasizing of the ideology at home. They had been largely successful, but at tremendous cost to the rest of the world – a fact that governments dependent upon Saudi oil and the wealth it had created conveniently overlooked.

Salma had married Mounir, one of Tariq's most loyal disciples, and had remained in deep cover for years. She occasionally managed to relay information to the Mossad about Libyan internal political squabbles and the increasingly large role the country was playing in recruiting for the most noxious of the terrorist organizations, though nothing specific to Tariq – Libya was now a magnet for those who viewed the West as a destructive force of evil that destabilized and destroyed the lives of millions in an ongoing game of geopolitical chess. Since the overthrow of Qaddafi, the entire country was a war zone, its infrastructure in ruins, its prosperity looted by criminal factions acting as quasi-governments, its population terrorized.

This was the environment Salma had chosen to live in, sleeping with a man she despised so that she could do her duty to the organization that had recruited and trained her for great things. Jet felt a pang of pain in her gut at the familiar story, which mirrored hers in too many ways – Salma had sacrificed the best years of her life to live in constant danger for an unclear objective, while Jet had done the same, becoming a ruthless killing machine sent as an instrument of destruction whenever her country decided that a situation could be best handled with only the most violent of means.

Jet tried to imagine spending over a thousand days married to a pig of a man whose touch nauseated her and whose beliefs were Neanderthal, and she shuddered as she perused the status report on conditions on the ground in Libya as of the prior week. While life had assumed a kind of tense normalcy in the capital city, the murder rate was still one of the highest on the planet, and the belief was that it was in actuality far higher, with the majority of cases going unreported as rival gangs exterminated anyone who opposed them, and the authorities remained ensconced behind thick, fortified walls. But bad as that was, the situation further degraded once out of Tripoli. South of the city there was no pretense of law or governance, and it was one armed faction against the other, making their own rules as they went, safe in the assurance that the world had abandoned Libya to an awful fate, as had been the history of all of Africa since the Europeans colonized it and spent centuries harvesting its resources, leaving the populations to existences of misery and horror.

Jet considered again her agreement to go in for Salma, which had seemed necessary and appropriate the night before, but now, with dawn still hours away, appeared rash and thoughtless. She was again leaving the safety of Matt's embrace and her beautiful daughter to put herself in harm's way in one of the most dangerous hellholes on earth.

She finished her first pass and slid the folder into the black backpack that was her only luggage. A private jet, its lights winking in the darkness, sat on the runway just past the gate. The sound of its turbines spooling up was practically deafening as she opened the door and stepped from the SUV, clad in a dark blue long-sleeved robe and colorful hijab, the better to fit in with the locals in Tripoli. Beneath the traditional garb she wore her usual cargo pants and ops shirt, their special material cool but stunningly durable, their multiple pockets and compartments making them perfect for any situation other than a cocktail party or royal wedding.

A hard-looking man with a crew cut opened the gate for her and she walked to the plane. A pilot waited at the top of the steps and offered a professional smile before wordlessly moving to the cockpit to join his copilot, leaving the battening down of the fuselage to a woman about Jet's age, who seemed equally uninterested in anything about her, and who also spoke not a word to her as the aircraft prepared for takeoff.

The plane taxied to the end of the runway and then shot forward as though fired from a gun, and after several moments of bone-crushing acceleration, soared into the sky, its wings leaving streaks of white in their wake. Jet retrieved the file from her backpack and read it again, ensuring that she was familiar with every aspect of it by the time she landed.

The trip would take two and a half hours, and after she was done with the file, she slid it into a burn bag that had been thoughtfully left on the seat beside her for her use, and reclined the seat. The hostess approached and offered her juice and her choice of breakfasts, which she declined, her stomach tense and the thought of a prepackaged meal unappealing. She spent the rest of the flight with her eyes closed, snatching what sleep she could before her adventure began in earnest.

Jet was awakened by the pilot, whose face bore a worried expression.

"There's a problem," he said. "Tripoli airport is closed down."

"Closed? Why?"

"Security problems. Some sort of terrorism alert. Not many details, but they're diverting all commercial arrivals."

Jet thought for a moment. "Commercial. What about private?"

"There won't be any ground crew or immigration officials."

"Never much cared for them anyway. Can you get me on the ground? I can take it from there."

"We can probably land, but it's questionable whether you'll be able to clear customs."

"Don't worry about that. Have you filed a manifest with the airport?"

"Nobody's asked for one yet."

"I'm not here."

The pilot considered the situation for a moment. "It'll be light out soon after we touch down."

"I'll only need a few minutes. Do you have enough fuel to turn around quickly?"

"Of course. No way we'd fly into Libya without enough to get home."

The pilot returned to his station and the plane began a gradual descent, banking over the Mediterranean as it approached the airport. When the jet's wheels hit the tarmac, it almost immediately began to decelerate, and Jet was pushed forward against her seatbelt as the little plane slowed.

The sky was painted lavender and tangerine by the rising sun as the plane rolled along the runway, and Jet could see the wreckage of damaged jets destroyed during the battle of Tripoli Airport still sitting where they'd been bombed, there being nobody equipped or motivated to move them. A few commercial airliners were parked at the main terminal, whose lights were burning bright in the predawn, and Jet pushed herself to her feet and moved to the cockpit door to instruct the pilots on where to go.

She swung it open and eyed the surroundings through the small windshield. "There are some private jets over at the far end. Get ready to swing the fuselage door open, and I'll jump out. Then turn around and take off. You can tell air traffic control that you didn't realize the strip was closed, and apologize for the mistake. Not like they can do much about it once you're in the air."

"I hope you know what you're doing," the pilot said.

"Me too."

The jet slowed near what passed for the private aviation terminal, and the hostess released the door, and the stairs swung toward the ground. The pilot came to a full stop, and Jet dropped to the tarmac; and then the plane was in motion again as the steps retracted and the aircraft swung around in a wide circle to return to the runway. She glanced around and then ran toward the other jets in a crouch, grateful for the remaining darkness but aware that she'd be fully exposed within a matter of minutes.

Truck headlights materialized from the opposite end of the airport and approached the private terminal as Jet's plane began its takeoff run with a roar. She continued toward the darkened building and ducked along the side as the truck arrived. It did a slow patrol of the private aircraft area, engine barely idling, a single orange roof emergency light strobing the planes. Jet flattened herself against the wall as the lights swept past the building, and then she was moving again, running along a strip of pavement that led to the passenger terminal, her robe flapping around her, the drone of the truck engine behind her goading her forward.

A voice called out from the darkness ahead of her in Arabic. "You. Stop!"

Jet cursed under her breath and slowed. A uniformed guard brandishing an assault rifle stepped from the shadows. "What are you doing here? Running like that?"

"I got lost. I walked here from the main road, but I'm all turned around. I don't want to miss my flight."

"All the flights have been canceled today."

"What? How am I supposed to get home?"

"Not my problem. The airlines can handle that. The passenger terminal is the big building."

"It sounds like I don't have to rush now."

The man looked her up and down. "Where were you flying to?"

Jet didn't hesitate. "Egypt. Cairo."

The guard shook his head. "Well, good luck. And don't run. You're lucky I didn't shoot you."

Jet dipped her head passively and averted her eyes so she wouldn't seem too aggressive or otherwise memorable. "Thank you. I was so afraid I would miss my flight."

The guard grunted and returned to his station, and Jet resumed her trek to the terminal, now walking at a normal pace, an anonymous woman caught in an aviation purgatory in a city under siege.

CHAPTER 9

Jet approached the terminal and found herself in a throng of travelers and scattered groups there to welcome new arrivals, all agitated by the news that flights had been canceled until further notice and everyone was effectively stranded. A host of voices echoed from the crowd, and Jet easily made out Italian, English, and German in addition to the pervasive Arabic.

She was to meet a Mossad head of station named Leo inside the terminal, and would know him by his red windbreaker if she didn't recognize him from the photograph in her briefing file. When she shouldered through the oversized doors, it was pandemonium, the high ceilings amplifying the worried and outraged voices of passengers who were being told by airline personnel that they were stuck in Tripoli until flights resumed. Clumps of business travelers stood in confused huddles, trying to make sense of conflicting instructions and announcements by personnel who were clearly being tasked with dealing with a situation far above their pay grade.

Jet felt a pang of empathy for an airline employee in a rumpled uniform at one of the counters, who was trying to maintain a dispassionate tone as she patiently explained for probably the hundredth time that the aviation authority had temporarily shut down traffic to the airport, both arriving and departing, and that she expected to have more information shortly but couldn't do anything other than wait along with the travelers. A pair of tall Germans were peppering her with questions in accented English, their Teutonic annoyance manifesting as cynical invective and demands for answers she obviously couldn't provide.

Jet looked around the hundreds of people in the building, searching for the telltale red windbreaker, which would have probably been a fine differentiator under normal circumstances, but was inadequate in a packed terminal filled with every color vestment in the rainbow. She wished the director had thought to equip her with a cell phone, but the plan had been for Leo to provide any necessary gear, in order to keep questions to a minimum when she passed through customs and immigration.

She spotted the back of a red jacket on a dark-haired man who could have been Leo, and pushed through a sea of passengers, only to reach him and see that he looked nothing like the photograph. Jet continued past him, eyes roaming over the mob, and saw another red top twenty meters away by one of the entryways. She edged past a line of local car hire agents pitching stranded passengers on their wares, and made her way toward the man, who was turned away from her, watching the scene outside through the heavy glass doors.

He stiffened as she neared, and she saw that he'd spotted her in the reflection and so was unsurprised when she put her hand on his shoulder. He turned with a fatigued smile, and crow's feet crinkled in the corners of his eyes.

"Omar! It's been too long," Jet said, using the introductory phrase from the file.

"The years have been kinder to you than to me," he replied, finishing the sequence. He briefly surveyed the chaos surrounding them and cocked his head at the door. "Come on. I have a car."

Leo led her outside and guided her through the loiterers to a parking lot only a third full of vehicles, most of which appeared to be ready for the junkyard. Soldiers ringed the lot with Kalashnikovs, and as the sun broke over the horizon and warmed her skin, a sense of impending danger was palpable.

They stopped in front of a rusting Renault sedan that was at least forty years old, and she eyed it dubiously.

"So what happened?" she asked.

"Terrorist attack on the naval base. Some kind of nerve agent. That's all I know. Nobody's claimed responsibility, and any of a dozen groups could be behind it. But what makes this worse than the usual mayhem is the bioweapon. Usually we see bombs. This is way different. Hundreds dead, although the reports have been shut down by the government." He paused. "That number comes from one of my sources."

He unlocked ,the door for her and she shrugged off the straps of her backpack and climbed into the car. He rounded the fender and slid behind the wheel, and the engine cranked over with a reluctant shudder before settling into an uneasy idle that sounded like monkeys banging on a pan with hammers.

"This thing will actually get us where we need to go?" Jet asked.

"Hope so. It's one of the better rides in town."

He slammed the shifter into gear and they rolled off in a cloud of blue exhaust, past a trio of soldiers by the entrance, who stared at them impassively. Once on the road, Leo filled her in on the current situation, where you didn't travel anywhere in town by night, and there were armed militias controlling whole swaths of the outer city, where the districts were outside of government control.

"Which isn't saying much," he continued. "What passes for a government here would make a Moroccan carpet merchant blush. You've never seen levels of corruption like this, and there's no end to it. Whenever one group gets tossed out, the new one is even worse." He cleared his throat. "But that's not your problem. We got a coded communication from Salma a few hours ago. She'll be in Sebha by this evening."

"Sebha? That's in the middle of the desert, isn't it?"

Leo nodded. "A ten-hour drive, assuming you aren't stopped by one of the militias."

"How are we supposed to extract her from there?"

"She'll rendezvous with you tomorrow. You'll recognize her by a headscarf she'll be wearing. You'll be dressed as a Berber woman, unless you prefer what you've got on."

"Why Berber?"

"Less chance of being assaulted. The Berber tribes are more feared the deeper into the desert you go."

Jet frowned. "What's the situation in Sebha like?"

"Imagine as bad as you can get, and it's worse. There are active slave markets, and half the population is armed at all times. There's no rule of law, and there are three different warlords who squabble over territory, massacring anyone unlucky enough to be in the line of fire when they're fighting it out." He gave her a sidelong glance. "Not a pleasant place. You won't want to spend too much time there."

"How am I supposed to get all the way to Sebha if the roads are death traps? I'm guessing you've thought that through?"

"Absolutely. We got you wheels."

"Wheels," she repeated. "To travel…over six hundred kilometers of war zone?"

"Headquarters indicated you were the best. They had high confidence you could get to Sebha and help with the extraction."

"For which there's a plan, I presume?"

"They're working on it. Depends on what you encounter. There's an airport there, although it's not in use. But they might be able to get a helicopter in, depending on how locked down airspace is over the next few days."

"A helicopter from where?"

He kept his eyes on the road. "To be determined. Might also be able to get a light jet in from Greece."

"Then why not simply fly me to Sebha?"

"We can't get any intel on what you'd be walking into. For all we know, one of the militias would blow you out of the sky, or take the plane out on the runway. That's part of the reason you need to go overland – to scope it out and report back on your preferred extraction method, based on what you see."

"Sounds like I have to come up with the plan," she stated flatly.

"No. Headquarters will come up with something. But the situation's…fluid. They need eyes and ears on the ground."

Jet was silent for a few moments. "Where are we going now?"

"To a warehouse on the south side of Tripoli. I've got a kit for you. Weapons. Comm gear. Your wheels."

"You keep saying wheels. What kind?"

His grin widened. "Motorcycle."

"I'm supposed to ride halfway across the country on a bike?"

"It's the only way you'll be nimble enough to avoid any roadblocks. And it's not just any motorcycle. One of my cousins builds special-purpose dirt bikes for the rich. This thing will do a hundred over sand. You've never seen anything like it."

"And that's not going to attract attention?"

"Negative. It looks like a junker. Plenty of locals, including women, ride bikes. Best way to deal with traffic in a place like Tripoli."

She sighed heavily. "I'm going to ride all day through some of the harshest desert on the planet? Where do I refuel, for starters?"

"Qaryat has gas. As of the last reports from truckers, it's relatively safe. That's about two hundred seventy-five kilometers from here. But you'll also carry some fuel. It's got a five-hundred-kilometer range, depending on how hard you run it."

She did a quick calculation. "Not enough to get to Sebha."

"Which is where the extra fuel will come in. But if you can, fill up in Qaryat. It isn't clear what you'll encounter in Sebha."

She looked out the window at the scrubby bushes and concrete rubble. "This just keeps getting better and better."

"You might want to lie low until late afternoon and ride in the evening and at night. Your choice. The heat's going to be extreme during the day, but your headlight will give you away at night."

"I don't suppose you have any NV gear."

"Sorry."

The warehouse was in a wretched area that would have given the worst of Brazil or Venezuela a run for their money. Leo waved to a man with an AK who was guarding the entrance to the yard, and the man tossed him a half-hearted salute before continuing his observation of the street. Another gunman, also with an AK-47, was waiting inside the walls and came to meet the car as it rolled to a halt in front of a wide steel door. He pulled it open, and Leo escorted Jet around pallets of crates to where a motorcycle was sitting beside two forklifts.

Leo patted the seat with a smile. "I told you. It looks like it's at the end of its life, but the engine's new, and so's the tranny and the suspension. We painted it to look half corroded, but it's a land rocket and can take you anywhere you want to go. 500cc motor bored out to 650, trick gearing, knobbies for sand, the works."

He showed her the saddlebags, which contained a 9mm Beretta pistol and three spare magazines, a Heckler & Koch MP7A1 submachine gun with four spares, a survival knife, a sat phone, six liters of water, a box of energy bars, and two robes in different colors. He tossed her a roll of dollars, which she caught without blinking.

"Ten thousand dollars," he said. "It's the preferred currency here. Nobody trusts the local dinars. Worse than worthless, although the exchange rate is close to one to one outside Tripoli. I put a few hundred dinars in there, just in case."

"Thanks. How about a map?"

"There's only one road to Sebha. No map required. Head south."

Jet removed her dark blue abaya and donned a beige one from the saddlebags, and Leo handed her an off-road helmet. "You going to do it daytime or night?"

"I don't like the idea of announcing my approach with a headlight, so I'll suffer through the heat."

Leo depressed the starter button and the engine purred to life. "You do know how to ride one, right?"

"I'll figure it out. Awfully quiet, isn't it?"

"We modified the muffler. Figured you didn't want your motor giving you away in the desert."

"Any idea where I need to start worrying about ambushes and roadblocks?"

He shook his head. "The truckers say that some days, the road's wide open. Others, there'll be one or two random stops where they have to pay a 'toll.' No rhyme or reason to it. But I'd stay alert from the time you leave the city limits. With the attack, we may be entering a new phase – someone making a major move."

"Good to know." She slipped on the helmet, lifted her robe, and wedged the pistol into the waistband of her pants along with the spare mags in her various pockets. She retrieved the knife and flicked it open, examined the blade, and pocketed it before climbing on the motorcycle. "Anything else?"

"You've got three liters of gas in the left saddlebag, which you'll know from the color. Other than that, good luck. My number's programmed into your sat phone. Speed dial one."

"Super." She toed the bike into gear and eased it forward to the roll-up door. Leo raised it by pulling on a chain, and Jet twisted the throttle. The motorcycle lunged forward like an attack dog, and then she was streaking from the warehouse, throwing a cloud of dust behind her on the deserted street.

CHAPTER 10

La Línea de la Concepción, Spain

A white cargo van crept along the Calle Canarias, its exhaust a low rumble. Traffic was sparse at the early hour, with the dimpled surface of the Alboran Sea to the southwest gilded by the rising sun.

The driver was a heavyset man with a dark complexion and a kinky black beard; the passenger was gaunt, with a goatee and a NY Yankees baseball cap perched sideways atop his head. Music that sounded like a cat being stuffed into a wood chipper howled from the radio over the motor's steady drone, and the driver tapped sausage-like fingers on the steering wheel to the polyrhythmic beat as he drove.

"What's that?" the passenger asked, squinting at the road ahead. They were nearing the marina, where a car was half over the curb, its hood crumpled.

"Looks like a drunk hit a tree," the driver said with a laugh.

"It probably jumped in front of him."

A siren whooped behind the van, and the driver's gaze flitted to the side mirror, where the flashing lights of a police car were coloring the rear doors. The driver's expression darkened and he reached for the volume control to turn down the music. "Trouble."

The passenger raised a two-way to his lips. "Just stay cool," he warned. "Our paperwork's in order."

"Why are they pulling us over?" a voice demanded from the tinny speaker.

"Don't know. Maybe bored. Routine check. Nothing to worry about."

The driver braked and pulled over just ahead of the wreck. The police car stopped behind it, and a pair of uniformed cops got out and approached either side of the van, hands on their holstered pistols. The one on the driver's side stopped by the window and regarded the driver with a sour expression.

"Driver's license and registration," he demanded in Spanish.

"Sure. But what did I do?"

"Papers," the cop repeated gruffly.

"Okay. Here," the driver said, pulling his wallet from his rear pocket while the cop watched, and handing him his license. "Registration's in the glove compartment," he said to the passenger, who opened the hatch to retrieve it.

"Nice and easy," the other cop said from the passenger window.

"Right," the passenger said.

"You have any ID?" the first cop asked the passenger.

"Um, yeah. But why? I'm not driving."

"Let's see it."

The passenger froze. "Which do you want first? My license or the registration?"

"Registration. Keep your hands where we can see them."

The passenger passed the registration to the driver, who handed it to the cop on his side, and then withdrew his wallet from his back pocket and extracted a Spanish driver's license. He gave it to the officer, who joined his partner a few meters from the van. They had a brief discussion, and the first cop called in their ID on his radio while the second stood with his arms crossed, staring at the van expectantly.

When they returned to the vehicle, their faces were hard. "Right," the first said. "Out of the car. Both of you."

"What have we done, officer?" the driver asked.

"Shut off the engine and step out of the vehicle. We're checking your documents."

The driver and passenger exchanged a glance and opened their doors and climbed out. The first cop pointed to a spot by the parked patrol car. "Sit over there."

"Why are we being detained?" the driver demanded. "Everything's in order. We weren't speeding. What is this?"

"Routine check. I'm sure you'll be on your way shortly."

The second cop radioed in the crashed car behind them and walked over to examine the wreckage while his partner watched the two from beside the van. The driver's side door was unlocked and the car was empty. The cop shook his head in weary resignation. "Driver bolted. Might be stolen."

"Nothing back on it yet?"

"Nope. Must be slow at headquarters."

A second squad car swung around the corner and parked behind the first. Two more officers stepped from the cruiser just as the first cop's radio squawked and a female voice spoke in rapid-fire Spanish. The cops listened intently and then looked to the driver and passenger before approaching them.

"The docs checked out. What are you doing on the road at this hour?"

"Driving, obviously," the driver said. "Making deliveries."

"What's in the back of the van?" the second cop asked.

"Dry goods for the boats. We're on our way—"

The driver's explanation was interrupted by the rear door of the van bursting open and Tariq opening fire with an FN P90 bullpup submachine gun. The first rounds caught the two closest officers in the torso and sent them sprawling backward as the driver and passenger dove for cover. A stray round caught the driver in the throat, sending a wash of blood onto the asphalt, and a ricochet wounded the passenger in the shoulder as Tariq emptied the fifty-round magazine, cutting down the remaining pair of cops while they scrambled to free their pistols.

The bolt snapped open, the magazine spent, and Tariq leapt from the van and sprinted to where the first cops lay. He unholstered one of their pistols and fired a round point-blank into the nearest man's head, and then did the same to the second, who was gasping for breath. He then strode to the other fallen cops and executed them the same way before returning to where the driver and passenger were sprawled on the pavement.

The driver was obviously dead, lying in a small lake of blood, but the passenger was still breathing, though his chest was laboring and his face drawn from pain. His eyes widened when Tariq raised the pistol, and he held out his hands defensively and managed a "No!"

The sharp crack of the handgun echoed down the street, and then Tariq was running as fast as he could, making for the marina half a kilometer away. He reached it in minutes and raced down to the docks, where an eighteen-meter commercial fishing scow was waiting with its lone diesel engine burbling. Tariq jammed the pistol into his waistband at the small of his back and descended the gangplank to approach the boat. When he reached it, he called to the captain in the wheelhouse.

"Morning. I'm your passenger," he said.

"Heard shooting just now," the captain said.

"Did you? Probably a car backfiring. You ready to cast off?"

The captain nodded and called to the two deckhands. "Let's get underway. Untie and stow the lines."

Tariq stepped onto the rear deck and watched as the men quickly unfastened the dock lines and tossed them onto the deck before climbing aboard. The captain put the engine in gear and twisted the wheel while he pushed the throttle forward, and the heavy boat eased away from the dock and puttered toward the harbor mouth.

"How long will it take to get to Morocco?" Tariq asked.

"Two, two and a half hours. Should be smooth sailing. Weather's clear, with hardly any wind, so the crossing between Gibraltar and Ceuta should be an easy one."

"That's good. I get seasick."

"You can go below if it'll help."

Tariq shook his head. "No. I'll stay up here. The fresh air will do me good."

"Whatever you want." The captain glanced over his shoulder at his men and then back to Tariq. "You have the other half?"

Tariq pulled a wad of euros from his front pocket and handed it to the captain, who tossed it on the console beside the compass. "We'll be cruising at about twelve knots with the wind at our backs."

"Are there any patrol boats to worry about?"

He shook his head. "No. I guaranteed you safe passage. Nobody will stop us. They know the boat."

Tariq nodded. The captain had a nice sideline to fishing that included ferrying hashish and heroin from Morocco to Spain, as well as refugees who could afford his high fee. Business had been so good that it had been years since he'd actually tried to catch any fish, but he still maintained pretenses by keeping his nets in ready shape and going out multiple times per week with no destination or cargo in mind. The deckhands were cousins who shared in the spoils, and between them they made a handsome living in one of the oldest businesses on earth, even after paying off the coast guard and customs inspectors in both ports.

"Good to hear," Tariq said, and turned to gaze skyward, where four pelicans had taken up position a dozen yards off the stern. The birds hovered in the light breeze as though kites being towed by the boat, riding the updrafts with stoic calm. Tariq's lips tugged into a tight smile, and he sighed contentedly. "Nice day for a boat ride, I'll give you that."

"We've got coffee or tea down below, if you want some. And rum if you favor something stronger."

"No. I'm good. Thanks," Tariq said, and walked to the rear deck. He sat against a pile of heavy line, the sun on his face, the salt air and pungent aroma of diesel a kind of ambrosia after years locked in a cell. The pistol jabbed the base of his spine, and he shifted to get comfortable, there being more than enough time to decide whether to kill the captain and his cousins when they were close to their destination or allow them to live as reward for carrying out their task.

CHAPTER 11

Al Aziziyah, Libya

The sun was a fireball in the azure sky when Jet rode through Al Aziziyah, whose dubious claim to fame was as the hottest place on earth. She was keenly aware of eyes tracking her as she coasted along the highway that was also the main boulevard through the town. Her odometer told her that the entire stretch was no more than a kilometer of buildings that looked like they were in the final stages of collapse, many with windows blown out and bullet holes pocking the façades from battles waged as the Qaddafi regime had folded and the insurgency had gained traction.

Jet's overall impression was beige. Beige buildings, beige sand, beige soil in the agricultural plots that she'd ridden through from Tripoli, the road coated with beige dust, beige rubble lining the highway from where structures had collapsed during fighting that had never truly come to an end.

Men with assault rifles sat in front of shops, sipping tea at rickety tables, their guns leaning beside them, weapons of war as essential a part of their wardrobes as their sandals. The cars that lined the road made the rolling wrecks of Tripoli look like luxury vehicles, and she instinctively gave the throttle a wrench to speed her past the town center. The only undamaged buildings in sight were the minarets of the local mosques.

Once through the town, she followed the road signs to the continuation of the highway south, the name Sabha, the local spelling of Sebha, figuring prominently above graffiti and bullet holes in the metal slabs. As the sad string of dwellings that comprised the outlying portion of Al Aziziyah flew past, she inhaled a draft of arid swelter off the desert, which spread before her as far as she could see in an endless reach of beige sand dunes, some as large as hills. She squinted as she picked up speed, her lips dry and the vibration from the motorcycle's handlebars throbbing up her arms, the motor as steady as a metronome beneath her.

An hour out, she pulled off the road and checked her fuel against the distance she'd covered. She topped off the tank with one of the bottles of reddish gasoline and pitched it aside, and after a breakfast of desiccated granola bar washed down with a liter of coffee-temperature water, climbed on the bike and resumed her ride, scanning the road ahead for any sign of danger.

Jet rode through the town of Garyan, which looked like it had been even more devastated by fighting than Al Aziziyah, and didn't stop even though there was a lone gas station with a line of cars sitting in front of it. She hadn't burned enough fuel that it would be worth the risk to draw attention to herself, and opted instead to speed through as fast as possible, leaving the inhospitable berg behind as she headed into the unknown.

She passed only a few trucks headed north, their stacks belching black exhaust like steel dragons, most empty on the return trip from carrying goods to the desert. Several of the drivers sounded their horns or waved as she rode by, which Jet interpreted as friendly, the camaraderie of the road especially strong when at any moment the next traveler might be the one to save your life if you were stranded.

The heat rose as the sun climbed overhead, with the wind that had been at least moderately refreshing in the morning now the relentless blast of a furnace. She stopped again, drained another bottle of water, and removed her pants and shirt, taking care to fold and stow them in the saddlebags before continuing, willing to risk her lower legs being sunburned where the robe failed to cover them versus broiling alive. She debated for several moments and then wrapped her belt around her waist and slipped the pistol into it, unwilling to surrender the weapon to a saddlebag, where she'd be unable to reach it in a hurry.

The terrain changed from endless miles of desert to beige hills, the sides carved into canyons by the wind and long-forgotten flooding. Jet banked the motorcycle along the curves, slowing as they grew tighter, wary of ambush – on the long, straight road it would be easy to see a raiding party from far away, but here gunmen could lie in wait without being spotted until it was too late. She didn't think it was likely that anyone would be out in the blistering heat, but she didn't want to discover the hard way that she'd underestimated the desperation of a local force and ride smack into them. She downshifted and forced herself to be prudent, fighting her instinct to speed along as fast as she dared.

When she finally reached Qaryat, it turned out to be a scattering of mud-brick homes, a few roadside stalls, and a gutted building with a pair of men sitting beside an ancient Datsun pickup with a large plastic container in the bed. A sign announced gas for sale, and Jet coasted to a stop at the truck and bargained for them to fill her tank, which they did with a hose after considerable dickering, the exchange seeming to amuse them no end. Jet figured they didn't see many women on motorcycles riding through the wasteland, so she could appreciate their good humor, but if anything, the heat was more oppressive standing in the shade with no breeze than on the bike, and she was back in the saddle and racing away moments after handing them a fistful of dinars and restarting the engine.

After Qaryat she was truly in the desert, with nothing but sand to the horizons. The road ahead was distorted by shimmering heat waves that looked to her tearing eyes like ghostly dancing snakes. She blinked away the mirage and concentrated on maintaining her focus, aware that in the heat her dehydrated mind would be prone to wander.

As she approached the desert town of Ash Shwayrif, she spotted a truck stopped in the middle of the highway ahead, with what looked like ants swarming around it. She braked to a near stop and the chatter of an assault rifle reached her – the weapon was unlikely to hit her at the range, but it sent a reliable signal that the boring part of her trip had come to an abrupt end. Jet wheeled onto the sand to her right and gunned the throttle, sending a spray into the air behind her as she put Leo's claims about the bike to the test. After fifty meters she spotted a trail through the dunes that ran perpendicular to electric towers carrying power from north to south, and she pointed the handlebars at the strip as she fought to maintain stability on the uncertain terrain.

She reached the trail and the motorcycle stabilized as she found herself on a dirt road that had been forged by the power company to access the towers. The engine roared as she picked up speed, and she was soon flying along the flat surface, a beige cloud behind her the only evidence of her passage. Jet continued to accelerate until she was clocking a hundred and twenty kilometers per hour. She leaned forward over the handlebars to reduce wind drag, her breathing raw inside the helmet. The track was almost completely straight, and she continued at the insane speed until it doglegged toward the road almost ten kilometers from where she'd left it, Ash Shwayrif at least six kilometers back, and hopefully the militia that had blocked the road well behind.

Once on pavement again, she increased her speed to two hundred kilometers. There were long stretches that were straight as an arrow, and she urged the bike forward until thirty minutes had passed and any pursuit would have been abandoned.

She stopped and chugged another liter of water, her throat dry as a tumbleweed, and after a few moments' break to stretch, she was back on the motorcycle and racing south, her robe flapping at her legs like angry birds, the only sound the hum of the engine and the thrum of the knobby tires on the cracked ribbon of pavement.

CHAPTER 12

Sebha, Libya

An overloaded 1950s-era school bus creaked to a stop on the outskirts of Sebha, and three passengers got off in the darkness. The senile vehicle shuddered off toward the town center, and the two men, laborers from the fields southeast of the city, tottered off in the direction of a collection of shanties, leaving Salma standing alone in the moonlight with nothing but the cold desert wind for company.

She looked around and began trudging down the road, her feet blistered and hurting from her marathon walk from Al Ghurayfah. She'd covered almost forty kilometers the first night in bitter cold before collapsing and sleeping well off the road in a field for half the day, after which she'd continued walking in the late afternoon and through most of the second night. Her feet had been about to give out on the third evening when she'd finally been able to flag down the bus, which carried workers to the agricultural plots, and for the first time in almost three days was able to cover the remaining distance to Sebha on something other than foot.

Salma had gotten word of her plight to Mossad headquarters and was confident that they would do whatever it took to extract her. Now all she needed to do was avoid discovery should Mounir have figured out her deception, and she would soon be home in Israel, more than ready to start a new life that didn't involve sleeping with an animal she despised. Tomorrow she would go to the main square wearing the distinctive headscarf she'd saved for just such an occasion, and her ordeal would be over.

She rounded a corner and spotted a flickering sign for a hotel. Salma limped toward it before pausing to consider the exterior, which was as shabby as anything still standing. Plaster was peeling from the walls, all the windows had bars on them, and the steps into the reception area were crumbling. She debated continuing into town, but her feet disagreed with that option, so she approached the entryway and pressed a black button at the side.

Two minutes went by, and the desiccated front door opened and a short man with the face of a troll stared out at her. "Yes?"

"I'm looking for a room."

The man's eyes roved over her and settled on her face. "Just you?"

"Yes. Only for a couple of days. My husband will be joining me shortly."

"Well, you're in luck. We have something available."

"Not too expensive, I hope."

The man pursed his lips and inhaled as though considering a great philosophical dilemma. "Twenty dinars. In advance."

"Per night?" Salma asked, pretending the number was insane.

"For two. You said your husband was coming. Will you want to stay longer?"

"We'll have to see." She stretched her neck to look past him at the interior, where a woman was watching over his shoulder from behind a counter. "I suppose it will have to do. Do you have running water?"

"Of course. And if you want, you can have a room with its own bathroom for…twenty-five."

"That would be best."

"Then come in. Please. Meet my wife, Fatima, who handles the money. She doesn't trust me. Can't say I blame her."

He stepped aside to allow Salma into the tiny lobby, which was barely big enough to accommodate a sofa and counter. Fatima looked her up and down as she entered and nodded in greeting. "Welcome. You want a room?"

The owner pushed past Salma. "Yes, Fatima. For two nights. One of the ground-floor rooms with bath. Twenty-five dinars for the stay."

Fatima frowned at the number. "That's quite a discount you worked out, young lady." Fatima held out her hand expectantly.

Salma unfolded several bills and placed them on the counter until she'd produced the required sum. Fatima snatched them up and eyed them as though wary of counterfeits, and then turned to where keys hung from a rack. "One C. A lovely room. Quiet. We don't have many guests at the moment, so you're in luck." She hesitated. "What's your name, for the register?"

"Ben Shaban. Sakina Milad Ben Shaban."

"Do you have ID?"

"I…I'm afraid I don't. My wallet was stolen last week."

The owner made a sympathetic face. "How awful. Don't worry. It's only a formality. We can skip it, can't we, Fatima?"

"Whatever you say, Umar," Fatima muttered, looking away as she held out the key.

"I'll show you to the room," Umar said, taking the key. "Any other luggage?" he asked, eyeing Salma's backpack.

"No. Just this. I can carry it myself."

"Very well. This way."

Umar led Salma down a hall off the lobby to the third door and swung it open with a flourish. He switched on the lights, revealing a whitewashed room with a sagging bed on one wall, a nightstand made from clay beside it, and a dilapidated overhead fan. "Here you go," he said, handing her the key. "If you need anything, we'll be in the lobby for another couple of hours."

"I'm sure this will be fine," Salma said, her eyes drawn to where a roach was scuttling beneath the bed.

"Well, then. Enjoy your stay," he said, his gaze lingering on her lithe form evident beneath her robe, which was clinging to her.

"Thanks."

Umar pulled the door closed behind him, and Salma frowned at the cheap deadbolt that hung broken on the doorframe. She twisted the lock on the doorknob and tried it, and the knob didn't turn, so she tossed the key on the bed and sat on the edge to remove her shoes. Skin came off with them, and she winced at the pain and then pulled the robe over her head and tugged on the fan cord. It began orbiting with a hum, and air began circulating in the dank room. She backed toward the bathroom to switch on the light, and then killed the one in the room as she took in the tiny shower and cracked basin.

"Better than nothing," she muttered, and twisted the shower lever. A gush of warm rusty water spurted from the head, but it turned clear after twenty seconds or so. A tiny sliver of soap was stuck to the ledge in the corner of the shower, and when the water was bearable, she stepped beneath the stream and set to scrubbing the road dust from her, beginning with her hair and finishing with her brutalized feet, which burned like fire from the soap.

Salma shut off the water, dried herself with the paper-thin towel, and then padded gingerly to the room and ferreted through her backpack for a pair of cotton sweats and a long-sleeved blouse; the cold in the desert night was bitter at this time of year in spite of the day's extreme heat. She pulled her things on and then tossed the bag to the side and lay down.

The mattress was hard as a rock, in keeping with the rest of the lodging, but felt like heaven after long days sleeping on dirt. Her feet throbbed with each beat of her heart, and the fan was doing little but making noise, but it was still better than anything she'd experienced since leaving Mounir's squalid home, which was only slightly better than the hotel.

She burrowed under the blankets and eventually drifted off to sleep, and dreamed of running across burning sand, chased by some massive dark form just out of view, but whose stink was as rank as a sewage trench. Her heart rate spiked and she moaned in her sleep as it transformed into a gargoyle with Mounir's face, its claws clutching at her as she barely kept out of reach.

Salma tossed and turned on the hard slab, each nightmare worse than the last, all involving pursuit by malevolent forces too powerful to escape.

She jolted awake and looked around the room in a panic, and then fatigue leached the fright from her and her eyes closed. Soon she was back on the broiling sand, Mounir now a pterodactyl screeching hate as it dove at her, jaws snapping with razor-sharp teeth as she twisted out of its reach.

The sound of a poorly muffled engine outside the inn jarred her from her uneasy sleep, and the pounding of running boots on the street drifted from the window. She tried to orient herself and remember where she was, and after a few seconds she realized she was far from Mounir, safe in a hotel where nobody knew she was staying. Whatever was happening outside had nothing to do with her and was probably just more of the endless brutality that she'd witnessed since taking this cursed assignment.

A rush of footsteps from the hall made her rethink her assessment, and Salma was struggling to throw off the blankets and rise when the door burst open, kicked in by a tall figure. She screamed in shock as four men entered, two with rope and a cloth sack, the others with rifles hanging from shoulder slings. They rushed toward the bed in the dim moonlight from the window, and Salma shrank from the intruders, instinctively pulling the blanket up to her chin.

"Wha–" she cried, but the nearest intruder slapped her so hard her head whipped against the wall behind her. Dazed, she tried to fight back, but the men were too strong. One stuffed a dirty rag in her mouth, and the other pulled the sack over her head and bound her wrists. The sour stench of dried perspiration from her attacker overpowered her, and she tried to kick at him, but a punch to her solar plexus knocked the wind from her. She gagged inside the sack as the men hog-tied her, working in silence, the only sound the rasp of their breathing and the rhythmic squeak of the fan. When they finished binding her, she felt herself hoisted over a shoulder, facedown, and carried down the hall, her moans of protest and panic unanswered. One of the men called out in the lobby, and Umar answered with something unintelligible before Fatima hushed him, and then they were moving again, Salma bouncing against her kidnapper like a sack of potatoes.

Out on the street, the man tossed her roughly into the bed of a truck, and she nearly blacked out when her temple slammed against metal. She winced at the starburst of pain that lanced through her head and gasped as she tried to regain her breath. Her abductors piled in with her, and then they were bouncing down the street, the men laughing and arguing over who would get her belongings as they rummaged through her backpack. The truck made a hard turn and bounced over a pothole, and the last thing Salma registered before a blow from the bed knocked her unconscious was that she was soon going to wish she'd never been born.

CHAPTER 13

Sebha, Libya

Jet arrived in Sebha as dawn was breaking, having grabbed what sleep she could in one of the orchards north of town, well out of sight of the road. The wind chill was only somewhat abated by the multiple layers of her pants and shirt and all three of her robes. She'd been somewhat prepared for the extremes in temperature between daytime and night from her prior mission in Libya, but even so, the cold had been shocking after baking in unbearable heat until the sun had set.

Now, dressed in her Berber garb, with her pants and shirt on beneath the flowing abaya, and sporting a hijab with the ends wrapped around to cover much of her face, she walked from where she'd concealed the motorcycle inside the remnants of a bombed-out shack to the mosque where Salma had set the rendezvous, where she would find somewhere to sit and watch for Salma to appear at ten a.m. She shivered as she made her way along a dusty street to the mosque and pulled her abaya closer around her, although already the cold was transitioning into warmth that she knew would soon turn into blistering heat.

Men on their way to work in the fields eyed her as she passed, but the traditional clothing had its intended effect, and they quickly averted their eyes when she caught them looking. A beggar with a diseased stump of a leg sitting in a pool of filth with a swarm of flies for company extended a clawed hand to her and displayed a toothless smile, and she tossed him a coin, the flush of infection on his face and bloodshot eyes telling her that he wasn't long for this world. Two boys, perhaps five or six, kicked an empty can between them in a simulated soccer match before school, and Jet smiled behind her veil at the innocence of youth.

Most of the men she saw carried rifles, and she felt little comfort at the pistol in her waistband or the knife in her pocket. Sebha had an atmosphere of active danger more palpable than in most of the worst places she'd been sent, and there was a definite sense that anything could happen at any moment, a feeling of potential catastrophic violence lurking behind every corner. Jet chewed her lower lip as she walked, wondering what it must be like to live like the natives did, at the whim of whatever the local Islamic militants decided constituted justice or the criminal gangs that infested the country felt like doling out.

The briefing file had mentioned the lawless state of the city and had pointed to several open-air slave markets, where for the price of a few liters of gas, migrants were bought and sold to labor in the nearby fields until they died. Looking around her surroundings, Jet had no problem believing the dossier's most dire warnings, and again wondered to herself at her foolhardiness in taking an assignment that put her in such peril. With no backup and no plan other than to find Salma and call in a distressed extraction request, she was flying blind in a territory where the slightest miscalculation could be lethal, and she reminded herself to stay hyper-alert for threats as the heat rose to stupefying levels.

She rounded a corner and spied the minaret and dome of the mosque. Looking around, Jet spotted a tiny café across the street, where two men were seated at a small circular table on the sidewalk, sipping tea, seemingly unconcerned by the clouds of dust being thrown up by passing cars. In no hurry and with hours to kill, she ambled around the area by the mosque, looking for any other promising places to linger. Finding nothing, she continued past the mosque into a commercial district, the shops all closed but a few restaurants open, serving breakfast to early bird customers.

Jet entered one and took a seat at a table near the rear, and a man approached with a menu and asked what she wanted to drink. Jet ordered tea and, after skimming the menu, selected the shakshouka – eggs poached in a tomato and spice base that was also a popular dish in Israel. When it arrived with her tea, she sampled a bite and smiled to herself; the chef wasn't going to win any awards, but it was a reasonable rendition, given her low expectations.

She took her time eating and sipped the tea, and at 8:30 paid the tab and retraced her steps to the mosque. There were more pedestrians on the sidewalks now, but the heat was already increasing, and the café across the street had put out large umbrellas to provide some slim relief in the shade. The men were gone and the area seemed empty, so she crossed to the café and sat outside, where she would have a full view of the mosque entry. If all went well, shortly after Salma appeared at ten, they would be riding away to safety, or at least less danger.

Jet's tea was unremarkable, and as the sun continued its arc across the turquoise sky, she adjusted her robe to allow better ventilation, the pistol uncomfortable but welcome at her hip. Her gaze roamed over the few figures who were braving the blaze, mostly men with headdresses, some with guns. That was a constant in modern Libya since the fall of the regime, although before the weapons had rarely been seen in public, and certainly not as a standard wardrobe item.

At ten, Jet's pulse quickened as a pair of women made their way across the square, but neither wore the headscarf Salma had described, so she remained seated. More pedestrians appeared from around a corner and walked slowly to where a street vendor had set up a cart and was selling tagine – a Berber stew that had originated in neighboring Morocco but migrated west over generations. Jet studied all of the women in the vicinity of the mosque, but as minutes turned into an hour, Salma failed to show.

Jet resisted the urge to check her watch too often, but by 11:40 it was obvious that Salma wouldn't be putting in an appearance as promised. She paid for her tea and considered her options, which amounted to either hanging around the mosque during the worst heat of the day or attempting to find a decent hotel, preferably with air conditioning, and contacting Leo for further instructions. She wound up opting for the hotel, reasoning that it was possible that Salma had contacted headquarters again with word of some complication that had kept her from the meet, and asked the proprietor of the café what the best place in town was.

The woman pointed at a multistory edifice perhaps a kilometer away and named it, but looked at Jet doubtfully. "That's as nice as anything built before the crisis, but expensive. And it caters to a different kind of clientele than many of the other hotels here."

"Is it safe and clean?"

"I've heard it's very nice. But I've never been inside."

A cry went up from the mosque, announcing dhuhr, the noon prayer time. Jet thanked the woman and set off in the direction of the hotel, moving slowly to avoid overheating. The already bad neighborhood deteriorated as she walked, and after several blocks she registered a trio of men following her and an old station wagon matching their pace on the street.

She ducked around a corner into a narrow alley as the sound of the car's engine increased, and drew her pistol. Jet thumbed off the safety and shrank back into an indentation between two buildings, a round in the chamber, her hand steady.

The sound of running footsteps reached her, and the three men appeared at the alley mouth. Their clothes were sweat-stained and soiled, and two carried rifles, with the third wielding a knife. Their eyes widened when they saw Jet peering over the pistol at them, and the one with the knife muttered something to the others, his stare never leaving Jet's face.

"No point trying to fight us off with that popgun. Put it down and we won't hurt you," he growled.

Jet didn't say anything as she adjusted her aim to the man's crotch. Her lips curled into a smile. "A 9mm Parabellum in your manhood will slow you down, I'd think. You have five seconds before I start shooting. And yes...I know how to use it." She paused as her statement registered. "You two with the rifles, set them down by your sides and back off, or your friend will get the first round and you'll get the next ten."

The car pulled up, blocking the alley, and Jet's gaze flickered to the driver, who was staring at the scene in surprise. The momentary distraction was enough to embolden one of the gunmen to raise his rifle, and Jet pivoted instantly and shot him in the thigh, shattering the bone. He emitted a bloodcurdling scream and went down clutching his leg, the rifle clattering to the pavement. His partner with the rifle hesitated.

"You have two choices," Jet said. "You can drag your man there to the car and get out of here, or you can all die. I'll make the decision for you if you don't, although I'd prefer not to waste ammo on the likes of you."

The man with the knife looked to his companion with an unsure expression. The remaining gunman looked down at his wounded companion, blood spreading on his robe as he whimpered in pain, and slowly knelt and placed the Kalashnikov on the ground.

"You're going to regret this," he hissed.

"Really?" she countered. "So maybe I should just shoot you both for good measure?"

That didn't elicit a response, so she motioned with the gun. "Get him out of here. If I see any of you again, I'll put a bullet in your skulls before you can blink."

"You have no idea who you're crossing," the knife wielder warned.

"Want to make it three dead men instead of one who'll never walk again? I'm out of patience."

The thugs hauled the wounded man to the car. The driver glowered at Jet, who stood framed in the alley, pistol leveled at him while slowly approaching to keep everyone in range as the men dragged the screaming man away. They got him into the back seat and the driver roared away, leaving Jet standing in the alley, beads of sweat on her forehead.

She collected the AKs and carried them to a garbage can, ejected the magazines, and dumped the guns. She stopped a block away and dropped the magazines into another trash container, and then continued to the hotel at a moderate pace, her mind churning over who had just attacked her and why. Best she could figure was either slave traders or human organ traffickers, both of which were well known to operate in the lawless reaches south of Tripoli. Whichever the case, she'd just made new enemies and could add them to the list of threats while stuck in Sebha. She'd have to be even more careful if she was instructed to retry the rendezvous the following day, because there was a fair chance that they'd be back to avenge both their fallen man and their honor.

"Just great," she whispered to herself as the hotel swam into view, and she blinked away the perspiration and adjusted her scarf over her face in preparation for dealing with yet more Islamic fundamentalist nonsense there.

CHAPTER 14

Moscow, Russia

An anthracite Mercedes limousine rolled into an industrial park on the outskirts of Moscow, its powerful motor a growl. The limo was sandwiched between a pair of fully armored G-500 SUVs with windows tinted so dark they seemed opaque. All vehicles were equipped with run-flat tires, and the lead and tail trucks were filled with bodyguards and enough firepower to stop a battalion. The vehicles stopped in front of a three-story building with a mirrored glass façade, and the bodyguards spilled from the trucks to form a protective cordon for the limousine passengers.

The limo door opened and Nicolai Karev stepped from the car, followed immediately by his security chief, Sergei. The pair hurried into the building, where they were met by a thin man in an expensive black suit. He ushered them past a series of cubicles and into a computer lab, where three men were waiting in front of a wall of monitors, the tallest with his arms crossed and relaxed, the other two obviously ill at ease.

"Andrei, we're here. What do you have for us?" Sergei asked the tall man, his manner typically brusque.

"Mr. Karev, Sergei, glad you could make it, and thank you for taking the time to come out," Andrei said.

"No problem," Nicolai said. "Why are we here?"

"Grigor? Would you do the honors?" Andrei asked.

One of the nervous pair leaned forward and keyed in a command, and a grainy image of a woman appeared on the monitors.

"We were able to recover these from the CCTV cameras on the boat. It was difficult, given the level of damage they'd sustained, which is why it took so long. Apologies, but this would have been impossible to do five years ago. It's only recently—"

Sergei cut him off. "Right. So this is the woman?" he asked Nicolai.

Nicolai's brow furrowed. "Absolutely. I'd recognize her anywhere." He paused. "Although she's more stunning in person. Her eyes are luminous and green. Truly remarkable. The image doesn't capture that."

Sergei cleared his throat. "Now what?"

"We're going to manipulate the footage and get the best grabs we can, and then we'll enhance them and process them with a new proprietary algorithm we've developed that will create digital fingerprints from the images."

"Which we can then send to whomever we need to?" Sergei asked.

"Yes. Although, as you're aware, we have the most extensive database of CCTV images from around the world. Anything we don't have stored, we can get." Andrei paused. "I presume from our discussions that you want to find her."

"That's right," Nikolai said.

"Any way to narrow down where we'll be looking? It's a big planet."

Nikolai looked to Sergei, who frowned.

"Yes, actually. We believe that she's affiliated with, or works for, the Mossad. So we'd start with Israel."

Andrei's eyebrows arched. "Mossad? That introduces an additional level of difficulty. They're the best, and they don't exactly publish lists of their employees. You're sure?"

Nicolai nodded. "Absolutely. I was held by them. They were Mossad, all right. I recognized the accent. Although oddly, she didn't have one…" He hesitated. "Regardless of how good they are, everybody has to live somewhere. This digital fingerprint – can you use it to compare it to traffic cam footage? Airport CCTV? That sort of thing?"

"That's the entire point of it. Eventually we'll be able to do a cross-section match exactly like we now do with fingerprints. Although the technology is still in its infancy."

Grigor cleared his throat. "Correct. But we can run the characteristics through an AI front end, which will match based on hundreds of data points, and then–"

Nicolai turned to Sergei. "I'm sure it's fascinating. How long will it take?"

Andrei stepped forward. "We can have the images ready in a day or so. Then it's a matter of running the last month or two's data from the camera archives through the…through the computers…and waiting for matches to appear. It's an enormous amount of data, but with our systems…shouldn't be too long."

"That doesn't sound like a hard answer."

"Correct. It's unknowable. But we'll throw everything we have at it."

Sergei nodded. "Do so. Round the clock. Anything you need, anything at all, call me and I'll clear it with Nicolai."

"Very well. And budget?"

Nicolai eyed Jet's image and a muscle in his jaw flexed. He leveled a hard stare at the computer jockeys. "Whatever it takes."

Andrei looked at Sergei, who nodded again. "This is our top priority," Sergei said. "Make it yours."

"Of course."

"I want daily reports."

"Then you'll have them."

"Very well," Nicolai said, and looked to Sergei. "Are we done here?"

"Yes."

Nicolai spun and marched back toward the lab doors, leaving Sergei to catch up. When they were gone, Andrei exhaled heavily and turned to Grigor. "You heard the man. No limits. And when he says none, he really means it."

Andrei followed Nicolai and Sergei out, leaving Grigor and his partner staring at the screens.

"How'd you like to have that guy pissed off at you?" his partner asked.

"I don't know. The way he was talking about her, I'm not sure anger's his primary motivator."

"Really?"

"Call it a hunch. He sounds conflicted. Like he either wants to kill her or spend a month in a dacha with her."

"Maybe both. The order would be the only negotiating point."

They laughed nervously, and Grigor stabbed the monitors off and turned to his companion. "Call a staff meeting in fifteen. This is going to be a bear. You and I know that. But it will also be a jackpot if we can pull it off."

His companion squared his shoulders. "Will do."

Grigor felt for a package of cigarettes in his breast pocket and grinned. "This could make our careers. Remember that. And remember it could ruin us if we fail."

"We won't."

CHAPTER 15

Sebha, Libya

Salma awoke shivering, her arms and legs bruised from the bindings that had been used to transport her the prior night, her head splitting from the multiple blows. She blinked away tears of pain, resolved to deal with whatever came her way, and looked around the room.

She had been sleeping on a cold stone floor, the chamber barren except for a bucket to use as a toilet. The door was made of heavy wood of the type found in older homes, and locked from the outside, she presumed. All of her things had been taken, and she'd been left with only her makeshift pajamas. Her captors had at least had the presence of mind to untie her before they left her in the room, so she could move her fingers and toes, but only with considerable discomfort.

She forced herself to sit up and nearly passed out again from waves of nausea. The room seemed to tilt like the deck of a ship in rough seas, and she focused on controlling her breathing, fearful that she would hyperventilate, which would only make matters worse. A coil of anxiety burned in her gut, almost as severely as the blisters and raw patches on her feet, and if she didn't get a grip on herself, she could tell that she would slip into despair.

How had Mounir found her? That was the question that she'd repeated in her head over and over much of the night. She'd left no trail to follow. It seemed impossible that he could have, but her captivity was inarguable proof that he had.

Once the dizziness had passed, she examined the room in the morning light streaming through grimy panes of glass high up the wall. She was in a small chamber, perhaps three meters by four, with limestone floors and walls of local brick. She debated screaming, but what good would it do her? It would only announce to her captors that she was conscious, and would no doubt annoy them. There was no way anyone was coming to help, she knew. Not in Sebha, where every imaginable atrocity was a daily occurrence. The city's reputation was horrendous even in a country that was in complete breakdown.

She took a deep breath and struggled to stand, her feet protesting the weight, her head throbbing like the worst migraine she'd ever experienced. When she was upright, she hobbled to the door and tried the handle without hope. It turned, but the door didn't budge. As she'd surmised, it was bolted from the outside.

Salma swore under her breath but refused to give in to the urge to cry. She'd signed up for the most dangerous duty the Mossad had, and this was an unenviable part of the job description. She remembered her training, the sessions of meditation where she'd been taught to escape in her mind to a place where nobody could hurt her, and she slid down the wall and sat again, this time with resolve.

She closed her eyes and focused more intensely on her breathing, inhaling through her nose and exhaling from her mouth, allowing her lungs to completely empty before drawing the next breath as she repeated a mantra until she had drifted away from her body, disassociated from the lump of neurons and muscles and bones that was only her physical manifestation.

Time seemed to stretch, and she stopped the breathing exercise, going deeper and deeper into the recesses of her mind until she felt a sensation of complete emptiness and tranquility that lasted until the scrape of the bolt on the door pulled her from her state and she opened her eyes.

Two of the men from the previous night entered the room and leered at her, followed by a third man, who held a pistol in his right hand and an iPhone in his left. His sneer was more alarming than those of the other men; his eyes were cold, his nose hooked, and the deep lines in his face signaled unbridled cruelty. A scar traced across one cheekbone to his left ear, which was mangled as though it had been chewed by a dog, and when he spoke, his voice was devoid of pity.

"She is a pretty one, isn't she?" he asked no one in particular. The men laughed.

"I want her first," one of them said, grabbing his groin in an obscene display lest Salma miss his meaning.

"You had the last one," his companion complained. "It's my turn."

"What do you care? Not like you've ever been particular. She's not a goat, like you're used to."

"I don't know. I think she'll fetch a better price untouched," the first man said.

"Come on, Amir. She's no virgin. Nobody will complain if she's slightly more used than yesterday." The man smacked his lips and looked to Salma. "Isn't that right, princess?"

She resisted the urge to spit in his face, processing with dawning awareness that as bad as her situation was, she hadn't been taken prisoner by Mounir after all. No, these were slave traders, who sold women as sex slaves to deviants from all over Africa and the Middle East, as well as to bordellos in Tripoli and Morocco. Which meant there was the possibility of not only survival, but escape, given her skills. All she would have to do was bide her time.

She looked up at Amir, gauging what it would take to drive his nasal cartilage into his brain before the other two could react, but in her weakened state she didn't trust herself to move quickly enough. If she miscalculated, his pistol would catch her in the stomach, and she'd die the most excruciating death imaginable, bleeding out on the floor as the men watched and, worse, probably raped her as she died.

Amir seemed to sense the inner debate and stepped back. "Remove her clothes. I want to get some photos of the merchandise. She's fair skinned, so she'll bring a decent price, even if she's older than some."

The two men moved to Salma, but she didn't resist, knowing that all it would bring would be further abuse and possibly incapacitation she couldn't recover from. As it was, other than her head and feet, she was exhausted and bruised and possibly concussed, but she wasn't out of the game entirely. But that could change if one of them slammed her head against the stone floor or broke her jaw with a punch.

They pulled her pants and shirt off, and Amir whistled as they stepped away. "A nice price indeed," he said, his expression ugly. "Lie still or I'll break your ribs. Like that. Arms to the side, legs a little spread."

The snick of the iPhone memorialized her humiliation, but she felt nothing, no protestation of ego, no insult or offended dignity. This was only her body, nothing more. Not her essence. They couldn't reach that to hurt the true her. That was out of reach.

When Amir was done with the photos, he handed his weapon to the nearest man and proceeded to invasively examine her with filthy fingers. He licked his lips as he did so, and for the first time his eyes were animated.

He eventually stood and nodded. "I have a number of clients who would be interested, I think. You're right that she's no virgin, but I've sold worse, and she's still got a few serviceable years in her. No children, so that's a plus. All in all, a good find," he pronounced.

"So…we don't get her?" the shorter of the two thugs complained.

"Not unless we can't find a buyer. No point in throwing away money, is there?"

The men tossed her clothes onto her prone form and left. When the bolt had locked back into place, she slowly pulled them on, willing away the memory of Amir's molestation, telling herself that after years with Mounir, nothing could be worse. Once clothed, she considered her predicament – on the plus side, she hadn't been gang-raped or mutilated…yet. On the minus side…everything else.

She curled into a ball, knees to her chest, and a single tear trickled from her eye and splashed on the dusty floor. She'd come so close to escaping the nightmare of the last three years, and it had all collapsed on her in the home stretch. Worse, now the data that she'd copied from Mounir – details of a plan so evil that her quick reading of it while copying the contents of the files had sent chills through her –

would never make it to her superiors, and the fate of her country would be permanently altered for the worse. The unfairness of it was like acid in her throat, and she coughed reflexively, the spasm sending waves of pain through her skull.

Several hours went by, how many exactly she didn't know, and the room transformed from a freezer to an oven. Sweat coursed down her spine as she sat motionless, the air leaden and sweltering, her breathing exercise now painful with each scorching inhalation.

The door opened at one point and a grimy hand rolled a two-liter bottle of water into the room before it slammed shut again, leaving her to slow cook as the temperature climbed beyond unbearable. She meted out the water after gulping down half, stretching it the best she could, aware that she was losing minerals she would need if she was going to be physically able to handle an escape attempt should the opportunity present itself.

Her only advantage was the slave traders' lack of knowledge of her background and training. They assumed she was a typical civilian woman, and wouldn't be expecting a seasoned, capable fighter, capable of doing extreme damage, even if unarmed, in the blink of an eye. As long as she continued to react like a broken husk instead of a calculating operative probing for weaknesses, she had an edge. Maybe not much of one, but the thought heartened her a little.

The light from the window was fading when the door opened again, and this time it was Amir and a swarthy tall man wearing western clothes – jeans and a polo jersey with salt stains beneath each arm.

"Stand up," Amir ordered.

Salma rose unsteadily and the man looked at her like he was examining a horse.

"Turn around. Slowly."

She did.

"Lift your arms and do it again. Arms to the side," the man said.

Salma complied and almost fell down from another wave of dizziness. If either Amir or the customer noticed, they didn't care, because they began negotiating a price for her while she stood six feet away, Amir extolling imaginary virtues with increasingly implausible claims, the man snorting in derision, listing real and imagined flaws down to the size and shape of her nipples from the photographs and a mole on one buttock. Salma kept her expression slack and didn't react when they finally agreed on a price for her that amounted to three thousand dollars – the customer arguing that he could get younger and less spoiled for only a little more, Amir pointing out her creamy skin and athletic build.

The entire exchange sickened her, but it also meant that she would have a chance to escape, and she fought to remain outwardly calm at the idea. Amir was about to shake his hand when his iPhone beeped, signaling a text had come in. He read it and his eyes widened, and then he turned to the man and shook his head.

"I'm sorry, my friend. I can't go through with the deal. My apologies for wasting your time," he said.

"What! You agreed to my price. You can't renege now!"

"I'm truly sorry, but I have no choice. Come. I'll explain outside, where it's cooler and doesn't smell like dung."

"No. I don't want an explanation. I want my property. I bought her, as agreed."

"True. But you haven't paid. And we haven't shaken. So she isn't yours. Again, a thousand pardons, but I can't sell her."

"If you go back on this, you'll have to contend with me tomorrow, Amir. You know my reputation. I won't be cheated."

"I haven't taken a dinar from you, so you haven't been cheated out of anything but a few minutes of your time. Which I'll compensate you for with the first choice of our next batch, I swear. You'll have your pick for a giveaway price."

"Someone bid more than me? Is that it, you little conniver?"

"Of course not. I would never dishonor you like that." Amir glanced at Salma. "Come. Let's talk where there's a breeze. I'll explain everything."

The customer reluctantly agreed, and the door closed again, leaving Salma to her thoughts. Her shoulders slumped and she felt herself tremble in spite of the stifle, completely mentally exhausted.

She'd been so close to getting out of this prison, and at the last moment fate had intruded? It seemed impossible, but it was true.

Salma sat back down, her stomach growling from having not eaten for over twenty-four hours, and began her breathing again, eyes closed, refusing to speculate on what had soured the deal but determined to be ready for whatever came next, no matter how demanding.

CHAPTER 16

Tripoli, Libya

A dilapidated fishing boat sat in the middle of the harbor, loaded to the bursting point with refugees, the hull down well below the water line. Small wind waves lapped at the wooden planks as the packed humanity above, who had paid top dollar for the chance to get out of Libya, fidgeted, there being no space above decks or below to do much else.

What little moonlight there was seeped through the marine layer that blanketed the port, rendering the area dark except for ghostly shadows, the hulls of the far larger cargo ships jutting from the surface like islands. The fishing boat's single diesel engine burbled quietly as the captain idled near the breakwater opening, waiting for a dinghy that approached with two men aboard.

When it reached the boat, the rubber watercraft bumped to a stop alongside the stern, and the captain and one of his deckhands pushed through the crowd of refugees.

"Got your message," the captain said to the men in the dinghy.

"We've got a delivery for you."

The captain shook his head. "We're full up this trip, boys. Can it wait?"

"Afraid not. But don't worry. Only weighs maybe twenty kilos." The man patted a rough cloth sack in the dinghy.

"What's in it?"

"Nothing you have to worry about getting caught with. Why? You expecting to be stopped?"

"Shouldn't. Everyone's been paid off."

"Then why the twenty questions?"

The captain frowned. "I want to understand the risks I'm taking."

"There is no risk. We've done enough business together you should know that by now." The man tossed the captain a brick of euros. "That'll make it worth more than your while. Just pass it off at the other end and there's another half for you."

The captain sighed and nodded. "All right. Hand it up, and I'll find someplace to fit it."

The man hoisted the sack and the deckhand grabbed it and pulled it aboard. It clanked when it struck the stern, and the captain stared at it suspiciously.

"Wasn't expecting that. Most of your stuff is…softer."

"I told you – don't worry."

"If you say so."

The dinghy pushed off from the stern, and the captain looked to the deckhand. "Let's get it below and have a look."

"There's no place to put it."

"Worst case, we can stick it in the bilge. Sounds like it's metal, so we don't have to worry about it getting wet."

They elbowed their way through the refugees and descended into the cabin area, which was also packed with human cargo, the air almost unbreathable from body odor. Even the captain and crew cabins were occupied to capacity, the profit from each refugee they could carry far greater than the discomfort of a few days sleeping in the pilothouse. Besides, the crew were being paid handsomely for the hardship and had gladly signed up for the voyages, where they could make in a week what they might in a month or more of ordinary work.

They swung open the engine room hatch and ducked through, and the deckhand turned on the single overhead light and held the sack out for the captain to inspect. He took it and peered inside, shook his head, and looked around.

"We should be able to fit it there," he said, and laid it in the bilge near the engine.

"Might roll around in heavy seas."

"Won't hurt it, I shouldn't think."

They returned to the companionway and pulled the hatch closed behind them, and then made their way up to the cockpit, which was sealed off from the rest of the ship and had a tiny latrine and a single bunk in addition to the wheelhouse and the charting table. The captain and crew would dine on dry goods and drink bottled water the entire trip to Italy, and so wouldn't have to leave except to check on engine fluid levels and ensure nobody had clogged up the head below in the cabin area.

The refugees would eat whatever they'd been able to bring, and would drink metallic-tasting water from the tanks, which were only half full in order to compensate for the weight of the overloaded boat. Even though the craft had been designed to haul dozens of tons of fish, the captain was pressing his luck, and the craft was beyond its limits with hundreds aboard – something he was normally loath to do, but with the weather calling for relatively calm seas, a risk he was willing to take.

The trip would be over in forty-eight hours, assuming the boat could maintain a steady nine knots, which was more than doable, even given the crowded conditions. The hull topped out at just shy of twelve, but at nine would combine optimal fuel consumption with speed. If he had to go slower, he could, although conditions on board would deteriorate with each additional hour. After having completed countless runs, he knew the drill.

"All right. Let's get underway," he said to his three crewmen, and put the transmission in gear and eased the throttle toward the windshield. The boat hardly seemed to react at first, and then it slowly inched forward and pushed through the water until it was steaming along at jogging speed, rolling slightly from the swell as it rounded the breakwater into the Mediterranean Sea.

Nobody from the Libyan navy or its laughable coast guard would stop him, he knew, and certainly not after the terrorist attack that had shut down half the port. Nobody on the Tripoli side had the slightest interest in interfering with the refugee trade, which was a major source of income for many who worked the waterfront, including many of the families of the navy personnel. That, and the captain routinely paid off the coast guard, which ignored his nocturnal runs, he being one of the more reputable of the human traffickers – those in the nearby port of Zuwara were notorious for loading unseaworthy boats to the gills with the desperate, who paid anywhere from $750 to $2500 for a trip to Italy but would largely never make it. The strategy of the Zuwara smugglers was to pay several migrants who understood the basics of boating to guide the boats to international waters and then allow them to run out of fuel in the hopes of being rescued by one of the groups that patrolled the area to attempt to prevent senseless death that had become a staple of the trade.

The captain's craft was in far better condition and more sturdily built than the open-air craft favored by traffickers who had no intentions of attempting to make it to Italy. It had started its life as a real working boat in Tunisia, and unlike the disposable craft that the captain's competitors bought for single trips, was worth considerably more for its integrity and equipment. His operation charged top dollar for passage, but even so, with competition fierce and prices down, he was forced to overcrowd the craft past its safe limits.

The boat passed several other Libyan fishing vessels hauling in their nets, and the captain hailed each on the radio and exchanged pleasantries and gossip, exactly as he would under normal circumstances. The swell was three feet, and the boat so heavily loaded that it barely rocked, merely rising up and down on the inky water as the captain pointed the bow north, the breeze so light there was no whitewater at all as far as the eye could see. He switched on an old Furuno radar unit and set the range to twelve miles, and then turned to his crewmen. "I'll do first watch with Ramzan here. You two get some rest. We'll wake you when it's your turn."

"Okay, boss," one of them said, and turned to the other. "I'll take the bunk for the first half. You get it the second."

"Fair enough."

The men moved to the rear of the cockpit, and the captain climbed onto the seat while Ramzan took a seat at the charting table. The trip under the best of circumstances was a boring one, the worst that could happen a freak storm, which at that time of year was highly unlikely, or an interception by the Italian navy that wasn't going to happen given how underfunded and overtasked it was. That, and the captain had paid off the Italian coast guard to look the other way as he entered Italian waters, and busy itself with other more important matters than three hundred and eighty miserable souls willing to risk drowning at sea in exchange for a better life.

CHAPTER 17

Sebha, Libya

Jet traversed the dusty streets from her hotel, taking a different route to the mosque than the previous day in case her attackers had decided to return better prepared. Beneath her robe she had not only the pistol but the MP7A1 and several spare magazines in the event she got cornered and needed more firepower. She doubted that would happen – Jet was expert at reading character, and the men who'd tried to abduct her had been cowards – but sometimes cowards were emboldened in larger groups, and she didn't want to underestimate them.

She'd spoken with Leo, who had assured her that they hadn't heard from Salma and advised her to try the rendezvous again today in case Salma had been unaccountably delayed, and Jet resigned herself to spending another few hours baking by the mosque, waiting for the woman to show. Jet had no opinion one way or another – it was as good or as bad a plan as any she could come up with – but she wasn't optimistic. If an operative missed a key meet, there were few positive reasons.

Jet's hotel was adequate, nothing more, but well-guarded and fortified against attack, which meant that she could actually sleep without keeping one eye open. Even so, she'd gotten only marginal rest, and her eyes burned and she found herself yawning periodically on the way to the mosque, following two other pedestrians going in the same direction for a modicum of security in numbers.

When she arrived, it was the identical scene as the prior day, the sidewalk café empty and her table waiting. She took the same seat and the owner greeted her with a smile, which Jet returned as she ordered tea, her eyes already scanning the area for Salma, as well as any miscreants. Seeing nothing obvious, she settled in after checking her watch to confirm that she still had forty minutes before 10:00 rolled around again. The tea arrived and Jet handed the man a ten-dinar note, telling him to keep the change. That earned another smile and a curious look. Berbers weren't known for effusive generosity or wealth, so by those standards, Jet was an anomaly.

She'd barely taken two sips when she spotted a woman carrying a basket, wearing a headscarf exactly like the one Leo had described. Jet watched her amble down the sidewalk, stopping to inspect goods being sold from the shade of doorways along the way, her body language relaxed. When she crossed over to the mosque, Jet choked down the rest of her cup and rose to follow her, glad that she'd decided to show up early again.

Jet didn't want to run to catch up, but she increased the length of her stride, puzzled by why Salma wouldn't have stuck to the program and waited by the mosque. Maybe she'd seen something dangerous that Jet had missed? Perhaps she was planning to swing back around when it was closer to ten? Jet didn't want to speculate, and put her effort into closing the distance between them without being obvious about it.

The woman turned a corner, and Jet speed-walked to it. The street she found herself facing was full of people, but none wearing the telltale headscarf. So where had she gone? And why had she disappeared?

Jet saw that the traffic was headed toward another side street, and she went with the flow, picking up her pace as she walked. At that street she rounded another corner and almost ran headlong into a crowd of people – mostly women in robes much like Salma's, shopping at the sidewalk stalls of an outdoor market. Jet blinked at the vision of hundreds of robed figures examining fruit and nuts and exchanging views on their quality, and squinted to try to locate the headscarf in the throng.

She felt a tugging at her robe and looked down to find an urchin pulling at it, a dirty palm uplifted, begging. One of the boy's eyes was swollen shut and crusted over, and Jet looked away as she felt for a coin. He was perhaps Hannah's age, but with no chance of anything but a hellish existence. Her fingers found one, but she released it and instead pulled out a five-dinar note and handed it to him. His good eye widened in surprised delight, and he squealed and ran off at top speed after a shouted *thank you*. In spite of the urgency of her chase, Jet smiled and felt a pang of regret at not giving him more.

Up ahead a flash of color drew her attention, and she spotted the headscarf stopped at one of the stalls. Jet edged past groups of intently shopping women until she reached the stall, and stopped beside her quarry to study her more closely.

It wasn't Salma.

Not even vaguely similar.

Jet exhaled in frustration and then reached for one of the dates the woman was inspecting. "What do you think?" Jet asked.

"I've seen better. And he's asking a fortune for them."

"Ah. Then best to keep looking."

"That's my plan."

Jet flashed her a friendly smile. "That's a gorgeous hijab. May I ask where you bought it?"

The woman's hands flew to her head. "This? Oh…thank you. I…I don't know where you could buy one, honestly. But it is beautiful, isn't it?"

"Yes, it is. Was it a gift?"

"Not at all. I actually found it at my work."

"Really? And where's that?"

"I'm a housekeeper at a small hotel not far from here. I do their laundry, that sort of thing. One of the guests must have forgotten it. It was under one of the beds."

"I would never have left that. It's really nice."

"I know. My lucky day someone was in a hurry. You'd be surprised at the things you find over time."

"What hotel do you work at? Would I have heard of it?"

"Oh, no. It doesn't really even have a name. It's over on the corner by the old bus depot." The woman named a street, and Jet pretended to understand the direction.

"Sure. That place. Do you like it?"

The woman tossed the date back, suddenly unsure about the discussion. "It's a job."

"Listen. I love that headscarf so much, I just have to have it. Would you sell it to me?"

The woman looked confused. "You want to buy it?"

Jet gave an embarrassed laugh. "Well, we are at a market. Bargains everywhere. Would you sell it? I'll give you a fair price, and you could buy another one right here."

"I…I wouldn't know what it's worth."

"How about fifty dinars?"

Shock washed over the woman's face. "Are you serious?"

Jet felt in her pocket for her Libyan money and pulled out a handful of bills. She counted out fifty and gave them to the housekeeper, who removed the scarf and snatched the bills away before Jet could come to her senses for agreeing to pay almost a week's salary for a strip of fabric.

"Thank you. Thank you so much! You've really made my day."

"And you made mine. I appreciate you parting with it. It's really lovely."

Jet left the market as quickly as she could, and after asking directions at a corner store, made for the hotel where the housekeeper worked. By the time she arrived, the sun was high in the sky, and she spent ten uncomfortable minutes surveying the edifice before entering and walking up to the woman at the counter.

"Hello," Jet said with a smile.

"May I help you?"

"Yes. I have a friend staying here. But I don't know what room."

The woman's eyes bored through Jet. "Male or female? We don't allow male guests to have female visitors."

"Very sensible," Jet agreed. "Female."

The woman's eyes flitted away. "We don't have any female guests at the moment."

"She was here a few nights ago. Does that help?"

"I don't know what you're talking about."

Jet held up the hijab. "Does this refresh your memory? I just bought it from your housekeeper, who found it in her room."

The woman's sharp intake of breath was audible. "Oh. Of course. Her. She left the next day. Only stayed one night."

"Which night was that?"

"Um, the night before last, I believe."

Jet held her stare. "Do you have a lot of female guests, that you're not sure?"

"I'm afraid I can't help you."

Jet could sense two things from the woman: fear, and that she was lying. Which meant that Salma hadn't checked out, or at least hadn't voluntarily. Jet decided that the situation favored the direct approach rather than a continued game of cat and mouse.

She removed the pistol from her waistband, pulled it free of her robe, and pointed it at the woman's head. "Tell me what happened to her. Now. Or I'll splatter your brains all over the wall."

The woman cringed, and the color drained from her face. "No…"

"Yes. You're lying. She didn't check out, did she? Yet your housekeeper thinks she did, and in such a hurry that she left some of her things. That leaves only a few possibilities, none of them good. But I want to hear it from you, not guess. Where is she?"

"I…I don't know. They took her. That's all I know."

"They? They who?"

The woman swallowed hard. "Slavers."

Jet nodded, as though she'd known all along. "See? That wasn't so hard. We're getting somewhere. What slavers, and how did they select her?"

"I had nothing to do with it. It was…it was my husband."

"I see. And where is he?"

"Out. I don't know where."

"What's your name?" Jet asked.

"My name? Fatima."

"Fatima, you have a tell when you lie. Do you know what a tell is?"

Fatima shook her head.

"It's a giveaway. An involuntary tic that only happens when you lie. I won't say what yours is, but it's there, and you're lying. Now, where's your husband?"

Fatima shivered. "He's in the back."

"Show me."

Fatima led Jet down a dark hall to a door and swung it open. Umar was sitting on a pile of rugs, watching a television in a stained T-shirt and shorts, his belly round as a watermelon. He leapt up as best he could at the sight of Jet and his wife, and then saw the gun.

"Hello. Your wife here was telling me about slavers that took my friend the other night, and I was thinking that you might want a chance to stay alive one more day by telling me everything you know about them."

"She…she what?" he sputtered.

"Here's how this is going to go. I badly want to shoot you, or maybe cut you into little pieces and make you eat them before I do. But I'll resist if you tell me who took my friend. I can already piece together that you got paid to tell them. So all I need to know now is who, and where I can find them. You lie to me and I'll indulge my impulse to butcher you like a hog, at which point you'll have begged me to believe you. Because you'll tell me either way."

"I have no idea what my wife told you. She's…she's never been right in the head. I have nothing to do with any slavers. I'm a poor man who runs a hotel. Please…"

Jet stepped past Fatima and slammed Umar in the side of the head with the gun butt before spinning and leveling it at Fatima again. He tumbled to the ground, and Jet glared at Fatima. "Go over there by your husband," she ordered.

Fatima did as instructed. "I had nothing to do with any of this."

"Maybe. Maybe not. But you're in this together, so you'll both pay the price."

Umar groaned from the floor and felt his skull. His hand came away with blood. Jet shifted the gun to him and exhaled impatiently.

"That was your one lie. Now you tell me the truth, or I'll start by shooting off body parts, and then switch to the knife. If you want to test me, I can start on your wife to prove the point."

"I didn't do—" Fatima protested.

"Shut up," Umar snarled.

"You know what?" Jet said to him, cocking the pistol hammer with her thumb. "I think I'll just shoot you first and then start asking questions."

Umar shrank from her. "No. All right. I'll tell you. The trader's name is Amir. He's one of the biggest in town."

"And where can Amir be found?"

"I…I'm not sure."

"But you know how to get in touch with him."

"No, I just recognized him."

Jet shook her head. "And here we were, doing so well. Which knee do you want to lose? Left or right?"

"I have a phone number. That's it."

"Give it to me."

"I have to get it. I don't have it memorized."

"Let's go together. All three of us."

Fatima helped Umar stand, and the couple walked to the reception area. Umar opened a blue notebook to the first page and read a number aloud. Jet repeated it and then crossed to where the phone sat on the counter and jerked the cord out of the wall. "Very good. Now here's how this is going to work. I'm going to leave. You're going to forget I was ever here. You're not going to call anyone or try to tell Amir about my visit. If you do, I, or someone like me, will be back, and we won't be here for information – we'll be here to silence you forever. Do you understand?"

Umar and Fatima both bobbed their heads in agreement. Jet studied them like insects and allowed the disgust to show on her face. "Like I said. I'd deeply love to kill both of you right now, but I don't want to alert the neighbors. But make it worth my while and I'll be back, and nothing on God's earth will stop me. Do you believe me?"

More nods.

"How much did they pay you?"

"Two hundred dinars."

"That's the price of both your lives. Remember that when you're tempted to betray me. Two hundred dinars is what you died for."

Jet turned, phone in her hand, and left, tamping down the anger in her stomach as she walked back to the hotel. She tossed the handset onto a rubbish pile on the way, and repeated the number in her head so she could have headquarters trace it to an address. She walked fast, now a woman on a mission, aware that now every hour that the slavers had Salma, she could be being subjected to the tortures of the damned.

Chapter 18

Southeast of Murzuq, Libya

A four-wheel-drive pickup with oversized all-terrain tires cut a beeline through massive sand dunes as it approached an encampment of thirty-five large tents with a variety of vehicles parked in the desert around them. The sun beat down on the scattering of shelters with brutal intensity, but on hearing the revs of the truck's engine, figures emerged from the tents, assault rifles in hand.

The truck neared and the men gathered to face it, and when it rolled to a stop in front of them, they raised their rifles overhead and cheered. Tariq threw open the passenger door and stepped from the vehicle, and the cheering intensified, along with several gunshots fired in celebration. Tariq waved at the gathering, and Mounir stepped forward with open arms. Tariq embraced him and patted him on the back before saying a few words to the men.

"Today marks a special day – a day of rejoicing. Our plans are finally coming to fruition after we delivered a devastating blow to the navy in Tripoli. Those forces are in disarray and ripe for a takeover. The government itself is running scared – the bureaucrats who have been stealing everything that isn't bolted down are unsure how to respond. We have deliberately remained silent about our responsibility for the attack, as well as our objectives, and will continue to do so until the time is right. All they know is that they face an adversary that can slaughter hundreds of them whenever it likes, and is willing to do so."

More cheering, and Tariq held up his hand for silence. A hush fell over the assembled men, and he smiled.

"Right now, the first boat is headed toward Italy, where our allies will deploy a canister of the agent to cause maximum damage. That will bring the battle to Europe, which has been insulated from the devastation its agents wreaked on our homeland and continue to wreak on our brothers in Palestine and Syria. It is but the first step. We will hit them where casualties will be maximized, which will make continued support of Israel so painful that it will find itself isolated…and with isolation, vulnerable. It is then that we will strike at the heart of the beast and rain vengeance down upon the heads of the infidels. Within weeks Israel will cease to be the darling of the West, and its citizens will scatter to the four winds like the cowards they are."

The cheering was deafening, and Tariq basked in the attention before offering another wave and moving to where Mounir was waiting by one of the largest tents.

"An exciting time, Tariq. You're a genius. Truly," Mounir said.

"It is nothing compared to what is to come," Tariq replied with a glance at the sky. "Let's get out of the sun, my brother. It was a long and hot drive, and I could use some refreshment."

"Of course. This way."

Mounir raised the tent flap and Tariq ducked inside, where it was surprisingly cool thanks to a thin insulated coating of thermal material. Mounir offered him water, tea, and a variety of nuts and dates. They feasted while seated on the carpets that Mounir had brought from his home when he'd come to the encampment that Tariq's most loyal followers in southern Libya had established a few kilometers south of the oasis town of Murzuq, an ancient enclave on the trading route to Rome from across the Sahara, situated at the northernmost extreme of the most inhospitable desert on the planet.

"Tell me about your wife, Mounir," Tariq said when they'd finished their meal.

"The situation is under control. She ran to Sebha, but we located her, and she's being held by slavers there. I planned to go and collect her once you'd arrived."

"Why did she run, Mounir?"

"I suspect that she was a plant who infiltrated us to spy on us. She left right after I received your package, and we're positive that she copied the contents and was taking them somewhere."

"Who is she working for?"

"I intend to beat it out of her. By the time I'm done flaying the skin off her, there will be no doubt that she has told us everything."

Tariq considered his answer in silence and sipped the tea Mounir had prepared on a kerosene burner that sat in a corner of the tent. When he finished his cup, he sighed and fixed Mounir with an intense stare. "How many years were you married to her, Mounir?"

"Three."

"And you never suspected?"

"No. She was a good wife, as those things go. But now I have to assume everything she told me, every gesture, every act, was a ruse to earn my trust."

"How much does she know?"

Mounir frowned. "We have to assume that she knows everything. She's met or seen most of our men at one time or another, and she has the plan. It is Allah's will that she reveal herself now and be taken captive in a city where we have influence."

"Yes," Tariq said, nodding. "Fortuitous indeed." He selected another date and popped it into his mouth, chewed it with relish, and then stood. "Come, my brother. Walk with me."

"Of course, Tariq."

They moved to the tent flap and Tariq paused. "Who else knows where she is?"

"Two of my most trusted men: Mahmoud and Abdu."

"Very good. I like them both."

"I knew you would approve."

They emerged from the tent, and Tariq put his arm over Mounir's shoulder as they strolled toward the truck. The heat rising from the sand was blistering. They were almost to the vehicle when Tariq plunged the curved blade of a jambiya dagger into Mounir's abdomen. Mounir screamed in shock as the steel sliced through his intestines, and when Tariq pulled it free, Mounir tumbled onto the sand as the men who were still outside stared in surprise.

Tariq held the dagger over his head and turned to them. "This man, Mounir, is like my brother. I loved him like one, and he was as close to me as anyone can be. But he failed me, and the price of failure must be paid. He trusted a woman who now jeopardizes everything we have worked for, and it is his failure to see her true nature that has cost him his life."

Tariq leaned down and sliced the razor-sharp edge of the blade across Mounir's neck, and bright crimson arterial spray sluiced from his carotid before ebbing to a slow pulse.

"There is no need for him to suffer in pain any longer. It gives me no pleasure to end his life here. Today I have cut out a cancer from my heart, and I suffer just as he does, the pain just as real." He looked at the men. "Move his body before the sun can damage it. Wash it and then give him a proper burial. I will take his tent. His name is never to be spoken in my presence or you'll meet the same fate. Today my brother died as a lesson to you all. Nothing is more important than our cause. Nothing. And those who fail me will suffer the same end. We are all of us expendable, and as such, we must safeguard our secrets with our lives."

Tariq waited for any comments. When nobody said a word, he grunted. "Where are Mahmoud and Abdu?"

"Over here, Tariq," Abdu called from near one of the tents.

"You have a vehicle?"

"Yes."

"I want you to go to Sebha and bring me his wife. Now."

The men looked doubtfully at the sky. "It's over two hundred kilometers. By the time we get there and back, it will be well after nightfall. We won't be able to find the camp in the dark."

"Then drive faster."

Abdu swallowed but nodded. The road, once they connected to it, was a cracked and pitted ribbon of asphalt well beyond its prime, and would be boiling late in the day after absorbing the afternoon sun. To drive any faster than forty or fifty kilometers was to risk a blowout or broken axle – the potholes and gaps in the pavement from a decade of no maintenance and heavy cargo trucks chewing it up were lethal in places, deep enough to park an ATV.

"We'll do the best we can."

Tariq scowled. "I have a handheld GPS in my truck. You can take it. I have the camp pinned as a waypoint. You'll be able to find your way back even at night, so better to be prudent than reckless."

"Of course, Tariq. We'll leave immediately."

"Good. And men? I want her in one piece and unharmed, am I clear? It is up to me to mete out punishment, and only after I get answers. Do you understand?"

Mahmoud gave a humorless smile. "Perfectly."

"You know who is holding her?"

"Yes. Moun…we were told. And given money to buy her."

"Then go. And ride with the wind."

CHAPTER 19

Sebha, Libya

Jet watched from the shadows as a trio of Jeeps arrived at the apartment building that headquarters had identified as the slave trader's home, based on the phone number she'd provided. A two-story affair that looked relatively modern and more expensive than the surrounding structures, the exterior paint was in good shape, blinding white and obviously recent, and the design more contemporary than most she'd seen in Sebha. Which figured. Buying and selling human beings had to pay better than most local vocations, or why go to the trouble?

The front vehicle held four men, the middle just the driver and a passenger, and the rear carried four more. Jet surmised it was Amir in the middle Jeep, coming home after a hard day's slave trading, based on the vehicle types – Amir owned a Jeep, according to the Libyan registration database the Mossad specialists had hacked into. Her only hurdle was that Leo had pinpointed the building from the phone company but not the apartment, and it was up to Jet to figure out which dwelling was his.

The Jeeps stopped in front of the building, and all of the men got out and entered the complex through a locked gate. They continued along a central walkway before taking the stairs to the second level. Jet resisted the urge to rush them and gun them down while they were out in the open, and instead waited until they stopped at the fourth apartment on the second floor, where the squat slaver opened the door and led everyone inside.

Now that she knew which unit was his, it was just a matter of patience until she made her move. Hopefully at least some of the bodyguards would leave for the sunset prayer or dinner, but if not, she would bring the MP7A1 into play and wipe the floor with them. She didn't really care whether she wounded the slaver or not. As long as he was alive long enough to tell her where he was keeping Salma, that would suffice, and then his usefulness would be at an end.

The sun set, and the call to maghrib, the sunset prayer, wailed from the minarets. Jet checked the time and fingered the trigger guard of the submachine gun, anxious to get to work now that the long hours of tracking and waiting were over. She was considering the best way into the complex when seven of the entourage emerged and returned to the two Jeeps, leaving Amir, his driver, and one guard in the apartment.

Once two of the Jeeps departed, she worked her way across the street to the iron front gate, but it didn't budge. She looked both ways down the sidewalk, adjusted the shoulder strap of the MP7A1, and pulled herself up and over the gate, her robe an impediment but not an insurmountable one.

Jet dropped to the ground and landed in a crouch, and then was a blur as she ran to the stairs, which she took two at a time. At the second level she continued to Amir's door, and after removing her headdress, she tucked it into a pocket. Switching the firing selector switch of the submachine gun to full auto, she knocked on the door and stepped back, the combat knife clutched in one hand by her side and the gun in the other, beneath the robe.

"Who is it?" a voice called from inside.

"I'm here to see Amir," she replied, tensing in preparation for what was to come.

After a brief pause, the door opened and a man peered out at her. Seeing only a woman standing on the landing, he opened it further, and then he was flying back, knocked aside by a powerful kick to the door that nearly knocked it off its hinges.

Jet was through and slashing with the knife before he hit the ground, and blood fountained from his throat as she sliced through to the spine. She continued in a whirl to where Amir and the driver were rearing back from a dining table, both reaching for their pistols.

Jet threw herself over the table and speared the driver through his right ear, driving the blade into his brain while leveling a kick at Amir that caught him in the chest and knocked him into the wall behind him.

She was on him before he could recover, and delivered two powerful strikes to the sides of his neck with her fists, leaving the knife in the driver's head as he sank to the ground. Amir moaned and slumped over, unconscious. Jet rose and tossed the bodyguard's guns across the room, and pulled the knife free and wiped the blade clean on the driver's robe. She then moved to the front door and closed it after glancing out on the landing to ensure no curious neighbors had come to see what had caused the commotion.

The bodyguard lay nearly decapitated by the entry, and she stepped over him and walked to the sink to rinse the blood off her sleeves and hands. When the water had faded from pink to clear, she dried her hands, moved to where Amir was still out cold, and slapped his face, hard.

He grunted and his eyes popped open. She showed him the gleaming blade of her knife and gave him a murderous smile.

"You must be Amir," she said. "How's the slave-trading business, Amir? Going well?"

He tried to focus on Jet's face, with obvious difficulty, and his breathing was a rasp. When he spoke, his voice was hoarse from the damage she'd inflicted on his throat. His Adam's apple bobbed four times before he managed a response. "What do you want?"

She turned the knife blade to better catch the light. "You have one of my friends. I want to know where."

He blinked rapidly in confusion. "I don't...who?"

Jet sighed, her exasperation evident. "The woman you took from the hotel. There can't be that many of them. Where is she?"

Amir cleared his throat and swallowed hard. "She's your friend?"

Jet shook her head. "I'm asking the questions, Amir. If you want to see tomorrow, you'll stick to answering them."

His eyes moved to the driver and then to his bodyguard before returning to Jet and the knife. "You...you killed my men."

She nodded. "Which should tell you that I'm more than willing to kill you if you don't cooperate. Now, what have you done with her, and where is she?"

Amir sneered and uttered a harsh laugh. "You're too late. They're already on their way to get her."

"Who?"

"Her husband."

She moved the needle-sharp point of the blade a centimeter from his eye. "Where are you holding her, Amir? You can tell me now, or tell me when you're blind. Doesn't much matter to me which. In fact, I hope you do put up a fight, understand?"

He shook his head once and closed his eyes. When he opened them, he glared at her with startling intensity. "You don't have a chance."

Jet shrugged and moved the knife even closer to his pupil. "I'm sure it's all hopeless. Now where is she? Final time, and then I start cutting."

Five minutes later, Jet was back outside, her robe billowing around her as she ran to where she'd left the motorcycle. Amir had reluctantly given her directions to his facility before the knife had ended his stay on the planet, and she was now racing the clock to get there before Mounir could.

She straddled the motorcycle, depressed the starter, and the motor roared to life. Jet toed it into gear and twisted the throttle, and then she was flying down the darkened street, a dark form on a fast bike, the only illumination her bouncing LED headlight and the faint red glow of the taillight.

CHAPTER 20

The building where Salma was being held was a simple single-story storage facility surrounded by a three-meter-high wall. The district was mostly industrial, with a smattering of homes nearby, the middle of the Libyan desert obviously not big on zoning. Jet killed the engine and swung off the bike, and debated how to best approach it in order to maintain the element of surprise.

The walls were scalable for her with her parkour skills, in spite of the intentions of the builder. The question was what surveillance might be in place. Amir had insisted that there were only two men guarding the enslaved overnight, but there was a limit to how much she was willing to trust his statements, and she'd decided to assume the worst.

Jet removed her billowing robe so she would have full mobility. She didn't require it any longer for a rendezvous, and even though the temperature was already dropping, she felt more comfortable in her black pants and shirt than the unwieldy cloak. She stuffed it into the saddlebag and checked the time, and then took off at a run toward the compound, zigzagging as she approached.

She didn't slow at the wall, but rather ran up it at a diagonal. The two large steps she managed were sufficient for her to be able to grab the top and pull herself up. She surveyed the interior grounds, which appeared empty, and then dropped from the wall and continued to the darkened main building.

Jet paused at the entrance. If she went in through the front, and the innkeeper had decided to risk death and called someone inside, she'd be walking into gunfire. But there was no alternative, other than to hope that her knocking gambit, which had worked at the apartment, would work inside a locked, walled complex that nobody should have been able to penetrate.

She circled the building, looking for a window that she could access, but all were either glass block near the roof, or had iron bars over them. Frustrated by the security, she crept to the rear exit and tried it. To her surprise, it opened, and she stepped into a darkened corridor with doors on both sides that stretched half the length of the building, the walls unplastered and constructed of local brick.

Jet inched along the hall and paused at the first door, eyeing the heavy steel bolt that barred it. She reached out and slid it open and pulled the door wide. Inside was a naked girl, no more than sixteen, huddled in a corner, her coffee-colored skin covered with bruises. The stench of human waste was overpowering, and Jet backed away from the doorway and whispered to her, "You're free to go out the rear door. Wait for a few minutes. How many of them are there?"

She didn't seem to understand Jet's Arabic, but Jet tried again. "Your captors. How many?"

"I…I don't know."

"Okay. I'm going to ask you to stay quiet, and when I call out to you, run for the gate. I'm going to leave it open. Understand?"

"They'll kill me if I run."

"The dead can't hurt you. They'll all be dead in five minutes."

She stared at Jet in disbelief. "Who…who are you?"

Jet's expression hardened. "Their worst nightmare."

She continued along the hall, throwing open the cells, which contained mainly women from sub-Saharan Africa, and repeated her instructions to each. All were so broken she had no doubt they wouldn't budge until she told them it was safe, and many probably still wouldn't dare move, fearing some unknown threat if they did. The cruelty of the situation broke Jet's heart, but she didn't have the luxury of doing any more than she was doing, and couldn't risk discovery by taking more time to help than she already had.

Jet reached the end of the hall but hadn't found Salma. She pressed her ear against the wooden door and heard music from the other side, nothing more. Jet swung the submachine gun up and then slowly twisted the heavy handle until it was open. She took two deep breaths to steel herself and then pulled it open an inch to look through, gun at the ready.

Only two men were visible, sitting on a sagging couch in front of a television, AK-47s leaning against the wall by the main door. They were engrossed in some TV program that was the source of the music, and Jet raised the gun and stepped through the door, her boots silent on the stone floor.

"Tonight's your lucky night," she said.

The men stared at her like she was a demon, and the closest one dove for the rifles. Jet fired a quick burst at him that stitched through his rib cage, and he fell short of the guns, blood pumping from the wounds. The second man sat motionless, his mouth an O of surprise, ears ringing from the suppressed fire in the enclosed room.

The wounded man's breath gurgled from the bullet holes, and ruby bubbles formed and popped with each labored exhalation. Jet moved to him and put a single round through his forehead, and then looked to the other man with murder in her eyes.

"Where's the woman you kidnapped from the hotel?" she hissed.

The man tried to form words, but failed the first attempt. When he finally managed, his voice was gravelly and uncertain. "She's...not here."

Jet aimed the submachine gun at his stomach. "Yes, she is. Amir told me."

He shook his head. "No. They came and took her."

"When?"

"Twenty, thirty minutes ago."

"Where are they taking her?"

The man spat at her. "Why should I tell you anything? You're just going to kill me."

"Do you want to die gut shot, or do you want me to leave a gun with you to finish yourself off? Gut shot takes many hours to die, and is excruciating. So do you want to keep your friend here company for hours before the two of you go to hell? Or have the means to end it painlessly?"

He thought about her words, and when he spoke again, his voice was heavy with defeat. "They…they're headed south on the road to Murzuq."

"Where's that?"

"Two hundred kilometers."

"What kind of vehicle?"

"White pickup."

She eyed him. "Where are the keys for the front gate?"

He glanced over at the square table by the window. A key ring sat on top of it.

"Do you have a car here?" she asked.

He shook his head. "No."

She walked over and picked up the keys. A groan and then a long death rattle emanated from the wounded man on the floor. She scooped up the keys, and as she did so, the man on the couch lunged for the rifles.

Jet's gun barked death, and the man's head exploded as a dozen 4.6mm rounds tore through it and spackled the wall with blood and brains. She hurried back to the hall with the cells and called out in a loud voice, "The slavers are dead. You're no longer prisoners. I'm going to open the front gate. I have the keys. Anyone who doesn't have clothes, there are two dead men in the front of the building with robes. You're welcome to them if you don't mind a little blood. And there are some curtains on the windows that could work in a pinch." A head poked from around one of the doorways, and then another. "I wouldn't stay here very long. There's no telling when more of them will show up."

She ran the length of the corridor, repeating her message that the women were free. When she reached the last cell, she looked in on the bruised girl.

"I know it's been hell, but you have to get out of here now. Go. Don't wait. Get one of the men's robes and go."

The girl gave her a blank stare, but nodded. Jet checked her watch, calculating how much of a head start the truck with Salma had, and shook her head. She couldn't delay any longer.

"I have an extra robe if you want to come with me," Jet said.

The girl stood and walked unsteadily to the door. "This is real?"

"Yes. You're free."

She shuddered, partially from the night chill, and partially from adrenaline. Jet sighed and offered her hand. "Come on. Let's move."

The girl hesitantly reached out and took it, and then they were hurrying through the door and around the building to the front gate. When they reached it, Jet tried several of the keys until she found the correct one and pushed the barrier aside. She looked over her shoulder and saw a half dozen of the women following them, and smiled grimly. Damaged as they were by their ordeal, at least they now had a chance. Of course, the town was filled with predators, so there were no guarantees they wouldn't wind up in similar circumstances, but she couldn't save the world. She'd done what she could, and if it wasn't enough, it was because she had someone else to save.

"This way," she said, and winced at the thought of the girl having to run on the street with bare feet. There was nothing to be done about it, though, so she pulled her along until they reached the bike. Jet pulled the Berber robe from the saddlebag and handed it to her, along with a headscarf, and cranked the engine as the girl pulled the robe over her head and fumbled with the hijab.

"Be careful in town," Jet said. "My advice is to get clear of Sebha. Here's some money. Find a way to get to Tripoli, at least." Jet handed her two hundred dinars, which was a small fortune for a native girl, and her eyes welled with tears.

"Thank you," she said. "Thank you so much. I was trying to get there when they grabbed me." She swallowed hard. "It's been…horrible."

"How old are you?"

"Fifteen."

Jet's stare burned with anger. "Where are your parents?"

"Both dead."

"You don't have anyone you can turn to?"

The girl shook her head. "N-no."

"Well, now you have some money. Get some shoes, and talk to…

Find a woman at the marketplace who seems nice. Look for someone with a kind face. Ask her the safest way to travel to Tripoli. If she can't help, perhaps she could at least recommend someone or some way. There could be a bus or something."

"I...I will. I'll do that."

Jet looked at the waif, barely more than a child and already badly scarred for life, and her heart ached for her, but there was nothing more she could do. She donned her helmet and gave the girl a wave.

"I have to go. Be safe," Jet said, and roared off into the darkness, trying to remember what street would take her to the southern edge of the town, pushing the thought of the stranded girl from her mind, her mission now at the forefront of her thoughts.

She reached the limits of the urban area and turned onto the only road that led south. Jet increased her speed until the wind was tearing at her clothes, and she kept up the pace past orchards and planted fields. When she reached a fork in the road, she stopped to consider which leg of the branch to take. One ran west, the other south, and she spotted a small sign blown half off its support with Murzuq glowing in her headlight by the side of the latter.

Jet steered onto the road and had to slow considerably, the condition of the pavement so bad it was almost like riding over rough terrain. Eventually she discovered that the area by the shoulder was the least rutted and pitted, and was able to increase her speed until she spied taillights far ahead. She killed her headlight and slowed while her eyes adjusted to the darkness, which was offset by the light of a thousand stars and a waxing crescent moon. After a minute, when she felt confident enough in her vision, she sped up again and closed the distance between her and the truck.

As she did, she realized that she didn't have a strategy to stop the terrorists when she caught up with them. She didn't know whether they had Salma in the truck bed or in the cab, so she couldn't just pull up to them and empty the submachine gun into the cab. Even if Salma was in the bed, Jet couldn't predict what would happen if she shot the driver. The truck might gradually slow and roll to a stop, or the driver could stiffen and speed up, or twist the wheel and flip it, or run off the road and flip it when the front wheels hit the sand without anyone steering.

Which left Jet with only two options: follow the truck in the darkness and hope that it stopped at some point for the men to relieve themselves, or cut around it and lay a trap farther down the road. What kind, she didn't know, but if the men's bladders were empty and she didn't risk breaking her neck riding on sand in the darkness, the entire adventure would have been in vain. Jet eyed the gas gauge and swore – she hadn't bothered to fill the tank in Sebha because there had been plentiful gas available, and she hadn't banked on making a midnight run into the desert.

The slaver's words came back to her. The terrorists were headed over two hundred kilometers south. With under a quarter tank and no reserves left, there was no way Jet would be able to make it.

Which left her with only one choice: she would have to brave the terrain and make good enough time that she could cut the truck off and lie in wait for it, and do so within the next fifty to sixty kilometers, or she'd be without sufficient gas to return to Sebha. And there was unlikely to be anything resembling a filling station where they were heading, so when she ran out, it would be game over for good, especially if Salma were injured.

Resigned to spending the next hour or two in impossibly treacherous conditions, she twisted the handlebars and tore off onto the sandy stretch that ran parallel to the road, the dirt hard packed enough that she could steer but still so dangerous at speed that if she made a single miscalculation, it would be the end of the bike and, with it, her life.

Chapter 21

The bridge of the Comandanti-class patrol vessel *Foscari* was bathed in red light from the instruments as it navigated calm seas a hundred and twenty kilometers east of Sicily. The night watch crew had been on deck for four hours, and twenty minutes ago they had picked up a bogey on the radar twenty-eight kilometers away that was failing to respond to repeated attempts to hail it.

The crewman assigned to plotting its course looked up from his chart. "It's making ten knots, on a direct course for…Le Castella."

The watch lieutenant frowned as he watched the blip on radar. "Still a long way from it. Maybe he's heading for warmer water?"

"Anything's possible, sir. But then why isn't he responding to our hails?"

"Maybe he's got his radio off. Or he's drunk and singing along with it."

The crew laughed at the image, and then the lieutenant grew serious. "Keep hailing him, and bring us about so we're on an interception course."

"Aye, aye, sir."

The eighty-eight-meter ship executed a gradual turn and then accelerated to twenty-two knots. At that speed it would intercept the blip in forty-five minutes, at which point it could ascertain whether it was an innocent fishing boat or something more ominous, like one of the increasingly regular smugglers plying their trade on the route between Africa and Italy. While the Italian navy technically didn't have jurisdiction outside its twelve-nautical-mile claim of territorial waters, due to a special charter, the Italian government was performing patrol duties well off its coast and could stop any vessel it could show presented a clear intent to enter Italian waters. While this stance had been challenged by a number of countries, in the end pragmatism ruled, as it was Italy that was the gateway for much of the illegal immigration taking place from Africa, and as such it was within its rights to attempt to stop as much of it as possible.

Compounding its duties were the number of refugees who'd died attempting to make the crossing, which numbered in the tens of thousands over the last four years. The sheer magnitude of the deaths gave the Italians a valid humanitarian mission in the Mediterranean in addition to one of national defense. For this reason, it had been given latitude by its normally contentious neighbors and had taken de facto responsibility for policing the Mediterranean up to a hundred and sixty kilometers from its shores.

The big patrol boat sliced through the moderate swells with ease and, when it closed on its target, continued to hail the suspect craft with no success. A spotlight on the *Focarr*'s superstructure flickered to life when the boat was half a mile away, and locked on what turned out to be a fishing boat running without any lights – deeply suspicious under any circumstances, and more so with a navy cruiser approaching at high speed.

"Looks like an African vessel, all right," the lieutenant said.

The ensign at the chart table stood, moved to the windows, and raised his binoculars to get a better look at the craft. "The name's illegible."

"Probably scrubbed off. You know how this lot operates."

The lieutenant gave an order to slow to keep up with the fishing boat and approach from the port side so they could get a good look at it. The helmsman obeyed, and a few minutes later they were closing on it.

The ensign raised his binoculars again as the spotlight played over the trawler's hull, and when he lowered the spyglasses, his complexion was blanched.

"It's packed…with refugees. But…nobody's moving."

The lieutenant frowned as he made his way to the ensign. "Asleep?"

"I don't think so. They look...they look dead. And like they crawled all over each other."

The lieutenant thought for a moment. "Launch one of the RHIBs." He paused. "No. Belay that. Launch one of the drones, and let's get some footage. If they're dead, we don't know what killed them, and I don't want to risk any crew finding out."

The ensign did as requested, and when the drone hovered over the boat, it was obvious from the camera feed that his initial take had been correct. All of the bodies were twisted in agonized shapes, their orange life vests covered in vomit, their hands curled into claws clutching at the night sky. The spectacle was a glimpse into hell as the drone slowly pored over the length of the boat.

"Switch to infrared. Let's see if anyone's still alive," the lieutenant said, his voice hushed.

The operator complied, but the screen remained dark except for the heat signature from the diesel engine. He looked up at the lieutenant and shook his head.

"Nothing."

The lieutenant paced in front of the window before turning to the ensign. "Set up an emergency transmission. We'll need at least one helicopter with a bioteam on board equipped with hazmat suits and test gear. I've seen footage of corpses like that before. Looks like a nerve agent. But whatever it is, we don't want to get anywhere near it."

"Aye, aye, sir," the ensign said, and moved to the radio to ready it.

"I'll go wake the captain."

Three hours later, a Special Forces helicopter was hovering over the boat, keeping pace with it, as two commandos in hazmat suits shimmied down a knotted rope. They set foot on the deck, wherever they could find footing among the corpses, and one of them climbed over the mountain of dead to the wheelhouse to back off the throttle and kill the engine.

The boat slowed, and soon a transmission from the helicopter came in for the captain.

"Hundreds of migrants, all dead. Crew of the boat, too. No sign of what the source of the agent is, but it's got to be somewhere aboard."

"Good Lord…" the captain muttered.

"We're going to have to be careful, which means we'll need to wait for a ship with appropriate facilities for decontamination and quarantine to arrive. We don't want our men rummaging around the boat and tearing their suits. Worse, there are some agents that can defeat even hazmat gear, and we have to take precautions to safeguard everyone. We've sent out a distress call, and one of our frigates is in the area. Maintain position until it arrives. There's a biowarfare team in the air, on its way here."

"Roger that."

When the frigate arrived, another larger helicopter settled on its helipad. A dozen men spilled from the aircraft carrying metal cases, and the ship's crew moved in to help unload more of them. The men set up a mobile lab shortly thereafter, and four of the specialists donned hazmat suits and prepared to go aboard the fishing boat to relieve the commandos who were still on board – and who were still alive, indicating that whatever had killed the refugees wasn't penetrating the suits.

The captain and lieutenant waited on the bridge, watching the scene from several hundred meters away with dour expressions. Eventually a report came in.

"Looks like we found the source. There's a metal canister in the engine room. Looks like it rolled around and hit the engine enough times that it leaked. Markings are Chinese." A pause. "To be clear, none of your crew went anywhere near the boat, correct?"

"That's right. Just the drone, and it never got less than five meters away."

"Good. Then you can continue with your patrol. We'll take it from here. And, Captain? Keep a tight seal on this. Consider it classified until further notice. Ensure your crew understands."

"Will do. Best of luck."

"Thanks."

The captain and lieutenant exchanged a look, and then the captain turned to the night watch. "All right. You all heard that. Not a word, including to any of the crew who weren't awake for the fireworks. The lieutenant will handle those who were. This never happened. Am I clear?"

A chorus of *aye, aye*s and *yes, sir*s rang out. The captain pursed his lips and considered the fishing boat through the window for a final time before turning to the helmsman.

"Resume course for our patrol coordinates. Lieutenant? You have the bridge."

The captain moved to the door, hesitated for a moment as though ready to say something else, and then changed his mind and continued through it, yawning as he made his way back to his cabin, the sight of hundreds of tortured souls who'd died in unspeakable anguish forever seared into his visual cortex.

CHAPTER 22

Jet bounced along the sandy berms, now well ahead of the truck's headlights a half kilometer over her left shoulder, the road an inky ribbon against the desert beige. The bike bucked beneath her like a living thing, and it was all she could do to maintain control over the unforgiving terrain, navigating by starlight through a lunar and alien landscape. Her arms were aching from the exertion of keeping the motorcycle stable at speed off road, the periodic patches of deep sand treacherous between relatively hard sections with only a skin of grit on the surface.

She came over a rise and eased off the throttle at the sight of a cluster of tents – a Bedouin encampment, the shelters old as time itself, the nomadic tribes lost to the modern world and oblivious to it other than to upgrade their weaponry from muskets to assault rifles, courtesy of the unending war being fought for control of the country's resources. Jet twisted the handlebars and gave the camp a wide berth, not wanting to create an easy target for a zealous sniper amongst the tribesmen.

Jet poured on the gas as she sped by, throwing a rooster tail of sand into the air behind her, and hunched down low to minimize her profile in case the tribe had posted guards. She didn't know whether the Bedouin had any natural enemies in the region, but she didn't want to find out the hard way that they were aggressively territorial and liberal in their use of ammunition.

She glanced down at the fuel gauge again and frowned. The off-roading was consuming more gas than riding on pavement, which was to be expected – but still, the level was dropping at an alarming rate. There was no point in trying to calculate how much more range she had in the dark while trying to avoid slamming into something or dropping into a sinkhole, but her gut told her that if she continued much further, she'd be seriously pushing her luck.

A bend in the road ahead brought her on a course that intersected with it, and she avoided using the brakes to slow, instead downshifting and allowing the resistance of the sand to bring her to a stop beside a mound of debris. She quickly pushed the bike behind several abandoned fifty-gallon drums by the shoulder and eyed the pavement, a plan beginning to form in her mind.

Jet lifted one of the drums and carried it to the road. She laid it on its crumpled side, the bottom facing north on the pavement so its silhouette would be minimized as the truck approached, and then bolted for the rubble pile while gripping the Heckler & Koch MP7A1 with white knuckles. She threw herself behind the debris and brought the submachine gun to bear, wishing it had come with a night vision scope.

Her pulse pounded in her ears when the truck's headlights appeared at the far end of the bend, moving lazily along the abysmal pavement, swerving periodically to avoid the worst of the potholes. She estimated it to be rolling along at no more than forty kilometers per hour, which would make her task easier and lessen the chance of unintended consequences when the driver lost control.

The motor growled nearer, and she steadied the submachine gun and switched to single fire. She wouldn't get more than a few seconds to squeeze off several shots, but at the truck's speed that would be more than enough. Jet slowed her breathing, and her vision narrowed to the area around the oil drum, and her finger slid through the trigger guard and rested just over the trigger.

The truck approached the drum, and the driver only saw it at the last minute. He slammed on the brakes, slowing to a crawl as he swerved to avoid it, and then straightened and accelerated slowly past the obstacle.

She sighted on the right rear tire and squeezed the trigger. The little gun popped and recoiled against her shoulder, and she fired again and again. The brake lights flashed several times as the tire flattened, and the truck came to a stop by the side of the road.

Jet was up and running when she heard the tire begin to flap, and by the time the truck stopped, she was sprinting toward it as fast as her legs would carry her. The doors opened and both the passenger and the driver climbed from the cab carrying rifles, but not as though expecting to use them.

Which would be the last mistake they ever made.

She switched the fire selector to full auto as she neared, and waited until both men were standing by the flat tire, far enough from the bed that she wouldn't run the risk of hitting it. She opened fire, careful to avoid hitting the bed, and aimed for their legs. Her first salvo caught the driver in the shin, and he screamed in pain as he pitched forward, his tibia shattered. The passenger was quicker on his feet and threw himself flat on the gravel shoulder, but Jet was closing too fast and emptied the remainder of the magazine at his silhouette.

A few of the rounds struck his skull and shoulders, and he died facedown by the side of the road without ever seeing his killer. Jet whipped her pistol free as she strode toward the driver, who was groping for the rifle he'd dropped, his fingers just shy of the stock. He had almost reached it when Jet stopped three meters from him and raised the pistol.

The driver's eyes were white in the moonlight and wide as saucers at the apparition of a woman, dressed entirely in black and standing like an avenging angel, backlit by the stars. His mouth worked without making any intelligible sounds, and Jet pulled the trigger, planting a 9mm Parabellum round through the center of his forehead.

She lowered the gun and moved to the truck bed. A woman clad in filthy sweatpants and a torn top lay there, her wrists and ankles bound crudely with white cord, and a dark scarf tied around her lower face to muffle any screams. She stared at Jet in shocked surprise, and Jet slid the pistol back into her waistband, removed the survival knife, and flipped it open.

"Hold still," Jet said in Hebrew, and went to work on the rope around her wrists. The blade sliced through the cord with ease, and when her hands were free, Jet did the same with her legs while Salma pulled at the gag covering her mouth. The rope fell on the bed, and Jet nodded in satisfaction at her work. "Salma, I presume," she said softly.

"Thank God you found me." Salma looked around. "How did you get here?"

"Motorcycle. Are you hurt?"

"My head took a hit, but I'm feeling better by the minute." She paused. "Do you have any water?"

Jet smiled. "Of course. And some of the worst energy bars you've ever tasted."

"Where's the motorcycle?"

"Back by that garbage heap. You can walk with no problems?"

"I could walk all the way back to Israel if I have to."

"Let's hope it doesn't come to that." Jet's nose wrinkled and she looked around. "Damn. Gasoline."

Fuel leaked from the bottom of the truck, pooling into a small lake around Jet's feet. "A ricochet must have hit the tank. That's not good."

"There's no fire. We should be fine."

"It's not that. We could have used some of the gas. I'm almost out."

Salma frowned. "Seriously?"

"I wasn't planning on a late-night desert run."

"How much do you have?"

"Don't ask."

"Enough to make it back to Sebha?"

Jet glanced at the spreading pool of liquid glimmering in the starlight. "Let me help you out of the truck. We'll see if I can catch some of the fuel with one of the water bottles."

Jet eased the tailgate down, careful not to move quickly lest she cause a spark that would ignite the gas, and Salma climbed from the bed and stood barefoot in the fluid.

"No shoes?" Jet asked.

Salma shook her head. "They kidnapped me while I was sleeping. I didn't have time to take anything."

Jet nodded sympathetically, but her expression showed her worry. "If we have to walk, that could be a problem."

Salma held up the rag that had been used as a muzzle. "I can tie this around one of my feet. Or…"

She padded over to where the driver lay and eyed his sandals, and then moved to the dead passenger and did the same. Salma returned to the driver and pulled them off his feet and, after grimacing at the filthy soles, slipped them on.

"Grab his rifle and see if he has any extra magazines or a pistol," Jet said. "Then do the same for the other one. I'm going to get a bottle."

Jet ran back to the motorcycle, opened one of the saddlebags, and removed a container of water. She took several long swallows as she retraced her steps to the truck, and then handed it to Salma. "Drink fast."

Salma took it from her and chugged half the contents in a few gulps, and then poured the rest out and gave it back to Jet, who crouched down to peer beneath the truck. The steady stream that had painted the road slick with fuel had abated to a few drops, and Jet cursed as she straightened.

"Great idea, but lousy execution," she said.

"Not so bad. You're here and I'm alive." Salma looked at the dead men. "They work for Mounir. My husband. Or rather my tormentor – one of the most loathsome terrorist scum in existence."

"Did they let on where they were taking you?"

"They just said to him. Nothing more." She looked around. "Where are we?"

"South of Sebha, about…ninety kilometers."

"Are you sure?"

"Positive. Why?"

Salma frowned. "Mounir must have moved after I left. He was west of Sebha a couple of days ago."

"It doesn't matter. He can't hurt you anymore."

Salma shook her head. "It's not that. It's the USB drive I copied his data on. It was in my backpack. The slavers took it when they grabbed me."

Jet exhaled heavily. Of course she wouldn't have it with her. "Did they…are you sure you're okay?"

"They didn't rape me, if that's what you're asking. But they searched me top to bottom. Besides which, I didn't have time to…hide it on me."

"Right."

Salma thought for a moment. "If we can find them, it may be where they were keeping me…"

"I know where they were keeping you. But by now it's swarming with angry slavers. I killed their chief and a few of them, but cockroaches like that always have a bunch more to fill in their shoes. There's not much chance we can get in to look around. That, and it's likely one of them took the drive to see what was on it. There weren't any computers in their prison." Jet shook her head. "So that part of all of this was a waste."

"Maybe not. I had a chance to read some of the material. Enough to know the broad strokes. I already told headquarters most of it. They've gotten their hands on some Chinese nerve agent and are planning to release it in Europe and Israel. It's something like the Russian stuff – Novichok – only worse. Aerosolized."

"Do you know where they're storing it?"

"No idea. It didn't say. Or if it did, it wasn't in the files I got a glimpse of."

Jet looked up at the moon and couldn't escape the sense that it was mocking her. She shook off the thought. "Let's see how far the motorcycle will take us."

"I know this area. There isn't anything out here until we get closer to Sebha. Then there are some farms. But those are a long way from here. We were on the road, what, two, two and a half hours?"

"You're lucky they didn't drive any faster." Jet eyed the Kalashnikov in Salma's left hand and the two spare magazines in her right, a pistol stuck in the waist of the sweats, and looked to the truck. "Let's see if they have anything useful in there."

The two women walked to the vehicle and stared into the filthy cab, which was strewn with wrappers and trash. Jet smiled and reached for a handheld GPS unit that was resting on the center console. She regarded the screen and nodded. "There's a waypoint another hundred klicks from here. That's where they were headed."

"Where?" Salma asked, puzzlement etched into her face.

"South of the only town down there."

"Never been, but that's just desert. There's nothing there."

"Not nothing. That's where they were taking you. So that's where Mounir's holed up."

Salma shrugged. "Strange. But nothing should surprise me anymore. Although…"

"What?" Jet asked.

"I overheard him talking. When I left Mounir, he was expecting Tariq, his terrorist god and the one who hatched the nerve-gas plan, to arrive at any moment. So it could be that's where he went. Maybe Tariq has a camp in the desert. That's about the only thing that makes sense. There's nothing but sand there."

"Not our problem right now. I'll call in the coordinates to headquarters, and they can make a call on what to do. My job's to get you safely home."

"You're not going to get a fight out of me over that." Salma hoisted the AK. "I'm ready."

"Follow me."

The women walked to the motorcycle, and Jet removed one of the robes Leo had given her and handed it to Salma. "That will help keep you warm. It's going to get a lot colder."

"Believe me, I know. Weird how the desert can be blazing all day and then freezing at night." Salma pulled the robe over her head and arranged her clothes underneath. "Perfect. So what now?"

Jet straddled the bike and depressed the starter button. The engine turned over and purred softly. "Climb on behind me."

Salma did as asked, and Jet eased the motorcycle to the road and switched on the lights. She saw immediately that the gas situation was worse than she'd feared – it had been impossible to read the gauge in the dark, but now, illuminated, it was showing just above empty.

"What do you think?" Salma asked, peering over her shoulder.

"I hope those sandals are comfortable."

"Compared to what I've been through, they're like walking on clouds."

"Good. Because they're going to get a workout. With two of us to carry, this thing isn't going to make it very far."

Jet twisted the throttle and the bike rolled forward, leaving the truck and the dead men for the buzzards, the chill of the night suddenly colder as the magnitude of the challenge facing them sank in.

CHAPTER 23

Washington, D.C.

The meeting room where the joint chiefs of staff were gathered was hushed as a tall man with close-cropped gray hair and a wizened face gestured at a screen to his left. The members of the joint chiefs sat in stunned silence as the senior intelligence officer finished delivering his briefing. When the presentation concluded, he stood by the head of the table, the screen behind him now dark, and waited for the questions to begin.

"Let me get this straight. The Chinese sold some Libyan terrorists banned weapons?" asked Admiral Kinsey, the chief of staff of the Navy.

"Negative, sir. We can't make that assumption. All we know is that the canisters were marked with Chinese script and are consistent with their bioweapons program. Beyond that, we're guessing — although I'd say it's highly unlikely this was officially sanctioned."

"Then how the hell did they get their hands on it?"

"Unknown at this time."

"It's the damned North Koreans," growled General Bishop, the chief of staff of the Army. "Has to be."

The chairman of the joint chiefs frowned. "I think our friend here is saying not to jump to conclusions."

"Correct," the intelligence officer said. "All we know at this point is that there have been two releases of the agent, and both occurred in, or on a boat coming from, Libya."

"And you have no idea how much more of this stuff is out there? Or who's behind it?" General Williams, commandant of the Marine Corps, barked.

"Regrettably, no, sir. Our total G2 at this time is limited to intel coming from the attack site in Tripoli and from the Italian navy, which is working closely with our people. As to how much more there is, or where it's stored, if there is more, or who's behind this, we don't have sufficient information yet. But we're working on it."

"What does that mean?" the chairman asked.

"It means we're squeezing every contact, every informant we have, for anything that could answer the outstanding questions. But at this point we can't make any definitive statements with any degree of confidence other than that a bioweapon threat appears to be in the hands of terrorists, who have yet to make any demands or identify themselves."

General Williams shook his head. "Jesus. We're relying on the Italian navy? You've got to be kidding."

The admiral cut Williams off. "If we know it's Chinese, why don't we put the pressure on them to figure out how the terrorists got it?" He paused. "Seems like you find out who sold it to them, and you're only a step away from finding them."

The chairman nodded. "We've already sent for the ambassador. He'll be with the Secretary of State this morning. Believe me, there will be pressure applied."

"Which is unlikely to yield many, if any, results," the intelligence officer said. "The Chinese are typically very tightlipped, and a scandal of this proportion...this is a banned agent. The fact that they even developed it violates a host of treaties, as well as international law. So they're going to play dumb and circle the wagons. It's possible we'll never learn how it made it into terrorist hands. But make no mistake. This is the nightmare scenario we've feared for years – a WMD in terrorist hands."

"More than one," Kinsey corrected.

The chairman sighed and put both hands on the table. "Here's where we are. The president was briefed just before we were. He's approved a complete shutdown of Libya. Nothing moving in or out. We're going to order warships into position to enforce a blockade, and we'll have air support from our bases in the area, but it will take at least forty-eight to seventy-two hours to cover the entire coast." He paused. "Unfortunately, as we all know, the borders in that region are notoriously…labile. So sealing the land perimeter will be harder than the sea. We're already working with Tunisia and Algeria to do so, and are in contact with Egypt, although our confidence level in their ability to lock down the border is minimal. The real problems are Chad, Sudan, and Niger. None are particularly friendly toward us, nor do they have any real kind of central command. And they lack the resources to do much."

"If the terrorists want to gas half of Africa, that's not our problem," Kinsey snapped.

"Racist bastard," Williams grumbled jokingly.

"Well, sir, I respectfully disagree," the intelligence officer said. "We have personnel in all three countries that must be considered targets. Worse, if they were to ship the gas south once the vise starts to tighten to the north, it could make it to Europe, or here, by any number of routes. We all know Africa is the wild west." He hesitated. "We're preparing to cut off all internet and cell phone traffic in Libya. That will make it difficult to impossible to communicate, assuming whoever is behind this is still in-country."

"The government's agreed to that?"

"We didn't ask. But they tend to do whatever the highest bidder tells them to. And we're always the high bid."

"The cost to the Libyans will be enormous. If nothing's allowed in or out, and there's effectively no communication…"

The intelligence officer shrugged. "Not my problem."

"The humanitarian cost alone, if this stretches more than a few days, could be disastrous," the chairman said. "We'll have to go to the UN in a closed session and explain."

"The plan is to communicate to all of our allies and alert them to the situation. They'll cooperate, of course."

Williams laughed grimly. "Seeing as they've rubber-stamped every one of our campaigns so far, in the face of a real threat, I'd say so."

"The implications of the attack on the naval base in Tripoli are clear. That was a demonstration. It couldn't have been anything else.

Whoever is behind this wanted to fire a shot across the coalition's bow and get our complete attention," the intelligence officer said. "Which they have."

"Why gas a bunch of refugees on some boat?"

"Perhaps I didn't make it clear that the Italians believe that was an accident. The boat was transporting a canister to Italy. We believe the actual target was somewhere in Europe."

"To what end?" Williams demanded.

The chairman sat back and took a long sip of black coffee. "What's the goal of all terrorism? To instill fear. Imagine the public reaction if a highly toxic aerosolized nerve agent was released in the London Tube, or in the Paris Metro, or at a soccer match in Spain or Europe, or the opera house in Berlin. There are hundreds if not thousands of scenarios where thousands would die in the most gruesome manner possible. It would be the mother of all attacks, because we'd have no way of defending against more, since we don't know who's directing it or what their objective is or how much of the agent they actually have."

"What are the odds that we have to contend with this on American soil?" Kinsey asked.

"Unknown at this time," the chairman said, his expression sour. "But we have to assume the worst. We're all familiar with the national security scenarios of biowarfare attacks, or EMPs, or suitcase nukes. Assume the worst of them: an unknown amount of this stuff is smuggled in from Mexico or Canada or on a freighter or as air cargo, and whoever is behind it wants to bag the biggest elephant there is. It would make 9-11 look like a Boy Scout outing."

"Shouldn't we seal the ports?" Williams demanded.

The chairman shook his head. "Too soon. Just as Libya will be devastated by the blockade, we're also vulnerable. Imagine if everything just froze and nothing came into the country through official channels. It would be economically catastrophic."

"Plus it wouldn't work," the intelligence officer pointed out. "Every day tons of cocaine and heroin and meth make it across the border, as do countless illegal immigrants. The truth is that anyone with a real will could easily get anything they wanted across the border through any of countless smuggling networks. Don't even get me started on how impossible it would be to stop every high-speed boat in Florida from making the run from one of the islands, or for a small plane to land in the Louisiana Bayou or the Everglades with a load, much less how impossible it would be to stop something from coming in through one of the cartel tunnels."

"Well, hell. So all this expensive security can't stop a real threat?"

The intelligence officer smiled for the first time during the meeting. "We all know the purpose for it, and it has nothing to do with security. The only way to keep the population under control is to keep everyone afraid – of each other, of illegal immigrants, of Russia, of China, of terrorists, of North Korea, whatever. We've got three hundred fifty million guns floating around out there. Can you imagine what would happen if everyone wasn't at each other's throats or scared of their own shadow? They'd turn their attention on us and want to know what they're getting for tens of trillions of their money siphoned off. So no, don't expect the TSA or border patrol or customs to do anything meaningful. That's never been their function."

The frank assessment was permissible within the confines of the room. Everyone in the meeting understood that the Pentagon hadn't performed its mandatory audit for decades, and when it finally was forced to, failed at a hundred percent rate. The DOD was a money-laundering mechanism with no accountability and no bottom, and all concerned understood its role, and theirs, in the scheme of things. There were predators and prey, and they were the predators pretending to be guarding the flock. Still, the statement made the chairman visibly uncomfortable, and he was quick to adjourn the meeting after agreeing to keep everyone appraised and to reconvene another briefing meeting that evening.

On the way out, he stopped the intelligence officer. "Can we have a word?"

The other men trooped out, leaving the pair alone. The officer raised an eyebrow in anticipation.

"Cool it on the telling it like it is, will you?" the chairman snarled.

"Everyone knows the score. What's the point of pretenses in here?"

"It's like knowing your girlfriend is cheating on you versus saying it out loud. As long as it's not spoken, everyone can pretend. So just don't rock the boat. We have enough on our plates as it is. This could send the entire world economy into a tailspin if the situation gets out of control. We don't need any distractions."

The officer held up his hands in defeat. "Very well. No more unvarnished truth. My apologies."

He left, and the chairman watched him walk down the long hall with a bounce in his step, a man who knew all the secrets and slept well each night.

"God help us all," he whispered, and took a deep breath. Hopefully the Italians would provide some sort of meaningful information shortly, because the bottom line from the meeting was that nobody knew anything of substance, and all they could do was wait for the next atrocity to occur.

And the chairman had been in the position long enough to know that playing defense was a losing strategy for anything but the short term.

CHAPTER 24

South of Sebha, Libya

The motorcycle engine sputtered before continuing to hum along, and then coughed again. Jet steered off the road just as the motor hacked like an asthmatic four times and shuddered to a stop.

"Party's over," she said, and Salma hopped off the seat.

Jet swung off the saddle and pushed the bike into the desert, and continued until the tires became mired in the loose sand and she couldn't move it any more.

"Help me remove the saddlebags. We'll need the water and the rest of the stuff," Jet said, and she and Salma went to work on them.

"How far from Sebha do you figure we are?" Salma asked.

Jet did a quick calculation. "Maybe fifty, fifty-five kilometers. It's going to be a long walk."

Salma shrugged. "But it's doable. I did almost triple that to get to Sebha."

"Sure. But we can also expect Mounir to send someone to find out what happened and why you aren't there. When he does, we'll have pursuers. And the problem is that in sand, we're going to leave tracks."

"So we stay on the road."

Jet shook her head. "Too risky. We'd be sitting ducks. And not just for Mounir. Two women alone in the middle of sex-slave central? Not a great idea." Jet thought for a moment. "We can walk a little in the sand and then retrace our steps, using the same footprints, and move up the road some before getting off it again. There are patches of harder ground along the way. That will leave some false trails to throw them, and if we can find solid enough areas near the road where we don't leave any tracks getting off the pavement, they may not be able to pick up the real trail because they'll be looking for another one from the road."

Salma nodded. "Worth a try. But it sounds like we're racing the clock."

"That's right. So let's be quick about it."

The women walked a hundred meters through the sand and then painstakingly worked their way back to the road before shouldering the saddlebags and beginning their march north. Jet removed the sat phone from her bag and called Leo, who answered on the third ring, sounding half asleep.

"I've got her," Jet said without preamble.

His tone changed to one of full alertness. "You do? Where are you?"

"We ran into some problems." Jet gave him an abridged account of the men in the truck and the fate of the motorcycle.

"So you're on foot?" Leo asked when she finished.

"Affirmative. And it's just a matter of time until we have a hunting party after us. Now would be the time to pull a rabbit out of your hat. You were talking helos?"

"I'll let headquarters know and see what they can field."

Silence hissed on the line. "There's another problem."

"Which is?"

"The data that Salma copied onto a USB drive? The drive is gone."

"Define gone."

She told him about the slavers. "It could be anywhere at this point."

"Damn."

"I'm going to put Salma on so she can do a data dump of what she was able to glean."

Jet handed her the phone, and Salma took Leo through what she knew of the plan. When she finished, he asked a series of pointed questions and then asked to speak to Jet again.

"Yes?" she said.

"I'll get all of this to the director. What are your options for getting to Tripoli, worst case?"

Jet's heart sank at the question, which told her that Leo didn't have a lot of confidence in the helicopter rescue scenario.

"We don't have any options."

"I'm going to have to ask you to think of some. Things have changed since we last spoke. I just got word that Libya's going to be sealed off within the next forty-eight hours. The Americans are going to blockade it by sea, and its neighbors are closing the borders."

"Why?"

He explained about the gas leak on the fishing boat and the hundreds of dead refugees. Jet listened in stony silence until he was done.

"Where does that leave us?" she asked, her voice barely a whisper.

"I'll get back to you. How's your battery?"

Jet glanced at the indicator. "About fifty percent."

"Leave the phone on. I'll call as soon as I have something."

Jet stabbed the call button off and turned to Salma. "We're on our own for now. Let's keep going. Let me know if you see any promising patches of ground. You're more familiar with this area than I am."

"Will do."

They trudged along the road for a half hour, and then Salma grabbed Jet's arm and pointed to her left. "That looks promising."

Jet regarded the strip of darker terrain for a moment. "Let's give it a try."

They left the road and found themselves on reasonably solid footing, and Jet paused at the far edge of the harder ground. "This is as good as it's going to get?"

"I think so. Hard to say. The closer we get to Sebha, the better it should be. There are farms and orchards both to the south of town and the north."

"Would they have vehicles?"

"They might."

"Then our best shot is to find one and see if we can't liberate it."

"If we're that far out of town, it'll take some time to reach the orchards."

"Then let's pick up the pace."

The going got rougher once on the sand, and soon their legs were aching from the effort, the desert sucking at their feet with every step. Salma began falling behind, and Jet had to slow to let her keep up.

"Sorry," Salma said. "I lost half the skin on my feet on the trip to Sebha."

"Do the best you can."

"I will."

"But tell me if you need to rest. If you don't say anything, I'll assume you're okay."

"Fair enough."

Jet stared out over the desert before her gaze landed again on the younger woman. "I knew your brother."

"My brother?" Salma asked, sounding surprised.

"Yes. David."

"How...how do you know about us?"

"There are no secrets from the Mossad. You should know that."

"But why would they tell you?"

Jet considered how to answer and decided on the direct approach. "He and I were a couple for a while. One that produced my daughter. Our daughter. So you have a niece."

Salma stared at Jet like she was mad. "Are you serious?"

"Deadly."

Salma thought for a moment. "How old is she?"

"Four."

An uncomfortable silence followed. When Salma spoke, her voice was softer. "I didn't have much contact with him. He was a stranger to me."

"I think he was that way with just about everyone. It was his nature."

She appraised Jet anew. "Obviously not everybody."

"We fell in love. It was a long time ago." She hesitated. "Did you…hear about him?"

"What about him? I've been stuck in Libya for three years."

"He…he passed away."

This time the silence lasted longer. Jet decided to be the one to break it. "So we're the only family you have. My daughter. And by extension, me."

"That's a lot to absorb. You tell me I have a niece, and my brother's dead, in the same breath. I mean…hard to figure out what to do with that."

"I wanted you to know. That's why I took the assignment. I have a vested interest in seeing you get home safely."

"I don't understand. You volunteered to do this?"

"They asked me, and I said yes. I didn't want to leave David's sister stranded in Libya and hope they sent someone competent."

Salma frowned. "Now I really don't understand. The Mossad doesn't allow its operatives to have children. Not field agents."

"True. It's one of the reasons I quit."

"But you're here."

"I freelance for them on sensitive operations."

"And you left your daughter to come to this hellhole?"

"It wasn't an easy decision. But yes."

Another long pause. "How did David die? Do you know?"

"Yes. I was with him. It was a…a messy operation that wound up going wrong."

"Oh, God…"

Jet sighed and embraced Salma before looking away.

"He wasn't around that day."

CHAPTER 25

An arctic wind from the west cut through Jet's and Salma's robes like a knife as they pushed north, the moon now lower in the sky as dawn approached. Salma had been marching along without complaint, but was now visibly limping from sand grinding into the raw patches of her brutalized feet, and was struggling in silence to keep up with Jet's pace.

They paused at a firm patch of ground to rest, and Jet eyed the younger woman in the predawn glow.

"What size shoes do you wear?" she asked.

Salma told her, and Jet shook her head. "My boots will be too small for you. They won't do you any good. Sorry."

"I appreciate it. Don't worry about me. I'll do what I have to do." She paused and looked off at the darkened desert. "I always have."

Jet was silent for a moment. "This whole experience must have been…hard."

"You have no idea. Married to that filth. It was a…a nightmare. He was worse than a pig. He treated me like his property. And when he would come for me at night…I can't tell you how many times I wanted to slice his throat in his sleep, or kill myself to end it. The only reason I didn't was I knew he was involved in something big, and I was the only one who could do anything to stop him. Still, he's the most vile, disgusting…I'm so glad this is over."

Jet exhaled heavily. "It's not an assignment that most would have been willing to take."

"I know. I didn't want to. But there was an opportunity, and I was the right age, with the right skills. They convinced me." She hesitated. "If I'd known what it was going to be like, I probably wouldn't have. The reality of it was so much worse than anything could have prepared me for. And it wasn't just him. This country. It's…It's prehistoric. Like the last thousand years never happened. You've seen just a fraction of it. I've been living it for years. It's…there are no words to describe how oppressive and evil many of these places are."

"I've seen enough. Slave markets, armed militia, disgusting conditions."

Salma nodded. "Every abomination you can imagine is taking place here. There's a club in Sebha where you can sodomize a six-year-old boy for pocket change. Where you can murder a teenage girl after raping her, and they'll just cart off the body and charge you extra. Where they'll kidnap someone with the same blood type and kill them for whatever organ you need. There's nothing to depraved, too evil." She swallowed, unable to continue for a moment. "And that's what men like Mounir and his kind want to turn the world into. It's the water they swim in. The air they breathe. They would turn Israel into a hellhole like Libya for some twisted ideological sickness they want to infect everyone else with. Some medieval dogma that doesn't even make sense. It's just driven by hate. It's the currency they trade in."

"Which is why the gas attacks are starting."

"Yes. Their glorious leader is now out of prison, and he intends to remake the world in his image. Mounir's more than honored to help him."

"What do you know about him?"

"Tariq? He's insane. Like the kind of crazy that would gladly detonate an atomic bomb and murder millions of innocents if he thought he could get away with it. He hates America, and Israel, and Europe – mainly because they go along with whatever Washington wants. So he wants to destroy all three if he can, starting with Israel. That's his passion. He views our existence as blasphemy. And he holds England and the U.S. responsible for us having our own country. He views us as invaders, illegally occupying land that isn't ours, given to us by an illegitimate government that never should have had the power to do so."

"Sounds like a charming guy. Have you met him?"

Salma shook her head. "He was in prison the entire time I've been here. But I've heard hundreds of hours of his philosophy from Mounir. It's the most toxic mix of half-truths and anti-Semitism and racial hatred you can imagine. But it finds adherents. There are so many here who lost everything after the regime fell that they'll listen to anything, join any fringe group, if it gives them meaning and a sense of identity. That's the big danger. Mounir would gladly give his life to achieve Tariq's vision. And there are a thousand more Mounirs waiting to take his place." She took a deep breath. "I wish I hadn't lost the USB drive. It was all on there. Everything."

"Sounds like you saw enough. We know they're planning to launch gas attacks in Europe and transport the gas with refugee boats. That should be sufficient."

"Yes, but all the details would have been invaluable. Like…where are they storing it? How did they get it in the first place? What specific targets have they chosen? How are they planning to get it into Israel, and when? Those are a lot of unanswered questions." She frowned. "They should just turn this whole place into a crater and be done with it."

Jet got to her feet. "Ready to keep going?"

"Sure. Lead the way."

"I passed a Bedouin camp when I was following you. That's also up ahead."

"We don't want to get within a mile of them. Most stay to themselves, but there are plenty of malevolent groups that are involved in the slave trade."

"That was my thinking." Jet powered on the GPS, waited until it acquired a signal, and studied the screen. "Here's where we are. So yes, we're not that far from the first of the agricultural spreads."

Salma adjusted the shoulder strap of the AK she'd taken from Mounir's man and hefted the saddlebag as she stood. "Lead the way. Once it's light out, we're going to be sitting ducks for anyone Mounir sends, as well as for the local warlords."

Jet nodded. "Shouldn't be too much farther."

"I hope you're right. I'm going to need feet transplants after this."

"I wish there was something I could do for you, Salma. I'm sorry."

"Not your problem. I'm lucky you risked everything to try to get me out of here."

They began walking again. Salma cleared her throat. "I really didn't know David. Hardly at all. Now…I never will."

"He was complicated."

"You say you loved him?"

"Enough to have his child."

"And he loved you."

Jet thought about it. "In his own way. He was hard to read. Made a career out of being inscrutable."

"He obviously must have thought you were something special if he was willing to risk everything he'd built for you."

"I suppose so."

"What was he like?"

Jet gave a rough laugh. "God. Where do I start? He was…wickedly smart. One in a hundred million. And honorable, at least to his personal code. But also ruthless when he had to be. And cynical. A master chess player using human pawns, I guess you could say. He was the best at what he did. I've never seen anything like it. He had a gift." Jet walked in silence for several beats. "As a man, he was everything you could want. But there was a part of him at his core that you could never get to, that he never allowed anyone to see. I got glimpses of it at times, but I would have loved a lifetime with him to really understand him." She sighed. "Unfortunately, the universe had other plans."

"What's your daughter's name?"

Jet's emerald eyes flashed in the darkness and a smile tugged at her mouth. "Hannah. I see a lot of David in her. The good parts of him. She's…exceptional in so many ways."

"I'd love to meet her." Salma thought for a moment. "It must have been difficult leaving her to do this."

Jet looked away. "One of the hardest decisions I've had to make."

Salma touched Jet lightly on the shoulder. "Thank you."

Jet waved off the gesture. "Let's get you to safety. Then you can thank me. We're still a long way away."

"Not if we can find something to hot-wire."

"A lot has to go right for that to happen. So far, not a great bet. And with the sun coming up, we're going to have to start looking around for somewhere to lie low until dark again. We're asking for it alone out here during the day, even armed to the teeth."

"I still know my way around a gun."

"No doubt. But if a caravan of slavers spots us, that won't matter. Besides, my job's to get you out of here in one piece, not wage a small war. Which means we keep our heads down and wait out the heat of the day somewhere we won't melt. We've only got three liters of water between the two of us. That's not going to last long once it's hot out."

"You're right, of course. I just want this to be over."

Jet nodded. "I don't blame you. But we also need to give HQ time to arrange for an extraction. Didn't sound promising when I spoke with the local conduit."

Salma absorbed the news, her expression unreadable, and then sighed. "Okay. Let's get this over with. We'll do better in one of the orchards than on the sand once dawn breaks."

CHAPTER 26

Tariq's lead truck rolled to a stop at the abandoned pickup in the middle of the road, and Tariq stepped down and walked to where Abdu lay bloating from the increasing heat as the sun rose, his skin already blackening and mottled. He stepped back from the corpse and regarded the small army of ants circumnavigating the dead man's neck and shook his head.

Amel, one of Tariq's lieutenants, approached and glowered at the scene. Tariq moved to where Mahmoud lay. "Looks like they got out of the truck and someone ambushed them. The windshield's intact, and so is the cabin."

Amel pointed to the flattened rear tire. "There's what did it. See the bullet hole in the sidewall? It's shredded, but you can just make it out."

Tariq nodded. "Picture it. They waited there, by the garbage. Saw a vehicle, shot out its tire, and then there was a firefight once our men were in the open. They shot them and took the woman."

"And their weapons," Amel said, and then his frown deepened. "Only…no. Look," he said, pointing to Mahmoud's AK lying a meter from him. "That's strange. Why would anyone leave a perfectly good rifle behind?"

Tariq walked to where a plastic water bottle lay by the shoulder and knelt to pick it up. He sniffed and slowly rose to look to Amel. "Smells like gasoline."

Six more men joined them, and Tariq looked to Amel. "We need to find the woman. Get the Bedouin here and see what he makes of the scene. Maybe his eyes will see something we don't."

Amel retraced his steps to one of the pickup trucks and returned moments later with a short, wiry man with skin the color of saddle leather, draped in a traditional Bedouin robe and headdress.

"Faiz, they took the woman. We need her back. Do your best and see if there's anything that can tell us where to look."

The Bedouin took in the two dead men without expression, and then his eyes slowly surveyed the surroundings before settling on the rubble pile. He walked over to it and spent several minutes walking around the debris, and then made his way back to Tariq, pausing to kneel and scoop up several spent shell casings before he stopped by the truck. He held up a cartridge. Tariq took it from him and examined it.

"I've never seen bullets that small," Faiz said. "Not for anything but hunting rabbits or birds."

Tariq's eyes narrowed as he held the shell casing out to Amel. "I have. And they aren't for hunting. There's only one weapon that uses this round that I know of, and it's the Heckler and Koch MP7. It's a commando weapon. Small, lightweight, and deadly. There are many in Iraq and Afghanistan, from the cowardly coalition forces dropping them when they retreat in failure."

Amel took the casing. "You know all that from a bullet?"

"I spent enough time in Germany before they imprisoned me to be more than passingly familiar with the weapon."

Amel's forehead creased and he tossed the shell aside. "It would be next to impossible to find ammunition for this weapon here."

"Agreed," Tariq said. "Which means this isn't the work of some militia or robbers. Whoever used it brought it here, along with the ammunition. Which tells me that there's more at play than a simple robbery."

"You think…?"

Tariq looked to Faiz. "What else did you find?"

"There are motorcycle tracks by the debris pile."

"How many?"

"Looks like only one."

Tariq grunted. "A single operative? Interesting."

"The tracks lead from the desert. But they continue onto the road."

"How can you tell which direction they go?"

Amel stepped closer to Faiz. "He's a Bedouin. Tracking's in their blood from the time they're children. It's said they can follow anything in the desert. Anything."

"I know all this," Tariq snapped. "I want him to explain how."

Faiz motioned to Tariq and led him to the rubble. "You can see that is where the motorcycle was parked. And there are two sets of footprints around it, but far more of the smaller ones – boots, it looks like. The tracks leading to the road are deeper – so there was more weight on the bike than when it came from the desert. You are missing a woman. I would conclude whoever ambushed the men rode away with her. It is the only explanation that makes sense."

"Then they could be anywhere by now," Tariq said.

Faiz straightened. "This is true."

Tariq had mobilized half the camp when the men had failed to return from Sebha, and his worst fears were now manifest. Somebody had planned, and then executed, an almost impossible feat in the dead of night. And the woman who knew everything about his plan was still on the loose.

"I can't lead the hunt for this woman – I need to get to Tripoli by nightfall. But, Amel, take Faiz here and three of your best men, and see if you can pick up their trail along the way, or in Sebha."

"Why along the way?" Amel asked.

"They came from the desert. They may have had a reason to take that route. We can't assume that they stayed on the road."

"It will take time," Faiz cautioned.

"You have as much as you need. Do your best." Tariq eyed the old Bedouin and then shifted his attention to Amel. "As soon as you're in Sebha, notify our people there to be on the lookout for the motorcycle. Offer a bounty for whoever takes them."

"Alive," Amel finished.

"Only the woman, and I'm not particular about how alive. Just enough to answer questions would be fine. If they can take the driver, even better – I'm curious who they're working for, and how much they know. If they sent someone into Libya to help her get out, probably too much. But I don't want to guess, and I certainly don't want to alter the plan if I can help it."

"Very well," Amel said. "How large a reward?"

"As much as it takes. I want every free hand between here and Tripoli trying to earn it." Tariq's face darkened into a mask of fury. "They must not be allowed to escape."

"I'll put out the word," Amel assured him.

"Very well. I'll be in Tripoli soon enough. Do not fail me. If they turned off the road, find them. If they rode into Sebha, I'll tell everyone we come into contact with on the trip north about the bounty. That should make it impossible for them to make it out alive."

Tariq returned to his truck, a bead of sweat tracing its way down his face, his stride powerful and confident. Once in Tripoli, with his plan already in play, he would become the de facto leader of the fragmented country. The chaos he'd unleashed with his gas attack and the predictable draconian response by the infidels was serving his purposes better than he could have hoped. The reports he had received, of the borders being closed and the cell service and internet being disabled, would kneecap the already terminally hobbled capital, and the cowards who were robbing the nation blind as its putative government would be the first to fly their private jets to safety.

Which would leave Tripoli his for the taking. One thing that Qaddafi had understood, like Hussein in Iraq and Assad in Syria, was that in order to govern what amounted to lawless tribes of competing factions, a leader with an iron fist was required. The fools from Europe and America believed that their laughable form of democratic rule could function here, but Tariq knew better. Most only understood force and brutality and would only obey and respect a figure who understood their use. The revolution that had been engineered by the American intelligence services had been moronically obvious as a mercenary assault against Qaddafi's regime, using paid fighters posing as rebels – exactly as the same players were now doing in Syria in an effort to topple that regime. But in the process, they had unleashed pandemonium while creating a vacuum into which divergent extremist groups had poured, resulting in the current nightmare for the population.

The people of Tripoli would welcome his strong hand and would cheer for a leader who would govern by the Koran rather than some absurd mob rules theory imported from America's privileged shores. That the Americans and their lapdogs in Europe actually believed their own rhetoric of the superiority of a system that had never once worked in any of the countries in the region had ensured their eventual failure, and with the collapse of the puppets they'd propped up to rule the oil flows, had created the perfect environment for Tariq to assume his place on the throne.

"Bury them in the desert, and let's move. You have five minutes," he told his men, and then watched with satisfaction as they scurried to do his bidding, like schoolchildren eager to please their headmaster.

"Yes, it's time," he whispered to himself, and with a final glance at the bloating corpses, strode back to his truck, where the driver was sitting with the engine running, the air conditioner a frigid blast as the heat rose to triple digits.

After the convoy pulled away in a cloud of dust and exhaust, Amel leaned into Faiz and spoke softly. "You really think they might have pulled off the road?"

Faiz shrugged, his face a mask. "If they did, we'll see the signs."

"It's a long way to Sebha," Amel countered.

Faiz glanced at the two gunmen in the bed of Amel's truck, their beards scraggly, their headdresses wrapped around their faces to block the sun and filter the road dust. "Agreed."

Two and a half hours later, Faiz returned to the road from a sandy area he'd spotted after noting a disturbance of the gravel at the shoulder, and climbed into the oven-like cab with Amel and the driver.

"The motorcycle is abandoned just over that small dune. Gas tank is empty. Their footprints continue on the far side, but dead-end."

Amel thought for a moment. "How is that possible?"

"They're good, but not that good. I believe they walked back to the road."

"Then they're up ahead?"

"I didn't say that. If I were out here in the dead of night with a woman, possibly injured, I wouldn't want to be found by anyone dangerous enough to brave this road. So I'd get off of it as soon as I was able."

"Why wouldn't they have filled the motorcycle before trying to ambush our men?"

"I'm not psychic. I'm just telling you what I found."

"If they're on foot, they can't have gotten far."

"Depends on what time they started walking. Their tracks won't be easy to follow, but now that I know what we're looking for, they'll never be able to hide." Faiz looked up at the sun, a fiery distorted ball in a cobalt sky, and nodded.

"It will be a long day, but we'll find them."

Amel grunted. "We'd better, or Tariq will have us skinned alive."

CHAPTER 27

Tel Aviv, Israel

The flight from Munich to Ben Gurion Airport seemed to hover over the tarmac before the wheels settled on the runway, leaving a trail of white smoke as the front wheel kissed the ground and the plane began to slow with a deafening roar of reverse thrust. The passenger in seat 9A looked out the window until the plane began taxiing to the terminal, and then checked the time on his watch before sitting back and closing his eyes for the short remainder of the trip to the gate.

Yevgeni Saldovich was ex-Spetsnaz and now made a comfortable living as a highly paid assassin, an independent agent who worked for everyone from the Russian Mafia to clandestine groups within the Russian government. At thirty-seven years old he was at his peak earnings age, if slightly past his prime physically, although he still put in two hours at the gym every morning to attempt to stave off the effects of time. Utterly ruthless, with cold gray eyes and a moral philosophy that would have chilled a lamprey, he was expensive, entirely sociopathic, and efficient, having never taken an assignment he'd failed to successfully conclude.

The plane stopped, the Jetway docked to the fuselage, and the passengers rose and opened the overhead compartments for their luggage. Yevgeni remained seated until the line in the center aisle began moving, and then removed the laptop bag from beneath the seat in front of him, hooked a hand through the handle of his carry-on bag in the overhead bin, and made his way to the front of the plane, ignoring the hostess's smile as he passed her.

Immigration and customs was a nonevent. Yevgeni had been to Israel once before three years ago, but on a security assignment for a high-net-worth oligarch rather than in an offensive role – something he did when times were lean. Fortunately for him, the killing business was more robust than ever, and he hadn't had to stoop to that level since.

Two officials stared holes through him as they scanned his passport, but relaxed when they saw that he'd been there before. They asked him several perfunctory questions, which he answered in a friendly, neutral tone, and then he was through the security checkpoint and walking to the exit. The vetting that had taken place in Munich airport at the El Al counter had been far more thorough, so on this end the clerks were merely verifying that those who got off the plane were the same ones who'd gotten on. In Munich, the passengers' backgrounds had been checked long before they arrived at the airport, and anyone suspicious had been pulled aside for rigorous questioning before they were allowed to obtain a boarding pass.

He waited in line for a taxi, and once in the back seat and on the way to his hotel, he considered his current assignment. He'd been hired to locate a target, with instructions to terminate with extreme prejudice. No need to make it appear to be an accident, which was the typical way many of his clients preferred his executions of business rivals or cheating spouses or embezzlers. A straightforward wet job, but with specific instructions to follow once he'd reported in with a locate.

Yevgeni didn't mind the ambiguity present in the termination stage of the exercise. It wasn't uncommon for a special request to be floated once the client was sure that he had the target in his sights. This was usually the case when it was something personal. The killing of a competitor or an unhelpful bureaucrat who was standing in the way of a project didn't require the individual touch – it was business. But when the client had been wronged, that was where it got interesting.

He did his best to comply with the requests, and had done his share of filmed dismemberments, blowtorch roastings, decapitations, disembowelments, and acid baths. Once he'd even had a demand that the target be torn limb from limb. Yevgeni had satisfied the client by filming the victim with his legs and arms chained to four different vehicles, which Yevgeni dutifully drove in different directions, one car at a time, until nothing was left but a screaming torso.

He enjoyed his work, or rather the challenge of it. The actual sanctions were mundane. Once you'd watched the light go out of a target's eyes a few times, life's end was unremarkable. The way he saw it, billions had come and gone before him, everyone dead in the end, but all surely convinced of their exceptional status on the planet – that they were special and different from all the rest, and the laws of nature would be suspended in their case. He recognized the folly of such thinking. He was a hunter, and a hunter never hesitated or questioned his purpose. Some drove tractors, some performed surgery, some wrote computer code. He located and terminated people. That was the only difference, and if he weren't doing it, someone else surely would be.

The hotel was mid-level, neither sumptuous nor squalid, in keeping with his cover as a Russian in town for a week on business. After he paid the driver, he checked in, and once in the room, sat at a small table near the foot of the bed and powered on his cell phone.

When the indicator showed that he had a signal, he dialed a number in Ukraine, which rang twice before it beeped and then disconnected. He busied himself with his laptop, and several minutes later the phone chirped, indicating that he'd received a text message. He tapped the string of numbers and letters in the message into a password-protected PDF file that had arrived simultaneously in the dead-drop email account he'd set up, and the document opened to reveal a dossier with photographs.

He sat forward and studied the images – young woman, a man, and a child, and then read the content.

The woman was the target. The other two had been included because there was a high degree of correlation between them and the target; they had appeared together numerous times on the feed from which the images had been pulled.

He eyed the map of Tel Aviv that had been included and zoomed in on a pinned area that was the traffic camera that had captured their movements, and which appeared to be a regular stop for the woman, usually accompanied by the man and child. He memorized the location and flipped to the end of the dossier, where there was another photo of the woman, this time in the interior of a wood-paneled room…or a boat salon.

Once done reading the dossier three times, he sat back and stared at the last photograph and rubbed the stubble on his chin with the back of his hand.

"What did you do, sweetheart? You pissed off the wrong people, that's for sure."

The times from the traffic cams corresponded to mornings and afternoons. He checked his watch again and saw that he wouldn't have time to do everything he needed before the morning opportunity, but might be able to make the afternoon sighting.

He signed off from the computer and locked it, and then took the elevator to the lobby and asked about car rentals. The desk clerk gave him several options and offered to call whichever company he preferred to have them pick him up. He declined and exited the building, preferring the anonymity of a taxi.

At the rental office he provided a Latvian passport and driver's license in a different name, with matching credit card, and after signing the contracts, was behind the wheel of an innocuous econo-box that wouldn't draw a second glance from even the most suspicious. He saw that he still had an hour before the clock ticked over on the time range of the afternoon sighting from the traffic cam, and he navigated the clogged streets until he was down the block from the intersection.

His plan was to wait for the happy trio to put in an appearance, and then call the number the client had given him to report that he had the target in sight. He would receive instructions on how they wanted her taken down, and then would source the appropriate resources so he could do the deed the following day.

He found a parking place in a less than optimal view spot, and stepped from the car to make his way along the street to where he would be able to observe both sides without seeming obvious. A coffee shop with a display window that fronted onto the street was the perfect choice, and he ordered a cup, taking care to pay for it when the waiter delivered it so he could leave without any delay when he spotted his quarry.

Ten minutes stretched to twenty, and then he spied the man walking along unhurriedly.

But no woman.

Perhaps they met there each day?

Yevgeni pushed back from the table and was out the door in seconds. He walked at a slower pace, seemingly window-shopping while he waited for the woman to appear. When the man turned the corner ahead of him, he accelerated, eyes sweeping both sides of the street in case the woman was making her way along the sidewalk to meet the man.

The Russian rounded the building and found himself on a side street filled with adults who were meeting schoolchildren as classes ended. He continued walking so he wouldn't attract attention, and extracted his phone from his pocket and pretended to be engrossed in a conversation as he passed in front of the school, within a few meters of where the man was standing.

At the end of the block he stopped as though confused and looked around, squinting at the street sign while sneaking a peek at the school. The man was walking in the opposite direction, holding the hand of a little girl – the same one as in the photo.

He debated following them but rejected the idea. He had yet to procure a weapon, and as good as he was, there was always the slim chance that the man had spotted him. With the target nowhere in evidence, that didn't seem worth the risk, so he continued across the street and turned right, where he would circle the block and wind up near the car for his trouble.

Back in the vehicle, he mulled over his next step and decided it was time to get his hands on some hardware. He had the name of a contact who could get him anything he wanted, and even though he didn't know exactly what the client's special request would be, some things were perennial: a pistol, ammo, and a butterfly knife or switchblade. With those simple tools he was virtually unstoppable and would be prepared when morning came and his next opportunity at the woman presented itself.

CHAPTER 28

South of Sebha, Libya

Horsetails of purple and cinnamon streaked the horizon as the sun sank behind the rolling dunes. Jet nudged Salma awake and looked around the orchard where they'd taken shelter. The olive trees that an industrious farmer had coaxed from the earth south of the oasis city had provided welcome shade during the brutally hot day, but now, as the gloaming dimmed the light in the sky, they needed to move.

Jet had waited to call Leo until her sat phone battery had drained to below twenty percent, but he hadn't had anything substantial to say other than that headquarters was working on an extraction and to stand by. When she'd pointed out that they were stuck in one of the most lawless areas of the planet, where warring tribal factions and militia often shot first and asked questions later, he was sympathetic, but had no definitive news.

"I told you that Tunisia and Algeria have sealed their borders," he'd said. "Well, the news is reporting that an international task force is steaming toward Libya to blockade the coast. So all hell's broken loose. The government's nowhere to be seen, and there are reports of wholesale desertions from the army. Can't say as I blame the poor buggers. I wouldn't want to be wearing a uniform that made me a target for every bad guy in Tripoli."

"How is that going to affect us getting out of here?"

"They're working on it."

"Which leaves us in the middle of the desert with a couple of guns and swarms of miscreants surrounding us. This isn't what I signed up for, Leo."

"I know. But the situation's fluid. Nobody could have for foreseen the entire country would collapse in a matter of hours."

"Figure it out, Leo. We're badly exposed, and we don't have any friendlies to fall back on."

"I know. We're doing our best."

"I'm shutting the phone off. My battery's going to be into the reserve pretty soon. I'll touch base when we get to Sebha."

"When will that be?"

"Hopefully by tomorrow morning at the latest."

"I'll stand by."

Salma yawned and sat up. They had traded watch shifts every four hours, but sleeping in hundred-degree heat had proven difficult, and neither of them was well rested.

"Last of the water," Jet said, taking three swallows of the final bottle and handing it to Salma.

"That didn't last long," she said, and swished each gulp around her mouth the better to satiate her thirst.

"We'll have to find some soon. Even in the cold we'll be losing moisture." She eyed the trees. "They're getting water from somewhere."

"Probably a register nearby, fed by a well."

"Do you know what it would look like?"

"Sure. It will be near the road."

They had settled in as far from the asphalt strip as they could, and as the last of the light faded, they made their way between the rows of trees until they reached the barbed wire fence that served as the lot barrier. Salma indicated a concrete trough to the right, and they approached it.

"Help me move the cover," Salma said. Jet moved beside her and they used Salma's rifle stock and Jet's back muscles to shift the heavy slab aside so there was enough of a gap to peek inside.

Jet's nose wrinkled at the smell of rot.

"All the water's going to have algae in it. No point to purifying it for irrigation," Salma said.

"It'll make us sick as dogs. That's no solution."

"We'll just have to hope that one of these fields or farms has a proper well."

"How likely is that?"

"Very. If anyone's living on the grounds, they'll need drinkable water. Even if they have to boil it." Salma patted her saddlebag. "I don't suppose you have a lighter."

"I actually do. But no way to hold water to purify."

"We should fill the bottles, just in case we come across something we can use."

Jet drained the last of the one in her hand and submerged the bottle until it was filled with yellowish-green fluid. They did the same with the others and then skirted the fence and walked to the next field, which was newly planted and offered nothing obvious they could use. Darkness was settling in by the time they reached a stretch of plots with a small home off the road, and they made their way to it slowly, wary of drawing the attention of any residents.

They needn't have bothered. There was no glass in the windows, and the door was ajar, the home clearly abandoned.

"Looks like nobody's been living here for a while," Salma said.

"Doesn't really help us, does it?"

"Maybe there's a well."

"Let's see if we can find it."

They eventually came across a raised stone circle. Jet reached inside and felt for a rope and, when she found one, lifted it to the surface.

The metal bucket at the end of the rope was bone dry.

"Looks like we know why they abandoned the house," Salma said.

Jet untied the bucket. "We can use this to boil the water we have."

They found enough pieces of broken furniture to build a small fire, and Jet lit a small piece and placed it beneath the pile. Soon the desiccated wood was crackling, and they emptied their bottles into the bucket and used the barrel of the AK to support the handle over the flames.

When they'd sanitized the water, they carefully refilled the bottles with the hot liquid and set out toward the road again, at least confident that they wouldn't die of dehydration. They were halfway across the field when Jet grabbed Salma's arm and stopped her in her tracks.

"Look back the way we came."

Salma did, and her breath caught in her throat. They'd both seen the glint of metal in the light from the rising moon.

"Something's back there," Jet said.

"Could be workers finishing up their day."

"I didn't see any. Did you?"

"No."

Jet resumed walking, looking over her shoulder periodically, and when they reached the road, whispered to Salma, "They're tracking us."

Salma's tone hardened. "Mounir. He probably went looking for his men when they didn't return." She paused. "I'll die before I let them take me."

Jet pointed at another structure farther up the road. "There's another farm over there. You're going to have to move faster, Salma."

They hurried to the next field, and at this one there was the dim glow of a light in the windows, and more importantly, the dark outline of a pickup parked by a smaller outbuilding. Jet led Salma to an aged Toyota truck that looked like it barely ran, and tried the door, which was unlocked. Salma stood watch while Jet reached beneath the steering column and pulled wires loose from the ignition. She crossed two of them, and the engine stuttered to life, the unmuffled exhaust deafening. Salma climbed into the passenger seat and Jet slipped behind the wheel, and then they were bouncing along the gravel drive.

The house door swung open and a pair of men ran out. Jet stomped on the accelerator and jerked the wheel hard left just as gunfire exploded from behind the truck. She continued to zigzag to the road as rounds sent geysers of sand and gravel into the air along the drive. Several thumped into the tailgate as she neared the road, and then the rear window shattered and a hole punched through the windshield six inches from Salma's head.

"Get down!" Jet yelled, and accelerated in a controlled skid until the tires were on pavement, at which point she braked until the truck was stable and then floored the gas. The gunfire faded as the old truck picked up speed, but Jet's eyes were locked on the rearview mirror as Salma brushed safety glass from her lap and shoulders and sat up.

"That was too close for comfort," Salma said. She adjusted the AK between her legs and frowned at Jet's profile. "What is it?"

"I think I can make out something back on the road. But it's running without lights, like we are."

Salma twisted to look out the back window. After several moments, headlights blinked on a half kilometer behind them, and Jet urged the truck to higher speed as the little four-cylinder engine whined in protest.

"That's got to be Mounir," Salma said, hoisting the AK. "When he gets closer, I'll give him a surprise he's not expecting."

"Hang on," Jet said. "They're gaining on us. This thing's underpowered. We need to get off the road."

"You think it'll make it?"

Jet scowled at the landscape rushing past them.

"We don't have a choice. Next break in the fields, we're going to find out. So buckle up and get ready."

CHAPTER 29

Tripoli, Libya

Leo backed away from the window of his third-floor apartment and killed the lights. Outside on the street, gunfire echoed off the building façades, and an anguished scream pierced the night. A flurry of pistol shots cracked from below and were answered by the staccato bark of an AK-47.

Tripoli had rapidly descended into chaos since the attack on the naval base, as rival criminal and political factions used the disorder the assault had created to settle grudges and attempt to seize power over coveted areas of the city, resulting in an environment that was as close to a war zone as anything since the 2011 revolution. Roving groups of heavily armed militia roamed the streets, attempting to keep a semblance of order in their neighborhoods, but ultimately only adding to the pandemonium as gunfights ensued.

Leo lay on the wooden floor of his simple walk-up one-bedroom and pointed the antenna of his sat phone at the heavens through the open window as he attempted to lock on a signal. When the indicator flashed that he was locked, he dialed the Mossad headquarters contact number and waited for his control officer to answer.

The call activated and he gave his ID code and waited as his identity was authenticated. Once it was, the line clicked and he was transferred to the group that was responsible for the Libya extraction.

"Status?" a familiar voice asked.

"The situation's deteriorating. Since they shut the borders, Tripoli's a free-for-all. The airport's closed for the foreseeable future, so no chance of getting anyone out that way."

"That's unfortunate. What's the situation with the assets?"

"They're ten hours south. But if anything, it appears the environment there is even worse. As I told you the last time, they're requesting immediate evacuation."

"We've checked with Tunisia and Algeria. Neither is willing to violate the quarantine."

"You need to apply pressure. We can't leave them hanging out to dry."

"Understood. But it doesn't look like an airborne extraction's practical."

"Then what do I tell them?"

"They need to get to Tripoli. You'll have to arrange for a boat for the primary asset."

"And the operative we sent in?"

"Use your best judgment. It would be best if we didn't put all our eggs in one basket. We can't afford two of our operatives to be compromised if something goes wrong and the boat is intercepted."

"What's the status of the sea blockade? A boat won't do any good if it gets blown out of the water."

"It will be several days before the Americans are able to move sufficient ships into the area, and there are some issues with international cooperation. It's bad politics to shut down what's perceived as humanitarian assistance."

"There's no guarantee they can get to Tripoli safely."

"We can't do anything for them in the middle of the desert. They have to. They're both capable. That's our only option."

"I committed to an extraction from Sebha."

A pause. "Decommit. It's impractical. They're on their own until they reach the coast."

It was Leo's turn to pause. "That wasn't the arrangement."

"It is now. We don't have any choice. It'll be hard enough to ensure whatever boat you get the target on has clearance with the blockade ships that will be in place soon."

"Assuming they make it, what do I tell the operative?"

"We'll figure that out once the target is out of danger. The operative may have to go to ground until the situation improves."

More shooting reverberated from the street. When it fell silent, Leo continued. "It isn't stable here. They'll be walking into a minefield."

The voice on the line sounded tense for the first time. "There isn't much we can do that we aren't doing. You'll have to do the best you can with the available resources."

After another minute of contention, Leo signed off and sat with his back to the wall. Headquarters was basically saying that their hands were tied, and it would be up to him to solve his charges' problem. But with the streets a shooting gallery and anyone with any resources trying to get the hell out of Libya, finding a seaworthy boat to ferry Salma to safety would be far harder than under normal circumstances, assuming anyone was willing to do it at all.

As to the female operative, he had no suggestions other than to hole up with a mountain of ammo, food, and water, and wait for conditions to improve. Which was the equivalent of throwing her to the wolves. His job was to get his operatives whatever resources they required to do their jobs, and then ensure they made it safely home. Given the current conditions, neither was practical, and he dreaded the call he'd be making once he figured out how to filter what he'd just been told. He knew from his training that it was important to keep optimistic even when the walls were crumbling, but it went against his nature to flat out lie to people who'd put their lives on the line.

More shooting from outside sounded farther away, and he sighed. Night brought out the predators, and in times of crisis, especially so. He'd have to wait until morning to assess the situation and determine how to proceed, but he had to tell the operative something, and it was with a heavy heart that he raised the sat phone to his ear again and dialed the mystery woman's number.

Her phone rang six times and then disconnected without answering.

Leo frowned and checked the signal strength and tried again. More ringing, but no answer.

It was possible that her phone had run out of juice, or that she was in a location where she couldn't get a sat fix. The other possibility was grim. The only reason an operative would ignore his call was because she was out of the game.

He had to proceed as though there had been some sort of technical malfunction, of course. But an acid knot had formed in his stomach when the second call wasn't picked up, and it was impossible to shake the feeling that something disastrous had happened. Leo tried a third time with the same result and set the phone down just as another volley of gunfire from down the block announced that someone had gotten even with someone else, or had rid the world of a hated rival.

He dared a peek over the sill and saw a swarm of turbaned figures running toward another group that was standing over the bodies of three men, their Kalashnikov rifles scattered in the street. How he would be able to make it to the port without being killed was a good question, given the current level of lawlessness, which even for Libya was alarming. But he knew he would have to do it, so he crawled to his closet and removed a lockbox that contained a pistol, a box of ammunition, and the twin of the H&K submachine gun he'd sourced for the operative. Whatever he encountered, his chances of prevailing were high, given his training and the armaments, but even so it wasn't an errand he was looking forward to, and he gritted his teeth as he fed bullets into the spare magazines, his prospects of making it to the next day lower than at any point since he'd gone into the field.

CHAPTER 30

South of Sebha, Libya

Jet gripped the steering wheel with white knuckles and twisted it hard left. The ancient Toyota bucked like a bronco as it veered off the pavement and onto relatively solid soil along the side of an expansive field. The tires skidded along the sandy terrain, and it took all of Jet's abilities to keep the truck from flipping or careening wildly.

Salma watched through the rear window frame as the road receded from view, and then turned to Jet. "They made the turn. Must have seen our brake lights."

Jet cursed under her breath. It had been a risk – she couldn't use the emergency brake given that all that remained of it after decades was a metal shaft rattling by her knee, and downshifting had only slowed the truck somewhat, not enough to avoid tipping when she'd made the turn.

She increased the speed until the front axle was slamming alarmingly each time they hit a rut, the shocks long ago rendered useless by time and hard use. The moonlight was sufficient to make out the worst of the hazards, but at speed she couldn't avoid them all, especially given the uncertain conditions and the tenuous grip of the aged rubber. Jet grimaced at the fuel gauge and speedometer, neither of which worked, and slammed the gear shift lever with her hand.

"It's like driving on ice," she said, squinting to make out the terrain rushing at them.

The headlights of the chase truck were gaining on them, and Jet tilted her head at another farm to their right, with a trio of stone auxiliary buildings a hundred meters from the house.

"We're never going to be able to outrun them in this thing. We'll

161

have to shoot it out. I'll get us to those buildings, and then we'll need to take cover and hope they rush us without thinking."

"Knowing Mounir, they will," Salma said, clutching her rifle.

"Then they're dead meat."

Jet guided the truck along the perimeter fence for a bit and then crashed through it, knocking wooden posts and wire aside. They bounced across furrows in the ground, the wheel thrashing like a living thing in Jet's hands, and slowed as they neared the outbuildings.

The Toyota skidded to a halt and Jet was already out the door with her MP7A1 as Salma threw her door open and followed her between two of the structures, the AK and a spare magazine in hand.

"How do you want to do this?" Salma asked.

"Take cover behind that one," Jet said, pointing at the building to her left. "I'll take this one. Don't fire until I do, and wait until they're close enough that you can't miss. And try not to hit their truck – it'll be our way out of here if it's got good tires and decent fuel."

"I remember my training," Salma snapped. Jet had to remind herself that this was also a trained operative who'd undergone the same rigorous conditioning she had, not a civilian.

"Sorry. I want to avoid a crossfire, so I'm going to edge along the side to where that pony wall is."

"Got it."

Jet melted into the darkness and Salma hobbled to the building, rifle clutched in both hands. The roar of the chase truck's engine grew louder, and she crouched down low, the AK fire selector in the center position for full auto. The headlights brightened and then bounced giddily as the vehicle negotiated the field, and Salma set the spare magazine on the ground beside her and adjusted the rifle.

Jet closed her eyes as the truck neared in order to avoid destroying her night vision. When it growled to a stop by the abandoned Toyota, she dared a peek over the meter-high stone wall and watched as the doors on a newer four-wheel drive pickup opened and three men spilled from it, with another pair joining them from the truck bed – all with rifles. They took cautious steps, leading with their guns, until they were at the Toyota. They peered inside, and then one of them barked an unintelligible order and they split up to move on the buildings.

Two of the gunmen edged toward the right structure, one crept up the center, staying low, and the other pair inched toward where Salma was hiding. Jet waited, controlling her breathing to slow her heart rate, and when the two who approaching her were thirty meters away, she opened fire with the Heckler & Koch.

Her first rounds caught the nearest man in the chest and he fell backward with a scream. His companion's reflexes were lightning fast, and her fire only grazed him as he threw himself to the side. He rolled when he hit the ground and was shooting before Jet could tag him. Most of his shots went wide, but enough of them pocked the wall that Jet ducked down, allowing him to expend his ammo shooting at shadows.

Salma's AK rattled on continuous fire in six- and eight-round bursts, and Jet offered a silent plea to the universe that her shots were finding home. When the shooting from her target paused, Jet rolled a meter and poked her head and rifle over the wall. The gunman was changing magazines; the first well-placed round drilled through his skull just below his left eye, and the second shattered his jaw.

Answering fire from Mounir's men barked at Salma, their muzzle flashes lighting the night as they pinned her down and pummeled the building with lead. An occasional single shot from her position told Jet that she'd switched from the ammo-wasting full auto to single fire, which meant she was still in the game.

Jet shifted her aim to where the lone middle gunman had been moments before, but she didn't see him. A high-pitched ringing in her ears from the gunfire prevented her from being able to hear footfalls, so she rolled away from the wall and crawled toward the first of the buildings, grateful for her black clothes and the night camouflage they provided. She reached it and froze when the sour tang of dried sweat assaulted her – the man was only inches away around the corner, waiting for her or Salma to show themselves.

Jet drew her pistol and tossed it onto the dirt a few meters away.

The sound of metal on dirt drew the man's fire, and she rolled into view and stitched him from navel to throat, earning a bloodcurdling scream of pain as he crumpled and dropped his AK.

She ran to him and scooped up the assault rifle, reluctant to waste any more of her precious rounds, and after ejecting the half-spent magazine and replacing it with a new one from his satchel, made her way toward the building next to Salma's as the firefight between the gunmen and Salma raged.

Jet darted between the buildings, and rounds ricocheted off the dirt where she'd been running in a crouch only moments before. She swore silently at the moonlight that had enabled her to drive but now leveled the playing field between the shooters and herself, and stopped at the far corner, where she could see Salma kneeling, breathing hard, the barrel of her rifle pointed at the sky as she waited for a lull in the fire to continue plinking at the gunmen. Jet waved at her to get her attention, but she was fully focused on her task.

Jet eyed the wall she was leaning against and saw that it was poorly crafted brickwork with mortar gaps wide enough to easily create fingerholds. She slid the H&K strap over her right shoulder and the AK over her left, and reached for the highest crevice she could. Her hands found holds, and she pulled herself up, using the toes of her boots to feel for holds, repeating the exercise until she'd hoisted herself over the roof lip and onto the flat surface.

She dog-crawled to the far edge and surveyed the area in front of the trucks. From the higher elevation she could easily make out the two remaining gunmen lying on the ground, the shot from her perch laughably easy at no more than fifteen meters. Jet slipped the AK strap from her shoulder and switched the firing selector to continuous fire, and after drawing a bead on the first man, squeezed off half the magazine and then peppered the second with the remainder, the wooden stock of the assault rifle slamming against her shoulder as it discharged its lethal load.

When the gun was empty, she stood and eyed the scene below for a moment before calling out to Salma.

"Game over. We win. You okay?"

"Yes. That's all of them?"

"It is. I'll be down in a second. In the meantime, gather up as many full mags as you can find and empty their wallets. Don't leave anything we could use behind."

Jet lowered herself from the roof and moved to inspect the truck the attackers had arrived in. It was also Japanese, a Nissan, but a different generation, with oversized tires and a heavy-duty suspension for serious off-roading. Salma arrived with an armful of magazines just as Jet turned the ignition key and the engine roared to life. She regarded the fuel gauge, which was two-thirds full, and turned to Salma.

"Which one's Mounir?" Jet asked.

"None of them. He sent others to do his dirty work. Just like before. He's a filthy coward at heart."

"Most terrorists are," Jet agreed. "That everything? I want to get out of here. Even in Libya, this much shooting's going to draw attention."

Salma nodded. "Everything I could find."

"Then climb in and let's get going. We'll stick to dirt until we've gone a few kilometers. I don't want to have to worry about running into any of Mounir's friends."

Jet walked to the old Toyota and scooped up the saddlebags, and returned to the truck to toss them into the cab by Salma's feet. Salma held up a pair of binoculars and a wad of dollars and dinars. "We won't starve. And the spyglasses may come in handy."

"Good find."

Jet hoisted herself into the driver's seat, adjusted it, and jammed the transmission into gear. "We may be able to make it all the way to Tripoli without stopping for gas if I take it easy. We'll see."

"And then what?"

Jet opened her saddlebag and checked the sat phone. The battery indicator was dead, so the phone was going to be of little use to them until they could get somewhere to charge it.

"We'll figure it out once we're there. Anything's got to be better than Sebha."

Salma gave her a knowing look and a short, bitter laugh. "Damn right."

CHAPTER 31

Jerusalem, Israel

The streets of the old city were bustling in the late morning as Yevgeni walked unhurriedly toward his meeting at a sidewalk café on the way to Temple Mount. Tourists with cameras hanging from their necks gaped at the ancient buildings and stopped to pose on the narrow streets as the tall Russian ambled by, his expression neutral, to any bystanders just another foreigner making a pilgrimage to some of the most sacred spots on the planet.

He'd spent the previous day contacting the three arms dealers he'd been given as reliable, and had set up the meeting after the Tel Aviv dealer hadn't answered his phone. Yevgeni hated to drive to a different city and return carrying weaponry, but he'd seen no way around it and had resigned himself to losing yet another day securing what he'd need.

He rounded a corner and nearly ran headlong into a trio of Hassidic men arguing heatedly over something. They brushed by, barely registering him, and he smiled inwardly. He could have easily dispatched all three in as many seconds, but instead had slumped his shoulders and assumed a meek stance, his expression bewildered and unthreatening, and most importantly, completely unmemorable other than the pink hue of his skin from exposure to the Middle Eastern sun.

Yevgeni had been reluctant to speak on the phone, as had been the arms merchant, so they'd agreed on an in-person so he could tell the dealer what he wanted. He didn't think getting the goods would be a problem – his agent had given this dealer his full endorsement, whereas the others had been recommendations from other independents who'd worked the area within the last couple of years.

He arrived at the café and smiled at a pair of young women, one of whom was chatting on her cell phone, the other engrossed in her own little screen, seemingly completely oblivious to each other as their coffee grew cold. Neither acknowledged him, which he saw as a positive – he normally drew a reasonable response from the opposite sex, but while on a job he deliberately dressed down and stuck to outdated sunglasses and cheap shirts – their lack of interest was a testament to the effectiveness of his disguise.

Yevgeni took a seat at one of the open tables and removed his green four-leaf-clover baseball hat, the agreed marker that the dealer would use to recognize him, and set it on the table. A waitress appeared from the doorway after a three-minute wait and greeted him in English, her tone as bored as only the young working in jobs far beneath their self-images could muster.

"I'll take a double espresso," he said after a glance at a menu card she handed him.

"Anything else?" she asked, as though his choice had already disappointed her.

"No, thank you," he replied politely, his accent slight from years of careful practice, although his words were still tinged with the distinctive tonality of his native tongue.

She left to get his order, and he admired her charms as she strolled away, before returning his attention to the street. A pair of Japanese or Korean women walked by wearing ill-advised yoga pants and polyester multicolored tops, followed by a trio of schoolboys bickering as they hurried along. He removed his cell phone and set it beside the hat, and checked the time again on the screen. The man was now officially late – not an auspicious start to the new relationship.

Yevgeni's coffee arrived with a whiff of floral perfume from the waitress, and then a septuagenarian with wisps of white hair poking out from beneath a beret pulled the chair opposite the Russian from beneath the table and sat down. He looked at the waitress as though a jeweler appraising a fine diamond, and gave her a wolfish grin.

"Cup of house blend, if it won't break the bank," he said.

The waitress rolled her eyes. "That's it?"

"Unless you want to run off with me for the most disappointing eight minutes of your life."

That drew a half smile and a wink. "Let me think about it. Hope you're a big tipper."

"Are you kidding? You're lucky if I can cover my drink."

When the girl left, the old man appraised Yevgeni, the warmth gone from his piercing blue eyes. "Glad to see you made it," he said, and extended his hand in greeting.

"Likewise," the Russian said, and took a sip of his espresso.

"Nice day, isn't it? Days like this you can almost believe in your fellow man."

"If you say so."

The waitress returned with the dealer's coffee and set it down without comment. Yevgeni handed her several bills and offered a smile. "Keep the change."

She looked at the amount he'd given her and pursed her lips before muttering a thanks and returning inside. The dealer drained his coffee in two gulps and stood. "Thanks. Let's stretch our legs."

Yevgeni walked beside the old dealer as he led him along the narrow way.

"What do you call yourself?" the dealer asked.

"Joe."

"Great. Nice to meet you, Joe. I'm Saul, which you know. What can I do you for?"

Yevgeni named a brand of handgun and a rifle that he knew would be readily available in Israel. "Fifty rounds for each. Spare mags. Suppressors for both. Something nondescript to carry them in."

"You care about the origin?"

"Prefer if they're virgin, although it's not essential. But they have to be untraceable no matter what."

Saul spread his hands. "Goes without saying."

"Still, I did. So they have to be."

Saul turned a corner and picked up his pace, moving surprisingly quickly for a man of his years. When he reached the doorway of a narrow home that looked like it dated back to Roman times, he turned to the Russian and named a price in euros and in dollars. Yevgeni nodded – it was at the high end of the expected range, but then again he wasn't looking for a bargain.

"Perfect," he said.

"Good. Then come in and I'll show you the goods."

The interior of the home was simple, the furniture well crafted but modest, the hallway's smell musty and old – a fitting accompaniment to its owner. Saul guided him past a living room and kitchen to a service area with a garbage can, which he pushed aside to reveal a trapdoor in the floor.

Saul pointed at an iron ring imbedded in the wooden hatch. "Mind doing the honors? My back's killing me."

Yevgeni stepped forward, lifted the trapdoor, and a light clicked on below, revealing stairs leading into a basement. Saul motioned for the Russian to descend, and followed him down into a small chamber filled with dusty junk.

"This way," he said, and crossed the room to a door by a rusting coat of medieval armor on a stand. He brushed part of a stained tapestry aside, revealing a retinal scanner, and leaned forward. A heavy bolt clunked inside the door, and he pushed it open and offered Yevgeni a small bow. "Welcome to my little shop of horrors," he said, and flipped a light switch inside.

Glass cases lined the walls of a vault easily five times the size of the antechamber, filled with every imaginable variation of assault and sniper rifle on one side of the room and pistols on the other. Saul moved without hesitation to one of the displays and removed an IWI Jericho 941 pistol and tossed it to Yevgeni, who caught it and inspected it carefully.

"Semi-compact polymer," Saul said. "9mm. Never been fired. More virgin than Joan of Arc."

"Provenance?" Yevgeni asked.

"Went missing from a lot at the factory, and the serial number's been acid-washed away."

"Nice. I'll take it. What about a suppressor?"

Saul bent and removed a tube from the bottom of the case. "Custom made by yours truly. Again, never used. Coupled with subsonic rounds, barely louder than a smoker's cough."

"I trust you have some of those?"

"Of course. Box of fifty. Two spare mags. You need more?"

Yevgeni shook his head. "That should do it. I'll want to test fire it before paying."

Saul nodded and indicated the door at the far end of the room. "I have a range set up. Soundproofed, although it wouldn't matter with the suppressor."

"What about the Tavor?"

Saul pointed at one of the other cases. "X95 380 with a MARS sight, chambered for 9mm. Lightly used as a demo model only. Also with a suppressor and a hundred rounds, although I can get you as many as you like. You don't need to go subsonic with this one to fire quiet, although it would further silence it."

"Let's see it."

Saul walked to the case and opened it, and removed the wicked-looking bullpup assault rifle. He gazed at it fondly for a second and then handed it to the Russian, who hefted it approvingly.

"Clean. Also sanitized?"

"Of course. Completely untraceable. Came from an armory nearby where goods have a habit of walking away." Saul shrugged. "Human character is predictable. We're all cast from imperfect clay."

"Indeed."

The shooting range turned out to be a fifteen-meter-long chamber carved from bedrock and lined with thick sound insulation. The air was dank and cool, and Yevgeni put both weapons through their paces with practiced efficiency before turning to Saul and nodding.

"As advertised. Let's clean them up and get you paid."

Back in the showroom, Yevgeni stripped the pistol first, cleaned and oiled it, and then did the same with the Tavor. Saul rummaged in a drawer and brought out a carton of subsonic 9mm rounds for the pistol and two boxes of standard 9mm Parabellum. He set them on the workbench and grinned expectantly.

"Handloaded by yours truly. And while I love my work, it doesn't pay the bills," Saul said. "This is the part I live for."

The matter decided, Yevgeni withdrew an envelope stuffed with dollars and counted out five thousand in hundreds and handed them to the older man, who inspected each before folding the wad and putting it in his pocket.

Saul pointed at a pile of black nylon bags. "Pleasure doing business with you. There's a duffle you can toss the gear into."

Five minutes later Yevgeni was walking back to his car, toting the duffle and whistling softly. He checked his watch and shook his head – he wouldn't be able to make it back to Tel Aviv in time to intercept the target today, but there was tomorrow to look forward to, and obtaining the right tools for the job was an essential part of any operation. At the car, he put the weapons in the trunk and closed it softly, and then slid into the driver's seat, the outcome of his assignment now all but guaranteed.

CHAPTER 32

Tripoli, Libya

A crowd had gathered when word of Tariq's imminent arrival had spread, and the streets leading into the city were filled with his gunmen and ordinary citizens, some with homemade signs with his name emblazoned on them, some with assault rifles waving in the air as they chanted his name. The main junction from the southern Gharyan Road was clogged with humanity, and those loyal to Tariq had sealed off the area so no rivals could take a potshot at their leader as he arrived. From near a fountain, long out of use, a group of youths dressed in castoffs, their faces dirty and hair slick with oil, cried his name with the fervor of true believers.

"Tariq Qaddafi! Tariq Qaddafi!"

The Qaddafi name, contrary to the Western media's claims, resonated with a broad cross-section of Libya's population, and the fact that Tariq was distantly related now served as his faction's battle cry. Conditions in Libya had deteriorated precipitously since the revolution, largely funded by the CIA and carried out by hired mercenaries dubbed "freedom fighters" by the media for public consumption, and nostalgia was strong for the leader who had improved the standard of living for most in the country, providing every citizen with free health care and remarkable infrastructure projects that were now lying fallow.

Tariq's group had leveraged this warm regard and advanced him to be a viable candidate to lead the country out of the quagmire in which it found itself, installing Sharia law and operating the nation's oil industry for the benefit of the citizenry rather than the multinational oil companies that had swooped in within nanoseconds of Qaddafi being toppled. Whereas Tariq was perceived as a dangerous terrorist threat by the West, the internal perception was that he was a visionary who could lead Libya back to greatness by standing up to the imperialist forces that had installed a puppet government to rubber-stamp their agenda, and by ridding the country of the multinational corporations that were exploiting the natural resources while the population languished.

Whether it was true or not was immaterial. What mattered was how his faction could seize control of the city without serious opposition – something only a group that had the lion's share of the people behind it could hope to do. Tariq's clan had quietly spread the word among the disenfranchised that he would soon return to Libya to take his rightful position on the throne, and the reception had been enthusiastic; not surprising given the squalor most lived in since the regime change. The prospect of drinkable water and an environment where the lawless couldn't terrorize everyone was enough for most to support Tariq's group after years of misery and conditions that were beyond most people's comprehension.

A rousing cheer went up from the crowd when Tariq's convoy came into view, and several of the armed fired their weapons into the air in triumph. Some of the gunmen in the approaching truck beds did the same, and grown men had tears of joy streaming down their faces, so overcome were they with emotion.

The trucks rolled to a stop, and four gunmen descended from the two lead vehicles and took up position beside the third. That truck's doors opened and Tariq stepped out, his travel garments replaced by a pristine white robe so bright in the sunlight he appeared to glow. He basked in the adulation for a solid minute and then held up his hands to quiet the throng. The excited chatter and screams faded to a dull murmur, and he beamed at the gathering before speaking.

"My brothers, it has been a long road to Tripoli, but I am finally here! And it feels better than anything I could have imagined!"

More cheers and shouts, and he paused until the group quieted.

"In the last days I have been all over our country, and it is a shambles – rendered a disaster by those who have usurped our national power and are operating the nation as their own private plantation. I have seen girls barely as tall as my chest reduced to selling their bodies just to eat. I have seen boys doing the same. I have seen lifelong friends murdering each other for control over little more than nothing. I have seen suffering that defies the imagination, and I am here to promise that it is time for it to stop!"

The crowd roared its approval, and Tariq continued to smile at his acolytes until they fell silent.

"Today is the dawn of a new time. An era of boundless prosperity for all, where we can walk down the street without fearing for our lives, where our women can live lives of virtue and honor, where our children are safe and have a chance for a better future. But it will not be easy. No, our country has enemies that have become its masters. That must stop if we are ever to return to our glory days – glory days that took place under my namesake's rule. I am here to continue his work, to raise us as a whole to greatness, and to banish those who have turned our home into a hell on earth. My message to you is clear. The days of Libya being a prostitute to Western interests are over. We will not live like slaves any longer. Those days are done, and this is now our time to rise up and throw off our chains!"

This time the cheering went on for minutes, and Tariq allowed the gathered to express their support without interruption. He spent another ten minutes speaking of a new era, led by himself, and then looked to Akmal, who ran the Tripoli cell of his group.

"I am tired," Tariq said. "Overjoyed at seeing our people, but tired nonetheless."

"We have taken the royal palace. You will be safe there."

He shook his head. "No. That is one of the things my predecessor did wrong. I am Berber. I belong to the desert, not to edifices raised for obscene glory. I will stay somewhere that reminds me of my humility and good fortune, not of ostentatious displays under the old regime. The people must see that I am one of them, and that my power stems from them. So find me someplace simple that can be defended against all enemies, and that is where I will lay my head."

Akmal exhaled in frustration. "It will be difficult to safeguard you anywhere but the palace. We've made all the arrangements."

Tariq shook his head. "I fear nothing."

"Your adversaries will do anything to remove you. And the West..."

Tariq waved the comment away. "The West has no power over us."

"They have shut down all cell and internet communications and have threatened to cut the city's power. They are also warning that a blockade is going to be put into place, and we will be completely isolated."

Tariq lifted a hand as if to block any further objections. "I know all this. But I have a plan. Speaking of which, I want to see the boat that will carry the refugees north before it leaves tonight." He paused. "We can't afford another disaster."

"Of course. We can head there after we find someplace to use as our headquarters, if the palace is out of the question."

"We can occupy one of the surrounding buildings. Something utilitarian and simple. I don't want the people to think that I am going to live like a sultan. I am one of them, nothing more. They need to see that, or they will grow resentful."

"We shall make it so." Akmal turned to his gunmen and shouted orders in Arabic. The men scrambled to drive back the mob so the convoy could pass, and Tariq gave a final wave and walked back to his truck, his shoulders squared and his head held high.

His plan, preposterous as it might have initially appeared, was viable. Western countries had sworn never to deal with those they defined as terrorists, yet they had shown their hypocrisy time and time again, supporting the most brutal dictatorships in the world. What had determined his course of action was reading a book on Yasser Arafat while in prison, and how he'd gone from being one of the most hated terrorist figures in the Middle East to an elder statesman.

There was no reason Tariq could see that he couldn't achieve the same end. As long as the nerve agent wasn't directly traced to him, he had plausible deniability, while wielding the unspoken threat that if he *was* responsible for it, there was more where it had come from, and he wasn't afraid to use it. Much as the CIA-created ISIS and al-Qaeda had served as a pretense for the U.S. to wage devastating wars in Syria, Iraq, and Afghanistan, Tariq's militant group could be separated from his political form and marginalized as a fringe element that he had nothing to do with. Nobody would believe it, but that didn't matter – he understood from careful study that all government was a game of liar's poker anyway, and all history was the winner's account.

He climbed back into the truck, looked at the driver, and growled instructions. "Follow their vehicles. Once we're rested, we'll head to the harbor."

The convoy eventually wound up at a large private home near the French embassy, owned by a supporter of Tariq's who lived full-time in Algiers. It was a multistory building with eight bedrooms, solid as a fort, and although not ideally defended, adequate for the purpose. Tariq managed a few hours of sleep in one of the bedrooms, exhausted after the trip and a longer-than-planned sojourn in Sebha, where he'd spent a full day negotiating with the various warlords who controlled the area, and proposed an arrangement where they would have positions of influence in his new government versus being hunted down like dogs by his forces. By the time he'd concluded the discussions, it had been late at night, and they'd driven straight through to Tripoli, their progress slowed by several encounters with militia who'd attempted to charge them the toll they extracted from the truckers who braved the desert route.

A knock at the door awakened him, and he rubbed sleep from his eyes before sitting up and calling out, "What?"

The door opened and Akmal poked his head in. "There's a problem at the harbor. They're working on it, but it's unlikely the boat will leave tonight."

Tariq's eyes narrowed. "What sort of problem?"

"The engine. They need to source a part for the transmission. They swear it won't take long."

"What about another boat?"

"All the larger craft are gone. Anyone with money has left the country."

"How about Zuwara?" Tariq asked.

Akmal shook his head. "Nothing but small wooden fishing boats. They'd never make it with the weather kicking up."

"And the cargo? It must make it to Italy before the blockade is able to stop it."

"I know. We're doing everything we can."

Tariq nodded. "See to it that it's enough. This cannot fail. It's an integral part of my strategy."

"I won't let you down."

Tariq's eyes bored into him like lasers. "I hope for your sake you don't."

CHAPTER 33

Brussels, Belgium

The massive conference room at NATO headquarters on the Rue de la Fusée was packed with high-ranking officials from all the member nations. The atmosphere was tense, and the discussions that had been ongoing for the last hour were going nowhere – not unusual when contentious issues were under consideration.

The United States representative had made the case for a naval blockade of Libya and had waxed eloquently for fifteen minutes about its need. The U.S. Navy lacked sufficient resources to fully block the waters off Libya, and required international support to do so – support that had been withheld by several of the key members.

The French attaché sat forward and adjusted the microphone before him before speaking.

"That may be, Mr. Ambassador," he said, addressing his American counterpart. "However, reports from our sources on the ground are that your country's unilateral actions against Libya are already resulting in a substantial crisis, which will only worsen should there be a blockade. Whole areas of Tripoli are without power, looting is widespread, the local government has gone missing, and the situation is deteriorating. To impose a complete blockade would result in untold hardship, not to mention that the…the optics, I believe you call them, would be disastrous."

The American ambassador frowned before responding, "We've been through all of this, Ambassador Leroux, and we don't make our demand lightly. But if you don't want this nerve agent employed against European targets, a naval blockade is essential. Minutes count. Even now there are hundreds of boats making their way from

Libya, and any one of them, or most of them, could be carrying payloads like that discovered by our esteemed Italian partners. Do you really want to risk a terrorist attack with a bioweapon in, say, downtown Paris? Or Cannes, or Nice, or Marseilles?" He paused. "I can assure you that the…optics…of that would be far worse than anything you can imagine arising from the blockade. Which we wouldn't have proposed if it weren't necessary."

"What evidence do you have that there is any more of this agent in Libya?" the Frenchman fired back. "Is it not mere speculation that more exists?"

The American ambassador's lips tightened. "We have to assume that it does."

The Italian representative smirked. "Assume? How did that work out in Iraq? Frankly, it will be extremely difficult to convince my government to go along with any unproven assumptions given your recent track record. My superiors are against a unilateral blockade, and we have legitimate concerns about putting NATO's resources to work in a manner that will be perceived as tantamount to genocide by many in the developing world."

"Your government is the one that alerted us to the threat in the first place. Yet now you're reluctant to stop more of the agent from reaching your shores?" The American ambassador shook his head. "What would it take for you to cooperate and dedicate the required resources?"

"More than empty speculations," the French representative snapped. "We're already contending with a huge immigration problem caused by American adventures in Iraq and Syria. We don't need our interests in Africa to be jeopardized. My government would never go along with anything that could worsen an already precarious situation."

"Gentlemen, this isn't about appearances. We know that terrorists have this bioweapon. They've already used it in Tripoli, which is what is actually responsible for the current chaos, not our asking Algeria and Tunisia to close the borders. It was calculated to do maximum damage and to send a message. The fishing boat was an accident.

Had it not been, we would right now be discussing how to react to thousands dead somewhere in Europe, with the threat of more to follow. Ask yourselves what the reaction would be to that. Or imagine that the responsible parties decided to target the airport here in Brussels at a time when we're all on our way home. Or a meeting of the EU. Forget sporting events or mass transit – imagine if you were targeted, or your families." He paused. "How concerned with the *optics* would your governments be if their headquarters were at risk?"

"As a practical matter, it would take at least two days to get our ships into position," the Italian said. "We couldn't just pull everything from our coast. It would have to be thought through. And the logistics of trying to seal off over a quarter of the northern coastline of Africa are incalculable."

"Our people say that it would be virtually impossible to stop all traffic," the Frenchman added.

The American nodded once. "Fair enough. So what's your proposal? Just wait until you have the mother of all bioweapon attacks on European soil? I'm actually tempted to acquiesce and wish you well when it happens. It's not like I haven't tried to get your governments to see reason." He looked around the room. "This will be remembered when the time comes for my government to cooperate with yours on some important matter. But if you don't care about stopping a crisis in the making by taking prudent precautions, I won't force you. You can explain to your citizens after the fact about how you knew and understood the threat, but were willing to allow the catastrophe to occur rather than taking action."

He pushed back from the table and began gathering his things as his assistants fidgeted and studied their shoes. The Italian sighed and looked to his French colleague.

"The matter isn't settled," he said. "Allow me a few hours to convey your thoughts to my people."

"I shall need to speak with my superiors as well," the Frenchman added. "Please give us the time to form a consensus. Acting rashly will serve none of us well."

The American ambassador's face could have been carved from basalt. "A reasonable request. Shall we reconvene in…three hours?"

The room cleared, and the U.S. ambassador walked with his subordinates toward the main exit.

"What do you think?" he asked his chief aide.

"The French will get on board. They have no choice. They're just being difficult because they can."

The ambassador snorted and allowed himself a trace of a smile. "They always are, until Germany decides it wants Paris as a suburb, or Russia points missiles at them. Then all of a sudden we can't answer the phone fast enough. You think this will be it, or will we have to suffer through another round of this nonsense?"

"Hard to read the Italians. My gut says with the populist movement in play there, they don't go along. It's just a hunch."

"I hope you're wrong. They've got the most ships available in the region." He hesitated. "I shouldn't say this, but that smug prick always seems like he's lying through his teeth, even when he's agreeing with us."

"They're just taking orders, like we all are."

"As I recall, that wasn't much of a defense at Nuremburg."

The young aide's brow furrowed at the reference. "Pardon?"

The ambassador waved a hand as he pushed through the door. "Never mind."

CHAPTER 34

South of Tripoli, Libya

The truck rumbled along the road as it neared Tripoli, its oversized tires accommodating the miserable condition of the asphalt with ease. Jet yawned; the three hours of sleep she'd gotten before dawn were inadequate, but the best she was going to see until they reached the port city. Salma had dozed on the trip north, but Jet hadn't trusted her to drive while she slept given her weakened condition and the ordeal she'd endured escaping her husband, as well as at the hands of the slavers.

She was now awake, their latest run on the sand to evade a militia blockade having jarred her from her sleep, and she wiped the sweat from her face with the back of her arm as a sea of endless beige blurred by.

Jet studied the fuel gauge, which read just below a quarter tank, and nodded to herself. They had enough to make it, but just barely. She hadn't dared stop for fuel – if Mounir had the kinds of contacts Salma claimed, he could well have communicated with his kindred to the north and arranged for an unpleasant welcoming committee. But the truck sipped gas when kept to a reasonable speed, and her concern lessened as they reduced the remaining distance they needed to travel.

"How did you wind up with the Mossad?" Jet asked, curious about the parts of Salma's past that hadn't been in the dossier.

"I suppose the usual. I was doing my stint with the IDF, and they approached me. You know the drill. Probably much the same way they recruited you."

Jet thought back to the ultimatum she'd been faced with and shook her head. "I doubt it. But you said you hardly ever saw David? So he didn't play a part in it?"

"I suppose we'll never know, right? He took his secrets to the grave. I suppose he could have identified me as a possible candidate, but that seems pretty cold-blooded…"

Jet recalled David's decision to rob her of her daughter without telling her, and pursed her lips. "He could be that way. Part of the characteristics that make for a good control, right?"

"Maybe. But like I said, we weren't in any way close, so I don't know what he'd hope to achieve. Besides, when I got the offer, I was all pumped up on patriotism and duty. You know how it is when you're nineteen and the world's shiny and new."

Her tone was bitter, and Jet supposed she had a right to be, having spent a thousand days in unimaginable servitude to a monster she despised.

"So you went through training, and then what? Was this your first assignment?"

She laughed. "Hardly. I'd been in the field for almost two years when they came to me with this. It was all very impressive and terribly urgent. The director himself called me to his office and made the pitch. I have to admit I was starstruck. I would have agreed to anything." She hesitated. "I suppose I did."

"You did what you had to do, Salma. We've all been there."

"Really? Have you had to be a whore to a man who smells like a goat and whose idea of romantic fun is to hurt you and humiliate you as much as possible? Day after day, week after week, and all to get your hands on some data you wind up losing?"

"I've got my share of ugly stories."

Salma studied her. "I suppose we all do. Sorry. This is just…fresh. Plus knowing the bastard's still out there, walking around, after putting me through this…"

"He doesn't exist anymore, Salma. He was just an assignment. An unpleasant one, but he can't hurt you, and this episode is over." Jet gave her a sidelong glance. "What do you think you'll do after this?"

"After Tripoli? To be honest, I want to quit. Maybe backpack across South America or Europe for a year, drink too much wine, maybe meet a handsome stranger who can erase the stink of death from me."

Jet considered her own adventure and was forced to smile. "Doesn't sound terrible."

"Right. But I've always heard you don't get to quit. You're the first I've met who has."

"Which proves there are exceptions. If you really want out, I can put in a word for you." Jet paused. "I'd say you've paid your dues."

"Would your support make any difference?" Salma asked.

"Truthfully, it's hard to know with the director. But it can't hurt."

Her eyes widened. "Then you know him?"

Jet nodded. "We've met a few times."

Salma fell silent, lost in thought, until eventually they bounced back onto the road.

"Shouldn't be long now," Jet said. "Once we're in the city, I'll charge the phone and we'll get you out of here."

"Sounds like a dream. I'll believe it when it happens."

As they drew closer to Tripoli, traffic fleeing the city increased as a long string of decrepit cars, buses, overloaded trucks, and bicycles clogged the road south. A haze of smoke lingered over the distant horizon, and Salma frowned at the line of pedestrians, many carrying bundles of belongings in the heat like war refugees, trudging toward the desert.

"It wasn't like this when I was here a few days ago," Jet said, swerving to avoid an impatient van that had cut into her lane to pass slower vehicles. "This doesn't look good."

Salma shook her head. "Even by Libyan standards. Did somebody start a war while you were gone?"

"I don't know."

Salma raised the binoculars and studied the road ahead, and tapped Jet's arm. "There's a truck with a bunch of gunmen in it. Looks like they're robbing some of the vehicles." She winced. "One of them just gunned down a woman who tried to run."

Jet slowed. "This isn't our fight." She glanced around and pointed to some abandoned buildings to the right. "Let's get off the pavement before they spot us."

Salma had warned Jet that the truck was a target because of its relatively youthful age and its custom suspension. At night it hadn't been a problem, but now it stood out among the senile vehicles crawling their way south, and any miscreants would be drawn to it, especially once they saw that there were only two women standing between them and the ride of their life.

Salma continued watching the horrific scene ahead as Jet rolled onto the dirt and crawled toward the buildings, avoiding any kind of speed for fear of throwing up a dust cloud that would attract the thieves. When they reached the structures, which appeared to have been part of an abandoned fuel station and restaurant nearer the road, they remained in the truck, engine idling, AK-47s in hand.

"Let me see the glasses," Jet said, and Salma handed them to her. She scanned the highway until she spied the truck – actually a pair of them, with a half dozen gunmen in each bed, waving assault rifles at everyone they passed and occasionally shooting someone, seemingly at random. They waited twenty minutes until the killers were well past their position, and then resumed driving, favoring the dirt until they'd put a kilometer between themselves and the threat.

"If you had any questions about how it must be going in Tripoli, that answers them," Jet said.

Salma shook her head as Jet returned the spyglasses to her. "Long as I've been here, I've never seen anything like that. Even Sebha, at its worst, wasn't…this." She swallowed and switched her rifle's firing selector to safe before setting it by her knee. "I'm almost afraid of what I'm escaping into."

"Whatever it is, we'll get through it. My job is to get you to safety, and I came a long way to do it."

"But if it's complete anarchy…"

"There's always a way, Salma," Jet said, steel in her tone. "Always."

"I believe you," Salma replied, but her expression betrayed her doubts, and she quickly looked away before Jet could see her eyes begin to well with moisture.

CHAPTER 35

Tripoli Harbor, Libya

Leo wended his way down a side street that led to the harbor, avoiding the main boulevards because of the escalating violence. Occasional gunfire popped in the distance like fireworks, reminding him that his prudence was justified in spite of the pistol in the waistband of his pants at the small of his back, covered by a long linen shirt, and the H&K in a shoulder bag. The few pedestrians he saw appeared terrified, their faces gaunt and their movements furtive, and several toted assault rifles in plain view.

Another call to headquarters had finally resulted in what sounded like a reasonable plan: Leo only needed to find a boat that could make it to an oil rig in international waters, just past the twelve-mile Libyan territorial boundary, where a helicopter from Tunisia would pick Salma up. It sounded simple, but Leo had lived in Libya long enough to know that nothing was ever straightforward and that it was foolish to take anything for granted. Still, it sounded like headquarters had resolved the extraction hurdle, assuming the target wasn't already dead and could make it through one of the most dangerous hellscapes on earth.

He reached the end of the street and did a double check of his surroundings. Only one more block to the waterfront, and then the hard work would begin. Since the naval base attack, there had been a steady exodus of boats, and he had no idea what remained, much less whether anyone still there would be willing to risk a trip offshore. Nobody had any idea how the forthcoming blockade would work, but it wasn't a stretch to believe that any craft that attempted to exit

Libyan waters would be sunk, the risk of it carrying the nerve agent too great to chance a less drastic outcome. The smuggling trade had always been more of a game to the locals than anything, but the prospect of death was enough to blunt the avariciousness of even the most adventurous trafficker.

A lorry clattered by, and Leo darted across the intersection and hurried down the block in search of a less public thoroughfare. Before the power had gone out a few hours earlier, the radio had warned inhabitants to remain indoors until the government was able to contain what the announcer euphemistically referred to as "the unrest." Leo understood the implicit code in the broadcast – that nobody would be stupid enough to show up for duty if it meant a day of nonstop gun battles with criminals who had nothing to lose, so the citizenry was on its own while the government either retreated to its privileged enclaves protected by high walls and massive firepower, or had winged its way to safety with the wealth of the nation in Cayman Islands accounts.

He spotted another narrow byway between two buildings and made for it. When he reached it, he paused at the sight of a pair of men making their way toward him, their robes billowing, making it easy for them to conceal weapons. His hand moved to his pistol, and his fingers locked on the butt, and his thumb felt for the safety and flicked it off.

The men neared, and Leo could see they were as fearful of him as he was of them. He relaxed when he saw they were older, perhaps in their fifties, their beards streaked with gray; not the profile of the jihadis or militia that plagued the capital. Leo nodded to them as they walked by, and they returned the gesture, their faces tight with apprehension.

He crossed the wide boulevard that ran along the water, which was deserted. At the wharf, Leo's shoulders sagged when he saw the paucity of boats in the harbor. Where before there had been over a hundred craft that could have been suitable candidates for his trip, now there were only a couple of dozen, many of which were in various states of disrepair from neglect. He scanned the waterfront, wary of threats, but the walkway was empty, and even the navy barracks appeared devoid of life, the personnel carriers gone, the flagpole barren.

Leo made his way to the side of the harbor where most of the smaller craft were moored, and spotted several that might work for his errand. One, a fifteen-meter open fishing boat, appeared serviceable, and Leo waved to the man in the stern, who had the outboard motor tilted out of the water, its engine cover off.

The man waved back, and Leo cupped his hands and called to him, "How's it going?"

"Good, I guess. Except for the city coming apart. Soon as I get this thing fixed, I'm out of here."

"What's wrong with it?"

"Dies after running for a minute. I think it's maybe the fuel filter. Or something in the injection."

"How long you think it'll take to repair it?"

The man frowned. "If I knew that, I'd be a mechanic, not a fisherman."

Leo digested that and nodded agreeably. "You interested in making some money?"

The fisherman studied Leo more closely before answering. "Right now I'm more interested in saving my skin. But what did you have in mind?"

"A run out to one of the oil rigs."

"When?"

Leo mulled over the question. "Maybe tonight. Or tomorrow."

The fisherman shook his head. "I'm out of here by then, assuming this thing will run. Things are going nowhere but down. I don't want to stick around to see how it ends."

"I don't blame you. But maybe for the right price…?"

The fisherman went back to work on the engine. "Sorry. I'm not your man. Gotta be alive to spend it."

Leo continued along the waterfront and then spun with pistol in hand when running footsteps sounded from behind him. A man in his early twenties froze, hands in the air at the sight of the gun.

"Don't shoot!" he exclaimed.

"What do you want?" Leo asked, keeping the pistol trained on him.

"I heard you talking to Jasim. My father may be willing to help you."

Leo's eyebrows rose. "May? What do you mean by help? I need a boat."

"He has one."

"Which one?"

The man slowly lowered his hands and pointed at a Zodiac inflatable Leo estimated to be at least twelve meters long. "It's fast and stable."

"What business did you say your father's in?"

The man smirked. "Not fishing. Can you put the gun away?"

Leo looked at the weapon and replaced it at the small of his back. "There."

"How much are you offering?"

"You said your father owns the boat? Maybe I can discuss it with him."

The young man's eyes narrowed, but he nodded. "I can take you to meet him."

"How far is it?"

"Not very. My name's Ahmed."

"Lead the way, Ahmed."

They walked three blocks and arrived at a home in the old city across the street from a mosque. Ahmed held the door for Leo, who waited for him to lock it behind him. They walked up a flight of stone steps, and Ahmed invited him to sit at an antique Italianate table with four chairs. Leo did, and a minute later the young man returned with an older version of himself, their facial similarities and height confirming they were father and son. The older man sat across from Leo and scowled at him for a long moment before speaking.

"My son tells me you're looking for a boat."

Leo leaned forward. "Something seaworthy to transport a friend to one of the oil rigs."

"Why would anyone want to do such a thing?"

"What matters is she wants to."

"How many passengers?"

"Just one."

"Refugee?"

Leo shrugged. "Does it matter?"

The father studied Leo. "It will be expensive. And I only deal in gold."

That was typical of many of the merchants in Tripoli since the collapse. The local dinar was useful for daily transactions, but for storing wealth, gold was the preferred method, with the dollar and euro a distant second. Libyans had a healthy distrust of accepting debt notes and using them as currency, and the old ways had persevered.

"How much?" Leo asked.

"When do you want to leave?"

"Tonight or tomorrow."

The father's eyebrows rose. "You're not sure? I wouldn't wait if I were you. There are some big changes afoot."

"So I see."

The father considered Leo. "Ten ounces."

Leo debated bargaining with the man, but the expression on his face indicated that he understood that it was a seller's market, and wasn't going to engage in the usual dickering over price.

"Done." Leo felt in his back pocket and removed a single gold Krugerrand and set it on the table. "You'll get the rest when we're at the boat. How do I contact you?"

"There's no cell service, so you'll have to call the landline. My name is Mahdi." He rose and retrieved a pen and piece of notepaper from a nearby bookshelf and scribbled a number. "Call me three hours before you want to depart."

Leo took it. "Do you have a problem running at night?"

Mahdi grinned. "I do most of my best work in the dark."

Leo stood. "I'll be in touch."

"Only out to the oil rig. No farther, and no exceptions, understand?"

Leo nodded. "Perfectly."

CHAPTER 36

South of Tripoli, Libya

The truck bounced along the rugged terrain, its custom suspension dampening though not eliminating the jarring from the ride. Salma scanned the road to their left with the binoculars and then passed them to Jet, who took them one-handed, steering with the other.

"Looks like we've attracted some attention," Salma said. "A truck. Loaded with ugly. Up ahead."

"The dust must have given us away." Jet looked around. "See anywhere we can hide?"

"There's a bombed-out building to our right about a half kilometer. But if they've already seen us…"

"We don't know if they're using radios or not. If we're going to have to get into it, I'd rather contain it to one truck and one place."

"Good point. Thank God we've got plenty of ammo."

"Be better if we didn't have to use it."

Jet slowed so the dust cloud behind them was minimized, and headed for the ruins Salma had identified. As they neared, Jet could see that all that remained of the building were partial walls – the rest had been hit by explosives, judging by the damage and scorch marks.

She skidded to a stop behind the structure and grabbed her AK and saddlebag, which held five magazines taken from Mounir's men. Salma did the same, and then they sprinted for the rubble after a glance over their shoulders at the approaching dust from the enemy truck.

Jet hissed a warning to Salma. "Looks like they're on a mission. This time we'll hit them with everything we have before they get a chance to get too close. If we're lucky, we can take most of them out on their way in." She chambered a round in the AK and looked to Salma. "You ready to do this?"

Salma rested her rifle on a crumbled stretch of wall and sighted on the truck. "Say the word."

"Don't burn through ammunition unnecessarily," Jet warned. "Single fire. We're likely far better shots than they are, so distance will work to our advantage."

Jet waited until the truck was a hundred meters away. "Three…two…one…fire!"

Both women began shooting at the truck, which made an easy target since it was pointed directly at them. Rounds struck the windshield in starbursts of glass, and then steam exploded from the radiator where a bullet had punched a hole. They continued firing as the driver swerved to the side, obviously shocked by the unexpected attack, and the truck lost its center and seemed to tip in slow motion before landing on its side and throwing the gunmen in the bed clear.

Most landed hard, and Jet concentrated her fire on picking off the ones who were moving while Salma continued focusing her shots on the cab. Jet's magazine ran dry before Salma's, and she fished a fresh one from the saddlebag while Salma continued to pummel anything around the truck with jacketed rounds.

The surviving gunmen returned fire, and divots of mortar and brick blew from the outside of the wall Jet and Salma had taken cover behind. Jet yelled to Salma, nearly deaf from the rifle fire.

"Forget the truck. Pick off the stragglers. They're the low-hanging fruit."

Salma adjusted her aim and squeezed off two shots at one of the active gunmen. Sand fountained into the air near his head, but he continued shooting, her fire off by a hair. Jet swiveled her rifle toward the man and loosed three rounds in rapid succession, and one of them took the top of his turbaned head off in a geyser of brains and bone.

The gunman in the truck passenger seat managed to pull himself through the window and tumbled onto the sand, and Salma put a bullet through his torso, and followed with a second to the chest as he groped at his stomach with bloody hands. He fell face forward, and Jet nodded to Salma. "Good shooting."

"You were right about the range. They suck."

Automatic fire rattled from where a man who'd landed near the truck was spraying the building with bullets, and they waited until he'd exhausted his ammo to answer with a hail of death that shredded him while he fumbled with a fresh magazine.

The air grew still, and Jet and Salma exchanged a glance.

"What do you think?" Salma asked.

"There may be a few who are wounded but still dangerous. Or who are playing possum."

"Should we try to mop them up?"

Jet shook her head. "No. I don't want to find out that their friends are right behind them. Let's get out of here before our luck turns."

Salma gazed out over the scene in front of them. "Forget their ammo?"

"Not worth the risk. I'll cover you. Make your way back to the truck. After you get in, do the same for me."

Salma straightened, checked her magazine, and exchanged it for a fresh one before taking off at a run, zigzagging toward the Nissan while Jet scanned the surroundings. She was almost to it when shots rang out from one of the downed men, and Jet fired five rounds at him in half as many seconds. He fell still and Jet looked over to Salma, who was still in motion, nearly at the passenger door.

She swung it wide and climbed in, and moments later the snout of her AK jutted from the window, trained on the wrecked truck. Jet waited several seconds and then repeated Salma's maneuver, staying low, legs pumping as the sand sucked at her feet and slowed her to what felt like a crawl.

Jet made it and heaved herself behind the wheel. She started the engine with a blast of exhaust from the tailpipe and tromped on the accelerator, sending a curtain of sandy soil into the air behind them.

"What now?" Salma asked.

"We find someplace to ditch this truck and go the rest of the distance on foot. It's too tempting a target."

"But two women swimming against the current back into Tripoli isn't?"

"Not wearing filthy robes and carrying assault rifles. At least I hope not."

Salma gave a half shrug. "You may be right. If we look like we don't have anything to steal, everyone might leave us alone."

"If not, we'll deal with it."

The Tripoli skyline was thick with black smoke when they abandoned the truck behind a gutted commercial building, and they proceeded toward the city on foot, each with a saddlebag and an AK. The refugees fleeing the city eyed them with dull interest and looked away quickly, unsure why anyone would want to head toward a battlefield, but their curiosity was muted by the women's bedraggled appearance.

By the time they neared the outer limits of the metropolis, darkness was creeping across the horizon, made gloomier by the smoke from fires deep in the city. An occasional gunshot rang in the distance, and Salma leaned into Jet, her tone concerned.

"We're going to have a tough time finding someplace to charge the phone," she whispered.

"Maybe. But it's our lifeline to headquarters, so we'll do whatever it takes."

Salma regarded the darkened buildings. "Looks like the power's at least partially out."

Jet studied the skyline before turning to Salma. "Which will make it easier for us. All we have to do is head toward whatever's lit up, and that's where we'll go to ground until I can communicate with the head of station here."

"You have a lot of faith in him continuing to do his job in the middle of all this."

"I've met him. He will. He isn't the type to cut and run while he has agents in the field."

"I hope you're right."

Jet took another look at Tripoli and her mouth hardened into a thin line.

"Me too."

CHAPTER 37

Tel Aviv, Israel

The director sat forward at the conference table, where he was being briefed on the Libyan situation by three members of the crisis team.

"The report from the Italians is inconclusive – the agent had deteriorated by the time they were able to perform all the tests. Their best estimate is that it's related to the Russian Novichok, but deadlier, and dispersed as an aerosol rather than via physical contact. That makes it far more dangerous, obviously." He paused to tap a cigarette from a pack beside an ashtray and light it with a wheezing inhalation. "We need a sample. Or at the very least, we have to find where it's being stored and how much of it there is, and then arrange to have it destroyed."

"Which we agree with, sir. The problem is that right now we have virtually no assets there other than the head of station and your operative, who hasn't checked in for two days. Not exactly a robust network."

His mouth twisted in a humorless grin. "You don't know this operative. I would bet my life that she'll reappear shortly. She's the best we've ever produced. Perhaps we should have her nose around to see if she can find it?"

"And how would she do that in a war zone?" one of the analysts asked.

"The intel we received from Salma connects Tariq Qaddafi with the bioagent. Which doesn't surprise me in the least. He's a particularly nasty piece of business we should have terminated while he was in custody, if we'd been thinking clearly. And we're hearing chatter in some of the foreign networks that support this, that indicate he's making a move to take over in Tripoli. If that's the case, it may be as simple as locating him and his main supply depot and then taking it out."

Another of the analysts spoke up. "It's not out of the question that we could fly a squadron of fighters to Tripoli and destroy a target. We wouldn't have to take responsibility for the strike, any more than we did for hundreds of strikes in Syria. Just a surgical in and out, and we can let the world agonize over who did what, assuming anyone cares."

The first analyst smirked. "It is Africa, after all. They've been blowing each other up forever, and it rarely even makes the news."

The director nodded. "Exactly. So all we need is targeting data, and we can hit them hard before they know we're in the air. There are no defenses at this point – the armed forces have literally gone missing."

"Can our head of station on the ground do this if your operative doesn't surface?"

The director drew a long drag on his cigarette and blew a stream of gray at the ceiling. "I suppose we'll have to ask him to. But it would be better if we could have a seasoned field agent do so." His stare moved from analyst to analyst before settling on the screen on the wall, where a summary of the briefing was projected. "We'll get in touch with the head of station and tell him what's at stake. That's all we can do at this point. That, and pray."

The meeting broke up, and the director walked with heavy steps back to his office, lost in thought, leaving a trail of nicotine in his wake. When he arrived, he stubbed out the butt of his cigarette and lit another, and then stabbed a button on his desk phone to life and instructed the Libya control officer to patch him in to the Tripoli head of station.

Five minutes later, Leo's voice emanated from the speaker. The director coughed and leaned into the device to better be heard.

"Has the operative or the target surfaced yet?" he asked.

"No, sir. Nothing from them, although I've arranged transport, as agreed. I told the captain it was only one passenger, but the boat can easily accommodate two, if they show."

"Belay that. Only the target is to be transported. I have a redirect for the operative."

"The situation here is…chaotic, sir. Any assumptions that are being made about it are likely in error. I've filed a report."

"Which I've read with great interest. But it doesn't change the situation. You are to issue the following instructions to her," the director said, and then laid out what he wanted Jet to do. When he was done, he extinguished his smoke and sat back. "Any questions?"

"Given that neither of them have surfaced and we have no idea if they will, what's the contingency plan?"

The director sighed. "Fair question. You're plan B."

"Locating this Tariq won't be easy, sir. If he's making a move to take over the city, he'll be well insulated, and any competent group would keep his whereabouts secret so one of the local warlords can't take him out."

"Understood. I didn't assume it would be easy. It's necessary, not easy. I've described the stakes. Was I somehow unclear?"

A long pause. "No, sir. I understood. I'm just saying it may not be possible."

The director cleared his throat. "Leo, is that right?"

"Correct, sir."

"Leo, your job is to make the impossible happen. Not *best efforts*. Not *close, but no cigar.* You're to carry out your orders, or die trying. Now start putting out feelers on where Tariq may be hiding, and don't waste my time with probability assessments. Call back in when you have news. You have my permission to utilize any and all resources. There is no higher priority than locating him."

The director terminated the call and frowned at the speakerphone. What was it with this latest generation of operatives? In the old days, nobody would have questioned a direct order from the top. Now it seemed everyone felt as though following orders was a negotiation.

If there was ever evidence that the world was going to hell on skids, that was more than enough.

CHAPTER 38

Outskirts of Tripoli, Libya

A sea of weather-bleached tents stretched out endlessly, with migrants from the south milling around the shelters like ants, the heat of the day ebbing as the sun set. The desperate from all parts of Africa were drawn to Libya as their gateway to Europe and the unimaginable life of limitless opportunity there, if only they could somehow make it across the Mediterranean without perishing. Refugees from Chad, Sudan, Niger, and Nigeria waited in silent misery for their chance to brave the crossing, the human traffickers who could transport them to their new lives a necessary evil.

Children barely out of diapers ran between the legs of the residents, mouths gleaming with white smiles, joy radiating from oversized eyes in malnourished heads. Women stood by a hand pump with all types of containers, waiting their turn at barely potable water. The stench from the nearby open trench latrines made eyes water whenever a breeze blew over the camp. Black clouds of flies thick as ink swarmed the area, and the exhausted inhabitants merely waved them away, resigned to their presence as a constant.

A gaunt man with skin the color of charcoal squatted at the dirt track that led to the encampment, watching the road in the distance and the stream of humanity escaping the city. Any irony of his thousand-mile journey north ending in a camp at the edge of a town where the residents were becoming refugees was lost on him, and his world-weary gaze merely tracked their progress for lack of anything else to do.

A pair of split-axle bobtail trucks turned off the road and onto the track, and the man's interest piqued at the sight. Ordinarily nobody ventured over to the refugee settlement other than an occasional government functionary or aid organization worker, and neither came in cargo trucks. The vehicles grew in size as they neared, and then groaned to a stop at the mouth of the camp, diesel engines idling with a sound like rocks being shaken in a can.

Two men in traditional garb stepped from the cabs and walked to where the man had straightened, and regarded the tents. After a pause, one of them raised a bullhorn to his lips and began addressing the encampment.

"A boat will be leaving the harbor tomorrow. We have space for three hundred of you, no more. The cost will be five hundred dollars apiece, two hundred for children under the age of ten. Anyone interested form a line here, and bring your belongings and the cash."

The sedate camp transformed almost instantly into a mad scramble as refugees who'd been waiting weeks for an affordable trip to Europe grabbed whatever they had and rushed to where the men waited, jostling each other in an effort to be one of the chosen. A queue formed, and soon there were a thousand or more people waiting with their things while the men returned to the trucks and consulted with someone on a handheld radio.

They retraced their steps to the line, and the speaker raised the bullhorn again.

"All right. First come, first served. My partner here will collect the money. Once you've paid, move to one of the trucks and get in the back. No fighting or other nonsense, or you'll be disqualified."

He stepped aside and the first refugee approached them, a woman holding the hand of a small boy, crinkled twenty-dollar bills in her outstretched hand. The second man took the money and counted it, and then nodded to his companion, who pointed at the first truck. "Move all the way to the front to make room for the rest."

The loading took an hour, and by the time the trucks were full, the camp was immersed in darkness. The unfortunates who'd stood in line for nothing shambled back to their tents, defeated, another opportunity in a string of far too few having passed them by.

Headlights blinked on, and the trucks rolled down the track as their human cargo swayed in the beds, packed tight as sardines but nobody complaining. In the cab of the lead vehicle, the second man sat beside the driver with the first riding shotgun, and counted the cash with a smile before handing it to the other.

"We did well," he said.

His companion eyed the fat wad. "I'll say."

"Tariq will be pleased."

"More funds for the revolution. He should be."

Once back on the road, the trucks sped up and headed for an abandoned hotel in Tripoli, where the refugees would stay until the boat that would spirit them to Europe had been repaired. When the trucks arrived at the hotel, gunmen surrounded the vehicles and herded the refugees inside, where they were told to find whatever space they could and to wait for further instructions.

By the time the trucks drove away, the rooms on the lower floor were full and the refugees had settled in. They accepted the presence of the gunmen guarding them, or keeping them prisoners, as part of the price for their ticket north, their fate now in the hands of traffickers to whom their well-being was unimportant.

Late that night, Tariq stopped by with his henchmen and was given a short tour of the facility. He walked among the miserable and desperate for less than a minute, his face twisted in distaste, and quickly left the building and strode to his waiting truck.

"When will the boat be ready to leave?" he asked, glancing around the street, which was deserted other than his entourage and a score of gunmen.

"No later than tomorrow evening," Akmal said. "The repairs should be concluded by nightfall."

"We cannot afford the shipment to be intercepted by the blockade. It would be disastrous for us."

"I understand. They're working as fast as they can. But there's only one skilled mechanic, and it's a complicated project. We don't want them rushing it and breaking down halfway to Italy."

Tariq frowned. "Agreed. But if the blockade begins before we're past the point of no return, we will have wasted all our effort."

Tariq's supporters in other countries had been communicating the news of the forthcoming blockade to him via shortwave radio, and while they knew that it was still at least thirty-six to forty-eight hours away, their anxiety was considerable over how close they were having to cut the boat's departure. There was still time, but if anything else went wrong, it would stymie Tariq's plan, which he couldn't allow to happen. His rule over Libya depended on the West's belief that he was the mover behind the nerve-gas attacks, and that if they attempted to overthrow him, it would open the gates of hell for them. Without that deterrent he would be a sitting duck for a Western-backed revolution or coup, and he wasn't kidding himself that he could bluff his way to success.

"I want to go to the waterfront and review the progress," Tariq said.

"Of course," Akmal responded. "Although I would prefer it if you weren't exposed until we have a more complete hold on the city."

"I will not hide. Allah will protect me, as he has all along. Let us go to the harbor without delay."

Akmal nodded, but his expression revealed his concern. "I'll radio ahead and ensure we have sufficient security in place. We're still far from in control of the city."

"Do what you must. But I want to be at the harbor within ten minutes."

Tariq's convoy arrived at the waterfront and occupied the better part of one of the parking lots. A cordon of gunmen poured from the vehicles, and then Tariq exited and followed Akmal to where a twenty-meter-long fishing boat was moored. Three men were sitting on the back deck, passing a cigarette between them, and they stiffened at the sight of the small army that had arrived.

Akmal led Tariq to a dinghy and rowed out to the fishing boat. They climbed aboard the vessel, and a fourth man emerged from belowdecks and put his hand over his heart in greeting.

"It is an honor to welcome you aboard," he said.

"This is the captain," Akmal said to Tariq. "Nidal."

Tariq eyed the man. "How are the repairs going?"

"Slowly, but we will be done by tomorrow evening. I relayed all of this through one of Akmal's messengers."

"Is there anything you can do to speed up the process?"

"We have to wait for the parts to arrive tomorrow morning. There's nothing to be done until they're here. The mechanic already dismantled the transmission and the relevant part of the engine."

"How confident are you that when it's fixed, the boat will make it to Italy?"

"A hundred percent, or I wouldn't captain it."

Tariq studied Nidal for a long beat and then nodded. "Very good. We will have passengers and some cargo for you tomorrow."

It was the captain's turn to nod. "I know. Akmal's people already told me." He paused. "Can I offer you anything? Refreshment? A tour of the boat?"

Tariq shook his head. "No. Thank you. She looks seaworthy. I just wanted to hear for myself how you were faring, and to meet you."

"Again, it is a great honor. I am humbled."

"The work you are doing is very important. It is I who am humbled," Tariq replied.

Akmal and Tariq rowed back to shore and lashed the dinghy to the dock, and were clambering from the little skiff when a figure materialized from the darkness, startling them both.

"Are you Tariq?" he asked.

Tariq squinted in the gloom. The speaker was a young man.

"How did you get past our security?" Akmal snapped.

"I was down at one of the boats. Nobody stopped me."

"Well?" Akmal demanded. "What is it?"

"You put out the word that you wanted to be notified if anyone unusual was looking for a boat. Today I was approached by a man who wanted to charter one to take a woman out to one of the oil rigs."

Tariq frowned. "What man?"

"I've never seen him before. He was asking fishermen whether they would make the trip. Because of my father's boat, I offered to introduce them. I thought it was for himself or perhaps his family.

When your men said to be on the lookout for a woman, it clicked."

"What did your father say?"

"They agreed on a price."

"When are they going to leave?"

"In the next day or two. That was the other odd part, besides only going out to the rig. He didn't seem to be sure when. Who would go to the trouble of finding a boat in all this if they didn't even know when they wanted to leave? Everyone else wants to leave immediately and go to Tangiers or Italy or Malta, not some platform in the middle of the sea."

"What is your name?" Akmal asked.

"I am Ahmed. Everyone on the waterfront knows me. My father is Mahdi."

Tariq exchanged a look with Akmal.

"See to it that Ahmed is richly rewarded for his loyalty," Tariq said, and turned to face the younger man again. "How is this mystery man to get in touch with you?"

"He will call our landline phone."

Tariq gestured. "Akmal here will give you a number to call at any hour of the day or night. When the man notifies you, all you need to do is call and let us know where and at what time he is going to rendezvous with you. We will arrange a surprise for him."

Ahmed visibly hesitated. "He agreed to pay us…fifteen ounces of gold," he said, exaggerating the amount. "But only once we met him at the boat."

Tariq waved a hand dismissively. "I will make up anything you lose. That is not even a question."

"It will be for my father. He knows nothing of my visit to you."

Akmal nodded, his eyes slits. "We will never tell him. You will receive the gold, to do with as you will."

"Good. He would not be happy if he knew. He prides himself on his discretion."

Tariq offered a tight smile. "Our intention is not to come between a father and son. Your arrangements are yours. Once you make the call, your part in this is over."

"How will I get paid?"

"After our business is concluded, Akmal will take care of you. He is well known, as am I. You have our word on this. Our word is our bond."

Akmal removed a pen from his satchel and wrote a phone number on Ahmed's wrist. When he finished, he stepped away and gave the young man a knowing look. "Go now. Remember to call, or there will be problems for you and your father you don't want to imagine."

Ahmed melted back into the night, and Tariq watched him go without comment. Akmal leaned into him and spoke, his tone soft. "It must be this woman you seek."

"I know. She's working with an intelligence agency. It is her network that is arranging for her escape before we have consolidated our power and instilled order."

"What do you intend to do?"

"I would dearly love to take her and find out who she's working for, but in the end it's immaterial. She's either relayed her information by now or she hasn't. Either way, our plan won't change, and in some ways it might help our cause if they have confirmation of my role in it. But she will be made an example of. So come. Let us return to the trucks, and I will tell you what I want you to do."

CHAPTER 39

Tripoli, Libya

A haze of smoke blanketed the street Jet and Salma were working their way along. The buildings around them were dark; the section of the city that had power was still out of their reach a half kilometer away.

Their trek through the outskirts of Tripoli had been fraught with near misses with armed groups – some militia attempting to act as self-defense forces, others criminal opportunists out to take advantage of the mayhem, still others factions seeking to eliminate rivals before the rule of relative law returned. They'd managed to dodge them all, and as night had fallen, it had grown easier to make progress – not even the most reckless appeared eager to be out after dark, when predator could easily become prey.

The street they were following ran toward the town center, but the going was still slow, the smoke cutting the moonlight to a minimum. Occasional gunfire echoed in the night, but nothing near enough to alarm them. Still, between the absence of power and the constant threat of being shot, both women's nerves were raw, and they were visibly on edge, their weapons gripped tight.

A noise ahead stopped them in their tracks, and they froze, rifles at the ready. When after fifteen seconds they heard nothing more, they resumed edging forward. A dark form darted from the shadows, and Salma gasped and raised her rifle to fire, but Jet reached out to stop her with a whispered warning.

"It's a dog, Salma. Relax."

Salma exhaled heavily and lowered the AK. "Shit. I'll be glad when this is over."

"Tell me about it."

At the end of the block, they glanced along the intersection, trying to make out any potential threats. They didn't see any and were halfway across when a shout from their right rang out.

"You. Stop, or we'll shoot!"

Jet and Salma turned to where the voice had come from, and saw four uniformed police approaching, assault rifles in hand. Jet frowned at the sight – they looked disheveled and unshaven.

"How do you want to play this?" Salma whispered.

"Drop your weapons," one of the men ordered.

"Do as they say," Jet said, and slowly knelt to lay her AK on the street. Salma followed suit, and when they both straightened, the men moved toward them at a more confident clip.

"Well, well," the lead cop said. "Two women on their own on a night like this? And armed to the teeth, no less. What's this all about?"

"We're trying to make it to where there's power," Jet said.

The lead officer glanced at the others and then back to Jet before his eyes settled on Salma. "You're both lookers, aren't you? Not a good idea to venture out in this."

Neither woman spoke, waiting to see what came next. They didn't have to wait long.

"I want the one on the left," the man behind the lead cop said.

"You'll have your shot at both," he replied with an ugly laugh, gun trained on them.

"What is this?" Salma demanded. "You're the police. You're supposed to protect us."

"You're obviously dangerous criminals," another of the cops said with a twisted smile. "We're just doing what we can to keep the community safe."

The suppressed continuous fire of the MP7A1 from within Jet's robe was muted by the cloth, but the jacketed bullets shredded through the group of would-be rapists and cut them down like wheat. Some of the men screamed and others moaned as the wicked rounds tumbled through their tissue on impact, but all fell, dying or terminally wounded, their weapons skittering as they crumpled.

Jet ejected the spent magazine and felt for her last full one. She slammed it into place and hissed at Salma, "Grab your gun and move."

They snatched up their rifles and bolted down the sidewalk, leaving the cops in pools of coagulating blood. They reached another side street, and Jet slowed. "This is getting worse, not better," she said, surveying the surroundings.

"We only have to make it another ten blocks or so, and there's power."

Jet looked around. "Which presumably will be safer. But now, I'm not so sure."

"What other choice do we have?"

"None," Jet conceded, and inclined her head at the artery to the right. "Let's stay off the main drags. If those cops were any indication, we want to avoid everyone, no matter who they are."

They made the turn and then cut over a block down, on a two-lane strip of cobblestone that ran between ancient tenements and stank of garbage. Jet led the way, but after three blocks, she slowed. She grabbed Salma's arm and held a finger to her lips.

"Hear that?" she whispered.

Salma shook her head. Jet looked around and pointed to a darkened doorway that looked like the door had been kicked in. "Follow me."

They raced to the opening and were inside just as the sound of dozens of running feet on pavement reached them from the street. Jet pulled Salma deeper into the darkness, which reeked of urine and rot. The floor was littered with trash, and once they were far enough inside that they couldn't be seen, they stopped, weapons pointed at the entry, Salma breathing hard.

A group of young men ran by, some with assault rifles and others with handguns, several of them laughing. The sound of a car window being broken brought more laughter from the men and a few shouted curses from a window on the second floor, followed by a gunshot from one of the runners. The gang continued on its way, savaging more vehicles, and eventually the sound of wanton vandalism faded, leaving an uneasy silence in its wake.

Jet and Salma waited until the men had disappeared before cautiously returning to the doorway and peeking outside. The sidewalks were deserted again, the only evidence of the gang's passing shards of glass glittering like diamonds on the pavement.

"What do you think?" Salma asked.

"The sooner we're in an area with power, the better. This way."

Jet set off at a trot, tailed by Selma, who was limping but doing her best to keep up. They made it three more blocks and skirted a group of men in army uniforms who were kicking a youth senseless at a junction, their laughter harsh and ugly. Once past that nightmarish scene, the glow of electric lights beckoned from only a few hundred meters away, and they both exhaled sighs of relief when they made it to the first lit street, which while barely more inviting than the ones they'd traversed, at least held the promise of power to charge the phone that would connect them to civilization and, with it, escape.

CHAPTER 40

Tripoli, Libya

Leo met Jet and Salma at a safe house five minutes from the harbor – a one-bedroom apartment he leased in another name for just such events. He looked them up and down and frowned at the damage evident on Salma's feet.

"Looks like you've been through hell," he said, extending his hand. "My name's Leo."

Salma shook and closed her eyes for a beat. "You have no idea."

"Well, you're safe now. Make yourselves comfortable. The water's hot if you want to take showers," he suggested. "And we'll see if we can get you some clean clothes. Although not much will be open. Maybe some street vendors for a new robe."

"That would be wonderful."

He smiled at Salma. "There's a pretty comprehensive first aid kit in the bathroom. You name it – morphine, antibiotics, antibacterial ointment, stitches, bandages…whatever you need, just take it, or ask and I'll get it." He looked to Jet. "I need to have a word with you while she's showering, so, Salma, if you'd go first…"

"You don't have to ask twice. That and some sleep sound amazing right now."

"Perfect."

Salma disappeared into the bedroom, and Leo indicated a chair near the living room couch. Jet set her MP7A1 and AK down beside it and sat, her expression blank as she waited for Leo to debrief her.

"Why didn't you answer your phone or get in touch for the last two days?" he began.

"We ran out of juice, and there was nowhere to charge it until we

213

got here. As it was, it took everything we had to find someplace safe with an outlet to charge it enough to reach you."

He nodded. "Makes sense." He paused. "I spoke with HQ. We have a situation we need your help with."

"A situation," she repeated, her tone flat.

"That's right." He explained about the nerve gas, the forthcoming blockade, and the need to locate Tariq. When he finished, her emerald eyes bored into his without blinking.

"I didn't sign up for that. Sorry."

"The director asked you to do it. He wanted to make clear it's a personal request."

She stood and brushed dust off her robe before pulling it over her head and tossing it in a pile at her feet. "My assignment was to locate and facilitate an extraction. Which is what I've done, with almost no help from anyone, even after I was promised complete support. I'm not going to risk my life here for a moment longer because the director feels he can put me to more use."

Leo stared at her in surprise. "I didn't realize following orders was optional."

"It is for me. I'm a free agent. I have the right to refuse anything. And that's what I'm doing. I want to get out of Tripoli and go home. That's the extent of my involvement from here on out. The director's going to have to find someone else to do his dirty work." Her tone softened. "Look, Leo, you seem like a nice enough guy, and I know this isn't your doing. But my refusal isn't negotiable. I took this assignment for only one reason, and that doesn't include flag-waving or national security or the director's whims. So let's save some time. How are you getting us out of here?"

"I chartered a boat to take Salma out to an oil platform, where a helo will pick her up."

"Great. And then what about me?"

Leo looked away. "The director assumed that you'd take the new assignment, so there isn't a plan to extract you yet."

"There is now. I'm going with Salma."

"I…I'm not sure that's possible."

"Sure it is. Two instead of one. I won't take up much room."

"I'll need to get approval from HQ…"

Jet threw him a dark look. "Leo, I'm calling the shots. And I'm getting on that boat. I'm not going to allow the director to blackmail me by keeping me in-country, so no, you don't need approval from HQ, you need to do as you're told. Now break down how you found a boat in all this, and what the plan is for getting us safely aboard."

Leo described his interaction with Ahmed and Mahdi, and when he was done, Jet was frowning.

"How can you be confident that he'll perform? In this environment, what safeguards do you have that he won't have you jumped when you're walking down the dock with gold in your pocket?"

"He didn't strike me as that type. I did a little checking after our meeting. He's got a good reputation." Leo hesitated. "Plus, I'll be armed."

"Have you been out on the street recently? Everybody's armed. Doesn't seem like that will be much of a deterrent."

It was Leo's turn to frown. "You have a better suggestion?"

She thought for a long moment. "I'll hang back and watch for anything suspicious. If they're going to ambush you, it won't be from the front. Do you have any two-ways?"

"Of course."

"Then here's how will do it." She laid out her thoughts, and by the end he was nodding along with her.

"That'll work," he agreed. "One issue we may have is that the captain may want more gold to transport two instead of one."

"He may want it, but he's not going to get it. You're paying top dollar for the boat and his time, not by the pound. And it should be a short run. A couple of hours round trip if it's a rigid-hull Zodiac and the seas aren't too ugly." She eyed him. "Still, it can't hurt to bring a few extra ounces. I'm not price sensitive."

He eyed her skeptically. "You know the director is."

"Put it on my tab if it's a problem. After this he owes me more than a little."

Leo nodded. "Give me an assessment of Salma before she comes out."

Jet scowled. "She's suffered moderate physical damage and severe psychological trauma for three years. You saw her feet. That's just part of it. They'll heal. Not sure about the rest." Jet told him about the slavers and Mounir's men.

"God. She's lucky to be alive."

"That she is."

"But the USB drive is lost?"

It was Jet's turn to nod. "I'm afraid so. It wasn't practical to scour Sebha for it. A needle in a haystack."

"Given how things are degrading, that was the right call."

"And we know the broad strokes. They have a nerve agent they acquired through China. Tariq Qaddafi is behind it. He plans to take over the Libyan government and establish a caliphate based on extremist principles and Sharia law, backed by the threat of deployment of the bioagent as his WMD. I have to admit it's bold, and it could work – try to overthrow him and any number of bioattacks would be launched in retaliation. Mutually assured destruction."

"I don't have to tell you this escalates the terrorist game to a whole other level. Imagine a madman running an oil-rich nation and threatening everyone, including Israel, with untold calamity. Even if not officially." He thought for a second. "It could very well work. Which underscores the importance of what the director's requested you do."

Jet shook her head. "It's nothing personal, but I'm unavailable. The director's going to have to solve his own problems." She frowned. "What's the weather report for tonight?"

He shrugged. "Beats me. No internet, and nobody's broadcasting anything but music on the radio."

"An open boat like a Zodiac isn't all that stable if the seas kick up, and there were a lot of clouds on the horizon this morning. Maybe we should wait for something more seaworthy?"

"Negative. There's no second choice. All the decent boats are long gone. It's this one or nothing."

"HQ has confirmed the helicopter?"

"Yes."

"And there's no complications from using the oil platform?"

"The company that operates it evacuated all but a skeleton crew of maintenance staff when it became obvious that the country was coming apart. As far as the crew is concerned, your arrival is a humanitarian relief effort."

"How did you manage that?"

"Money's the ultimate lubricant." Leo chewed his lower lip. "I just have to figure out where I can get a second scooter for you."

Jet smiled. "The director's paying."

"Then all things are possible."

CHAPTER 41

Tel Aviv, Israel

Matt finished brushing Hannah's hair and inspected her school uniform. His face cracked into a smile. "You look beautiful as ever, sweetheart."

The little girl turned and studied herself in the full-length mirror, angling her head to confirm that Matt had done an adequate job with the brush before matching his smile and smoothing her blue skirt.

"Thanks." Her smile turned into a pout. "I miss Mama."

"Me too, my love."

She looked up at him, her eyes huge. "Will she be home soon?"

"Should be any day now."

Her pout intensified. "When?"

"Maybe in a couple of days."

Hannah thought for a moment. "Why don't you know?"

"She hasn't told me yet. But it won't be long," Matt said. "Now go grab your backpack or we're going to be late."

"Two boys pick on me at school," Hannah announced when she returned with her bag.

"What do they do?"

"They tease me. They're mean."

He knelt down to look her in the eye, his expression serious. "They probably like you, but they're too shy to say so."

She gave him a disbelieving look. "No. They're mean."

Matt relented. "Could be. But sometimes when boys are mean, it's because they want your attention."

"I don't like them."

"Right now I'd be surprised if you did."

Matt slipped on a light windbreaker and extended his hand. Hannah took it, and they left the condo and descended to the ground level.

Their walk together to and from Hannah's private school was one of the high points of Matt's day. For the first time in a life that had largely been spent in the field, he felt complete as the head of a real family, even if it was hardly traditional. Still, the routine of preparing the little girl each morning, walking with her to the school, and then helping her with her homework – she, in very unladylike fashion, was fascinated with astronomy and devoted reams of paper to drawing the solar system and coloring in planets – and finally, preparing her for bed was strangely satisfying for him even in Jet's absence, as though Matt was accomplishing something truly worthwhile.

The wonder of the transformation from a clandestine life into one of seeming mundanity amazed him at times like these, when the morning sun warmed his face as they strolled along the sidewalk. He'd gone from trained killing machine to a glorified nanny, and he couldn't have been happier with the change, especially after so many months on the run.

He'd quickly grown accustomed to the routine of living in Israel, which in many ways was oddly like living in America. Matt supposed that in a world of megacorporations that knew no national borders, it made sense that people everywhere would be wearing Nikes and Levis and Hollister while chatting on iPhones. He wondered what it must have been like in the sixties when Israel was still in its infancy, and imagined it as very different from what it had become.

Then again, he supposed nothing remained the same, and progress inexorably steamrollered forward, whether for better or worse.

They reached the main boulevard, and Matt stopped with Hannah. "What's the rule?" he asked.

"Look both ways. Drivers are crazy."

"That's right," Matt intoned. "Completely nuts."

Their heads swiveled to the right and left, and then the light changed and they crossed with a throng of pedestrians, some of whom were also escorting their children to the same destination.

They walked hand in hand and turned the corner onto the school street, where a line of cars was discharging tykes at a rapid clip while a pair of serious women waved the empty vehicles along to keep the file moving.

A horn honked just behind Matt, and he glanced over his shoulder to where a woman in a compact car was pulling her child's hand off the steering wheel. Movement in the corner of his eye drew his attention, and he zeroed in on a parked car, where a man had looked away when Matt had twisted at the honk.

The skin on Matt's arms prickled and he returned his attention to the school. His craft instincts immediately kicked in and he began walking back toward the boulevard, eyeing the reflection in the windshields of the waiting vehicles to see if the car followed him. As he neared the final car, he saw that the man was now following him on foot, keeping his distance like a competent professional would.

It had only been luck that the horn honk had triggered his glance, and he swallowed hard at the unexpected scenario. If a pro was staking out Hannah's school and following him, there was only one possible reason, and it wasn't good. Matt didn't allow his mind to worry over the possibilities, but instead focused on how to proceed – whether to lose the tail or try to get the upper hand and learn who he was working for.

A vision of Hannah made the decision easy. If it were only himself, Matt would have put his considerable skills to use and tried to corner the man. But that would entail risk to Hannah in addition, if he failed, or if the man was working with a team. Matt hadn't spotted anyone else, but he hadn't had the time to do a thorough scan of all the parked vehicles, much less of the surrounding buildings.

So he needed to err on the side of conservatism and call in the cavalry.

He fished his cell phone from his pocket as he turned the corner and selected one of the speed-dial buttons and, when the screen indicated the call was active, raised it to his ear.

"This is Bluebird. I'm at school, and I've got company. Following me now. I need you to send someone to pick up the package."

There was a brief pause. "I understand. Are you in danger?"

"No way of knowing. But I'm not the imperative."

"Roger that. We'll have a team get the package. In the meantime, I'm looking at your phone's location and you're four blocks from the condo, correct?"

"Yes."

"Take evasive action, but play it slow. We'll have someone pick you up in a few minutes. Leave your phone on and I'll call with details when we're close."

"Will do."

Matt terminated the call and held the phone up as though checking something on the tiny screen. The man was forty meters behind him and across the street, confirming Matt's impression of good tradecraft. Any closer, and he ran a greater risk of being detected; any farther away, he might lose his quarry.

Matt slowed and began window-shopping, the game now to run out the clock until the Mossad could bring him in. The boulevard had scores of shops he could linger in, so he wasn't worried about having to make a move. Rather, his mind was on Hannah. Matt was more than equipped to deal with whatever came his way, but Hannah was vulnerable, and anyone who wanted to get to either Matt or Jet would use her to do so. Which left a narrow window of opportunity to whisk her to safety. What he was doing was buying her time, nothing more.

He dialed the number again, and the same voice answered. "Pick up the package first. Then me. Do not reverse the order, understand?"

"I understood the first time. A team's been deployed. I'll call shortly to confirm pickup."

Jet and he had the same emergency number on their Mossad-issued cell phones – their last line of defense in case someone came for them. It had been part of her negotiation with the director: her family would be protected at all costs, no matter what happened to her. That was the arrangement, and Matt fully expected the Mossad to live up to its end.

He entered a store and browsed a rack of men's jackets, and then tried one on for size with the assistance of a fussy clerk, who assured him that it was the highest quality and he looked fabulous in it. Five minutes passed as he debated the purchase, and he decided to buy it as plausible cover for the time he'd spent in the store.

Paying for the jacket took another couple of minutes, and when Matt left the shop, he spied the tail farther up the block, gazing into a display window. Matt's cell vibrated and he took the call.

"The package is secure. Stand by for pickup in two minutes. We have your location from the cell. Any special instructions?"

"The tail looks to be about six feet tall, wearing a brown shirt and jeans. Caucasian. Fit. Maybe ex-military. He's at the junction on the west side of this block. Might want to see if you can pull traffic cam footage and identify him. His vehicle is a white compact car parked on the same street where you retrieved the package."

"Ten four. Your pickup will be a silver Nissan sedan," the voice said, and gave him a license number. "They're now ninety seconds out."

"Roger that."

Matt hung up and pretended to be fiddling with his phone so it would look to the watcher like he'd requested an Uber. He then checked his watch to further reinforce the assumption the man would have to make, and stared at his cell screen as though tracking his ride's progress. When the Nissan pulled to the curb in front of the shop, Matt opened the back door and slipped inside, and then they were off, leaving the watcher with no option other than to return to his vehicle – where he would get a reception from the Mossad that was more than he'd bargained for.

"Where are we going?" Matt asked the hatchet-faced man in the passenger seat.

"Safe house. We have to assume the condo is blown. We'll retrieve your personal effects this evening."

"That won't work. I want to go with you. There's a safe, and a few things stashed around the apartment I need to get."

"You can clear it with HQ. My orders are to take you to the house."

Matt exhaled sharply. "Okay. Where's the girl?"

"Already on her way there."

Matt sighed and closed his eyes. "How could this happen?"

The driver didn't say anything, preferring silence to responding to questions to which there were no answers, and left Matt to ride the rest of the way with his mind racing.

CHAPTER 42

Tripoli, Libya

Lights in the windows of the surrounding buildings twinkled as Leo and Salma climbed aboard Leo's Vespa and he cranked the starter. When the engine had settled into a steady purr, he rolled away into the dusk, leaving Jet, who'd gone downstairs ten minutes earlier to scout out the street on a scooter of her own, to follow at a discreet distance.

There was little traffic, although more than the prior days when pandemonium had ruled the city. A radio broadcast that afternoon had assured the population that order was being restored by the new interim governor of Libya, Tariq Qaddafi, and that violence or looting would be severely punished in keeping with Sharia law, where the penalty for theft was the amputation of the thief's hands, and for murder and highway robbery, summary execution. The announcement had apparently had the desired effect, because the pedestrians that Jet saw as she rode well behind Leo's scooter were unarmed, with the only gunmen those clearly acting as police on behalf of Qaddafi's group, standing on street corners with AK-47s and wearing red armbands to denote their authority.

Their route to the waterfront was circuitous, and night was falling by the time they arrived at the wide avenue that traced along the harbor. Leo had called Mahdi an hour earlier and told him to expect their arrival by dark, and the smuggler had confirmed the boat would be ready by then, and had agreed to meet them at the marina for payment.

Jet coasted to a stop well away from Leo's scooter and removed a pair of small binoculars from beneath the robe Leo had provided, along with a two-way radio and a box of ammo for the Heckler & Koch. She did a slow sweep of the waterfront, beginning with the deserted pedestrian walkway and ending at the jetty where the remaining boats were moored.

The Zodiac that would ferry them to safety was easy to pick out, being the only inflatable in the harbor. The sleek craft was lashed to one of the concrete docks, where an older Arab man was standing near the Zodiac with another man half his age. She watched as Leo and Salma made their way down the dock to the pair. After exchanging greetings, Leo paid the older man with a small cloth bag containing the gold and gestured toward the waterfront.

The older man counted the contents of the bag and, once satisfied, pointed to the inflatable. The younger man led Leo and Salma toward the boat as the older Arab left the dock, and then Jet gasped when she saw a figure climb from beneath a tarp that covered a dinghy near the Zodiac and follow the trio toward the larger boat.

She raised the radio to her lips and depressed the transmit button. "Leo, abort. Repeat, abort. There's a shooter behind you."

She released the button, but Leo didn't answer. As the figure closed the distance to Salma and Leo, Jet sprinted for the gangplank, the MP7A1 hanging from its shoulder strap beneath her robe bouncing against her ribs.

She was halfway to the dock and was transmitting another hurried warning when the figure called out. Salma and Leo turned, and then gunfire shattered the silence as he shot Salma three times at close range. Leo ducked and drew his own handgun as the shooter fired again, this time at him. Leo stumbled backward as the assassin's round slammed into him, and he slipped and fell into the water. Jet increased her pace, feeling for the submachine gun butt as she ran, her breath a snake's hiss between clenched teeth.

The shooter bolted for the dinghy as she pounded down the gangplank and onto the dock, and he was inside with the outboard roaring to life by the time she freed the MP7A1, and then the little boat was tearing across the inky water, leaving a white froth in its wake. Jet squeezed off three bursts at the dinghy, and then ran to where Leo was struggling to stay afloat at the side of the dock.

Jet set the gun aside and lowered herself onto her stomach, her arms extended toward him. He grabbed at her hands, and she latched onto him and heaved him onto the dock, noting a wound in his upper chest.

The young Zodiac captain stood frozen by the boat, watching the surreal scene with a shocked expression. Jet ignored him as she stood and scooped up her weapon and hurried to Salma's prone form.

"Oh…Salma," Jet whispered. The younger woman was clearly dead and lying on her back, the top of her skull blown off along with two bullet holes in her chest. Jet knelt beside her and closed her sightless eyes with her free hand, and then retraced her steps to Leo, who was grimacing in pain.

She examined his wound and looked up at the captain. "Do you have anything on the boat like clean towels and rope?"

The man nodded rapidly.

"Get them."

He raced off to do as asked, and Jet returned her attention to Leo. "Looks like it missed your lung. How's your breathing?"

"H…Hurts."

"I'll make a field dressing, but there's not a lot more I can do here. With the city like this, you're pretty much screwed – I doubt many doctors are working."

"I…how's Salma?"

Jet's face hardened. "Dead. She was obviously the target."

"God…"

The captain returned with a handful of rags and some yellow nylon line. Jet took it from him and eyed him. "Get your boat ready. We'll be leaving in two minutes."

Leo coughed, and blood trickled from the corner of his mouth. Jet selected the least dirty rag and folded it twice, and then placed two of the filthier ones on top before placing the makeshift bandage over the wound and uncoiling the rope.

"I'm going to rig a pressure dressing. It should keep you from bleeding to death until you get to the oil platform."

Jet lashed the rope around his shoulder as he winced in pain, and ran the line over the rags several times so it would hold the dressing in place. She finished by tying a pair of knots and then called to the captain, "Help me get him into the boat."

The young man did as instructed, and when Leo was in the bow, leaning against the rubber hull, she handed him her 9mm pistol. He took it, and she turned to the captain.

"Take him to the rig and your job's done. Try anything funny and he'll blow your head off. Understand? Now go. You're out of time."

Leo's eyes widened when she leapt back onto the dock. "What…where…are you…going?"

"You need to be evacuated, Leo. I've got some unfinished business to take care of," she said, staring out across the water at where the assassin's dinghy was half deflated and taking on water, its outboard silent. "Give me your keys. I'll need to get into the apartment."

He removed them from his pocket and tossed them to her, and she caught them in midair. Leo struggled to say something, but she cut him off and glared at the captain. "I said get going. Now."

The young man thumbed the starter, and the motor revved to life. Jet untied the bow and stern lines and tossed them into the boat, and then the craft was heading for the harbor mouth with a sonorous rumble of exhaust.

Jet looked around and spotted a five-meter-long wooden fishing boat with a battered Evinrude outboard that looked like it was older than the marina. She scooped up her submachine gun and dashed over, her eyes fixed on the shooter's dinghy. Jet climbed into the stern, and after four tugs on the starter cord, the motor coughed to life. When she was sure it wouldn't die, she cast off the lines and pointed the bow at the dark shape of the dinghy adrift in the middle of the harbor, its gray rubber form barely visible in the partial moonlight.

CHAPTER 43

The assassin heard Jet's approach and renewed his efforts to start the dinghy's outboard, pulling on the starter cable again and again as the wooden fishing boat bore down on him. When it was obvious that the motor wasn't going to cooperate, he shifted his wounded leg and felt for his pistol in the bottom of the dinghy, which had filled with water as the outer chambers had deflated.

His fingers brushed against the familiar shape and his face twisted in pain as he raised it and fired at Jet's boat. He had little hope of hitting her, but he wasn't going to go without a fight, and he continued squeezing the trigger until the magazine ran dry. He ejected it and groped in his pants for a spare, and had nearly fit it into place when the wooden boat rammed him, sending the pistol spinning through the air and into the harbor with a splash.

The impact knocked him from the dinghy, and he followed his gun into the water. He splashed as he tried to get his bearings, lances of pain from his wounded thigh blinding him as he fought to keep his head above water, and then he found himself staring directly down the ugly snout of a submachine gun held by a woman in a black robe.

Jet tossed the assassin the bow line and kept the MP7A1 pointed at his head.

"Pull yourself into the boat," she said, her tone flat. When he didn't comply, she glowered at him. "I can take your head off before you can get deep enough to matter, so don't even think it."

The man sputtered water and reached for the line. He snagged it and, using both arms, pulled himself close to the hull.

"I can't get into the boat without your help," he said. "Please."

She shook her head. "Pull yourself up and over, or stay in the water waiting for the sharks to come. Doesn't much matter to me."

"I…can't."

"Then hang on. I'm headed over to the breakwater," she said, the muzzle of the submachine gun never leaving his head. She backed across the bench seat and made it to the stern with the H&K pointed at him the entire time, and then shifted the transmission into gear and gave the throttle a small twist with her free hand.

A minute later they were at the rock slope of the long breakwater, and Jet cut the power and drifted the final few meters. The bow gently bumped against the boulders, and she eyed the assassin dispassionately.

"Drag yourself onto the rocks," she ordered.

Jet kept the gun trained on him while he pulled himself onto a particularly large stone's flat surface and lay on it, breathing hard, blood staining the rock beneath his wounded leg.

She moved to the middle bench seat and held the MP7A1 steady. "You killed my friend. Who are you working for?"

He glared at her. "What does it matter? I'm dead if I tell you."

Jet shrugged. "It's a matter of how you go. Quickly and painlessly, or in excruciating pain."

"I'd rather die honorably than as a coward."

The submachine gun popped once and the man's knee exploded. He screamed in agony, the wail loud as a siren, and Jet waited until he was gasping for breath before speaking.

"I know you were doing a job. This doesn't have to be personal unless you make it. Who are you working for? You have one chance to answer, and then you lose the other knee. So talk."

"You won't live to see tomorrow," he spat, voice strained from pain.

"Wrong answer," she said, and shifted her aim to blow his other kneecap off. The gun spit again and she was rewarded by another shriek of agony, followed by anguished whimpering. "I can keep at this for an hour if you want," she said. "Next will be your shins, then your hips, then your arms – and then I'll start on that embarrassment between your legs. This is your chance to avoid it. Who are you working for?"

He tried to speak, but it was nothing more than a strangled curse. Jet shook her head in obvious disappointment and fired again. This time he passed out from the pain, and she took the opportunity to climb from the boat and secure it to a smaller rock before moving to the unconscious man and sitting a few meters away, gun in her lap.

When he came to, he could barely focus from the pain. Jet was humming to herself, sharpening the edge of her survival knife against the rocks, the sound a soft scrape, methodical as the ticking of a clock. She held the blade up and inspected it, then eyed the assassin.

"You're not going to be of much use to your seventy-two virgins without your manhood. I've decided to save ammo and cut directly to the chase. Get it? Cut to the chase." She smiled. "So if you want to lose your eyes first, and then the family jewels, keep it up. Or we can stop all this, and you can tell me what we both know you eventually will. It's just a matter of time. And I've got all night."

Four minutes later Jet was back in the boat with the name and location of the man the assassin had been working for. She whispered the name as she made for the far dock, eyes roving over the empty waterfront, the suppressed shooting having failed to attract any curiosity after days of gunfire throughout the town.

"Tariq Qaddafi," she said, her expression grim. "Small world. Looks like Fate wants us to cross paths after all." The shooter hadn't known where Qaddafi was holed up, but before he died, he'd given her the location of his subordinate who'd organized the hit, and from there she would follow the crumbs to the great man himself and terminate him with as extreme a prejudice as he'd employed with Salma.

She throttled up, urging the old boat faster now that she had a target for her wrath. The terrorist had seen fit to murder Salma just as she'd been about to escape with her life, and Jet could think of nothing she'd rather do than return the favor. That the director had wanted her to go after him barely registered. No, Tariq had killed Hannah's aunt, and the only connection to her father that had existed. Now she'd never get the chance to meet her, and Salma's life had been cut short with little to show for it but misery at the hands of animals.

That would not go unavenged.

"Not as long as I'm in the mix," she murmured, and leaned forward to minimize her silhouette on the off chance that the assassin had been working with a partner who was lying in wait. He hadn't mentioned one, and she'd been very persuasive, but Jet wasn't about to take chances after seeing Salma gunned down before her eyes.

Jet was already in motion when the boat bumped gently against the dock, and bolted along the platform as the craft drifted away, the motor's rough idle the only sound on the waterfront besides the thumping of Jet's running boots as she made her way to the gangplank and the parking lot beyond.

CHAPTER 44

Tel Aviv, Israel

Yevgeni sat in his hotel room contemplating how to proceed since his botched attempt to follow the man that morning. He'd immediately been suspicious when the sedan had appeared to pick him up, and had taken evasive action when the target had disappeared, including leaving his rental car parked by the school in case it had been compromised. He'd used one of several alternative identities to rent it, so he wasn't worried about the ramifications of it being found, and he'd worn latex gloves while driving it, so an inspection of the vehicle wouldn't yield anything but dead ends.

He more than understood that if his intuition was correct, the man had spotted him, in which case he was blown. How the man might have managed to do so remained a mystery to Yevgeni, whose history was one of successes, not aborted assignments where he'd alarmed his quarry. He'd done everything by the book, taken no chances, hadn't gotten careless that he could see, yet he'd been detected within minutes of taking up the chase – a first in his career, and not one that augured well for his future.

He had few options that he could see if the Mossad was involved. He had nothing but respect for that agency, which, unlike the bumbling Americans or laughably inept MI6, was serious and effective. If they'd spirited the man away, as he suspected, his time in Israel was already over.

Yevgeni used his burner cell and dialed a Moscow number. When Sergei answered, he laid out the situation in flat, emotionless terms. Once finished, Sergei took a moment to respond.

"I expected better than this," Sergei said, the anger in his tone clear.

"I have no evidence that my suspicion is correct. But I wanted to keep you informed," Yevgeni replied.

"If you've tipped them off, they'll go to ground and disappear from the radar. We both know that."

"Yes, I would expect they will. But this is a small country. They'll turn up again now that we have their images. The little girl makes them especially vulnerable."

"There was no sign of the woman? The man was merely a means to that end. I can't believe it could have gone so wrong before anything of importance took place."

"Perhaps it hasn't. But my field sense is that he's taken himself out of play. If that's the case, the girl won't be showing up to classes any longer. So we're back to square one."

Sergei was silent again for a long beat. "Get out of Israel. Now. Take the first plane to anywhere. Assume the worst."

"I'm afraid it isn't that easy. There's a good chance they'll have my description from the rental car agency, which means they'll be stopping anyone who looks remotely like me at the airports."

"Not my problem. Our business is concluded."

"I understand. But I thought you would want to know all the details should you wish to deploy another contractor."

"Understood. Best of luck."

The line went dead, and Yevgeni removed the battery from the cell, tossed it into the garbage, and pocketed the phone. He stood and regarded himself in the mirror – he'd bought hair dye and was now a brunette, but his appearance was still too close to that on the passport he'd used for comfort. He'd thought about his next step all day and had concluded that the airports weren't an option, which left the worst of all possible alternatives: making it overland to one of the frontiers and crossing into either Egypt, Syria, Jordan, or Lebanon on foot.

He didn't like his odds traversing the country, where there were sure to be traffic stops, nor was he enamored with the idea of spending days trying to get out of Israel. The only other choice was the one he'd decided on in the last hour, and he'd seen no way that it could fail if he was careful.

Yevgeni retrieved his carry-on bag and the rucksack with the weapons, and took the stairs to the ground level. He walked to the rear of the hotel and departed through the service exit, and then walked eight blocks to the water and headed south toward the Carlton Tel Aviv hotel and its marina.

It was dark by the time he made it, and he studied the layout and the comings and goings of the two security men who were safeguarding the expensive yachts. One remained in the guardhouse near the main dock at all times, and the other roamed along the waterfront; a straightforward setup with no obvious surprises. He watched the pattern for over an hour from a bench overlooking the water, and once the last of the evening's couples out for a romantic waterfront stroll had vanished, he made his way down to the marina perimeter.

Another hour passed, but still he waited, patience being one of the virtues that had saved him many times in the past. At midnight, two new guards replaced the ones on duty, and he smiled in the shadows – as he'd suspected, the night shift would appear to spell the evening shift, and he'd have many hours to execute his plan.

The new guards got settled and repeated the pattern of their predecessors, with one remaining in the shack while the other roamed the marina. After twenty minutes, Yevgeni was ready to make his move.

He worked his way along the water behind the roaming guard and, when he was a dozen meters from the man, put a single subsonic round through the back of his skull. Yevgeni dragged the man's body to the rocks and rolled it halfway down the slope, where it came to rest as though staring eternally out at the water.

The guard in the shack was surprised when Yevgeni appeared in the doorway, and was pushing back from the CCTV monitors when the Russian's slug blew the back of his head onto the wall behind him. Yevgeni removed the set of keys on the man's belt and, after locking the door behind him and wiping the knob with his shirt, hurried to the gate that protected the docks.

The third key opened it. He descended to the water, where he eyed the long string of yachts before settling on a particularly hardy-looking twenty-meter sport fisherman in pristine shape, the dinghy on the front a hard bottom on a pair of stands beside a crane. He stepped aboard and tried the cabin door lock, and wasn't surprised when it didn't budge. A round from the pistol solved that problem, and he kicked the shattered lock open and entered the salon.

A set of ignition keys was hanging on a rack by the breaker panel. He switched on the blowers and all the operating equipment, set his bag on the expensive leather sofa, and mounted the ladder to the enclosed flybridge. After confirming that the fuel tanks were three-quarters full, he powered on the radar, autopilot, and GPS navigation systems, and then started the big diesel engines, which rumbled beneath his feet with satisfying intensity.

Yevgeni lowered himself from the bridge and untied the dock lines, and after tossing them onto the deck, climbed the rungs and engaged the transmissions. The heavy boat backed from its slip at a crawl and, once clear, made a wide turn and headed for the breakwater and, beyond it, the Mediterranean.

By his reckoning, he was seventy nautical miles from the nearest marina in Lebanon, where if he was lucky, he could use the dinghy to enter, and then vanish on foot toward Beirut well before dawn. He set a waypoint for a mile off the marina and eased the throttles up till the boat was slicing through the moderate seas at twenty-five knots. The radar indicated the course north was clear of threats, with any Israeli naval vessels farther out to sea than the kilometer from shore his route would take him.

When the lights of Tel Aviv had died behind him, he went through a mental checklist of errands to perform before he abandoned the boat on an autopilot course to nowhere. He'd ditch the weapons, as well as anything that could connect him to Israel, and would stick to back roads until he reached Beirut. From there he'd book a flight to Germany and then to Moscow, to make a refund of his fee to Sergei. Then he would drop off the grid for several months, the poorer for having failed for the first time in his career.

He cursed in Russian at the thought of returning the money, but quickly got his emotions under control. His contracts called for satisfaction guaranteed, not best efforts, and he would do what he had to do in order to keep the client happy. In this case, that might not be possible, but he didn't want his reputation tarnished, so in the end the price he'd have to pay might turn out to be a bargain.

CHAPTER 45

Tripoli, Libya

The night air was crisp, a wind off the sea blowing any lingering smoke inland as Jet arrived a block from the decrepit hotel that the assassin's boss was using for his base of operations. She left the scooter in the shadows at the side of a market whose display window was protected by a heavy layer of roll-up steel, and crept down the street until she stopped at the sound of big diesel engines rolling toward her.

Jet made for a building on the corner across the street from the hotel and pressed herself into the darkness of a doorway as a big truck ground its gears and lumbered past. Moments later, a second followed it to the hotel, where both vehicles entered through a wide gate, which a gunman closed behind them.

She tried the handle of the door beside her, and it didn't budge. She backed out onto the street and regarded the exterior of the building and spotted a drainpipe to her left, running from the roof. Jet moved to it and jerked on the pipe, but it didn't budge. She reached as high as she could and tested her weight and, when it didn't give, shimmied up the pipe and pulled herself onto the flat roof.

The lip on the far side provided sufficient cover for her to look into the hotel courtyard without being seen. She removed the binoculars from under her robe and studied the hotel. Inside the walled area, men were carrying crates to the larger truck while gunmen waited nearby, rifles in hand. Several imposing figures stood by the side of the building, watching as the laborers struggled with the crates, and the closest one called out something Jet couldn't discern, and everyone stopped while he inspected a container that was about to be loaded onto the truck bed.

A discussion ensued among the supervisors, who crowded around the crate and gestured at the truck, the men, and the courtyard. Eventually a consensus was reached, and the loading resumed under the watchful eye of the bosses. Jet wished the area was better illuminated, but she could make out enough. She recalled Salma's account about Tariq's plan to ship nerve agent to Europe, and a shiver ran up her spine. Was it possible she was witnessing the preparations for exactly that?

When six crates had been loaded onto the biggest of the two trucks, the supervisors held another quick conference and then barked orders to the men, who armed themselves from a pile of rifles near the gate and ran into the hotel. Several minutes dragged by before a group of civilians stumbled from the building and moved to the rear of the first truck, directed there by the gunmen. Still more joined them in a few moments, and soon there was a steady procession of young and old making their way to the trucks while the supervisors watched and the gunmen prodded those who seemed hesitant to climb aboard.

By the time the loading was done, Jet had seen enough. Between the crates and the refugees, she could see something big was afoot, and she resolved to follow them to wherever they were headed, her thirst for revenge set aside when she realized what she was likely witnessing. She ferreted in her robe and withdrew the sat phone and, after getting a lock on a satellite, placed a hushed call to headquarters and advised them of what she'd seen.

Jet finished her report, powered the phone off, and replaced it in the satchel with the binoculars. After checking the hotel one more time, she lowered herself back down the drainpipe and was nearly to the sidewalk when the roar of engines sounded from the street. She dropped the rest of the way and landed hard. Her ankle telegraphed pain up her leg, but she ignored it and retreated into the recesses of the doorway as four pickup trucks motored by on the way to the hotel.

This time the gate didn't open immediately, and the trucks pulled up out front, blocking the street. When it slid open, the gunmen from inside came at a jog and climbed into the backs of the pickups, rifles slung from shoulder straps, some of them smiling in the darkness. Jet waited until everyone was aboard and the gate had been opened wider before darting away to where her scooter was parked, the sharp spikes of discomfort from her ankle reminding her with each step that one small mistake could cost her everything.

Jet swung onto the seat, pausing to roll her ankle a few times before starting the engine and heading toward the hotel, her lights extinguished. She was sixty meters from the gate when the row of pickups began to move, their headlights bright at street level. They rolled away, and the pair of cargo trucks with the refugees trundled from the compound and followed, heavy and low on their springs from full loads, the larger one that contained the crates bringing up the rear.

Jet waited until the sound of their engines started to fade before setting out after them, their brake lights dim at an intersection two blocks away. She was determined to avoid detection, and at that distance she felt secure in the knowledge that she'd be able to hear them if they made a turn that she missed.

As she followed the caravan, she quickly realized it was headed to the harbor. When it reached the waterfront, there were likely to be more of the terrorists waiting for the trucks, which meant that she'd need to improvise a plan or risk being unable to stop them.

When Leo had been wounded, she'd understood that there would be nobody to stop the terrorists, but she hadn't thought through whether she was willing to risk everything in order to try. Now she was in the thick of it, and she couldn't in good conscience ignore what was taking place any more than she was willing to allow Tariq to get away with murdering Salma. Which meant that she'd have to come up with something extraordinary on the fly – preferably something from which she stood a decent chance of walking away.

Jet accelerated and drew within thirty meters of the truck with the crates. The MP7A1 was hanging from its strap beneath her robe, and she had her pistol, so she could shoot out its tires. But then what? She'd have to contend with at least thirty gunmen in the pickups, and there were the women and children in the cargo bays to consider. Even with her skills, the idea of taking on thirty gunmen was lunacy, and she knew it.

An idea leapt to mind, and she eyed the truck's tarp and ribbing. It seemed impossible at first sight, but she'd learned that nothing was if you approached it correctly. She kept pace with the vehicle as she thought the move through, and nodded to herself. It would be tricky, but relatively straightforward if she timed it right.

Jet pulled the robe over her head and tossed it onto the street, freeing herself up for the maneuver to come. If the driver sensed her rolling up on him, he didn't give any indication, and she goosed the throttle until she was parallel with the truck bed and only a few feet off the passenger side. She squinted into the darkness ahead to ensure that she wasn't about to plow into a parked car, and then edged closer until she could reach out with her left hand and touch the wood and steel ribbing of the bed.

Her fingers locked onto one of the planks, and then her right hand abandoned the throttle and grabbed a vertical steel rib that supported the tarp covering the bed. The scooter immediately began to slow, and Jet pulled herself off the bike so her legs were hanging in midair, her feet only a few inches off the street. The bike veered off to the right and smacked into a building, but by then Jet had scissored her legs up, and her feet were on one of the lateral metal beams of the frame.

The bobtail accelerated as it approached a larger thoroughfare, and Jet reached higher with her right hand and felt for a support. Her fingers found one, and she repeated the maneuver with her left, inching up until she was lying flat on the tarp near the cab. Cautiously she crawled forward, using the beams for support.

She glanced over the roof of the cabin at the truck in front, which was ten meters ahead. The streets were inky black from the power being out, so she had little concern over being spotted. She tried to recall whether the driver had climbed into the cab alone or whether one of the gunmen had accompanied him, but couldn't remember, and so prepared to contend with at least two in front, and possibly three.

Jet pulled herself forward until she was on the roof of the cabin, and then swung the MP7A1 forward and flicked the firing selector from safe to full auto. She thought through how she'd make her next move and, when she was confident she'd be able to pull it off, pointed the barrel down at the sheet metal of the cabin like a nail gun ready to secure a tarpaper roof.

Twenty rounds punched through the roof of the cab in a straight line along where the seats would be. She didn't wait for the outcome and instead slung the gun aside, pulled herself to the passenger side, and twisted and dropped onto the hood, facing the windshield.

Which was spackled with blood from the passenger and driver, both of whom had been hit multiple times.

As the truck slowed, Jet kicked in the windshield, which had been punctured by four ricochets and was a collage of starbursts. The glass crumpled inward on the wounded men, and Jet followed it in and kicked the passenger's head as hard as she could, slamming it into the side window. She followed through with a brutal elbow strike to the driver's throat as she twisted to face forward, and then yanked her pistol free and put a bullet in each man's head while gripping the wheel with her free hand to keep the truck from running off the road.

The immediate danger neutralized, she dropped the gun on the seat and reached across the driver's corpse to open his door. It swung wide with a clank, and she gave the dead man a powerful shove. His body seemed to hang in the doorway for an instant, and then it was gone, tumbling along the pavement as she took the bloody seat and stomped on the accelerator.

Jet glanced over at the dead passenger, and her nose wrinkled at the familiar stench of blood and bowels, offset by the wind rushing through the windshield frame. Safety glass littered the seat and floor, the chunks painted with crimson, and she felt for the pistol and slid it into the satchel before downshifting and shutting off the lights so her next maneuver wouldn't be spotted by the other vehicles.

CHAPTER 46

Jet slowed at the next intersection and took the turn as fast as she dared with a truck filled with human cargo and what was likely enough nerve gas to kill half of Tripoli. She ground the gears before finding one she liked, and accelerated again as a pair of headlights swerved into the lane behind her from a side street.

Two of the pickups filled with gunmen had peeled off from the convoy and come after her, which left Jet with few options but to fight it out on the run. Her MP7A1 only had ten rounds left in the magazine and a spare in her satchel, but the driver and his companion had carried AK-47s that were wedged between the seats. She pulled one free and waited for the pursuers to make a move.

It didn't take long. Gunfire exploded from behind her, and panicked screams rose from the cargo bed as she jerked the wheel back and forth to make her trajectory less predictable. The gambit didn't work for long, though, and one of the trucks sped up until it was nearly alongside her. She watched it approach in the side mirror and yanked the steering wheel hard left, driving the side of the big truck into the lighter pickup, which sent it skidding out of control and into a parked van.

The second pickup driver was more patient than the first, and kept just off her rear bumper on the passenger side, where it was hard for her to keep tabs on it. She tried running it off the road twice, but both times the driver avoided the slam that would have ended its run.

Another intersection brought the pickup closer, and she simultaneously stood on the emergency brake and turned the wheel hard right. This time the pickup's driver was an eighth of a second too slow, and the smaller vehicle's hood plowed beneath the side of the cargo bay. The big truck yawed precariously before righting itself and coming to a stop, and Jet leapt from the driver's seat with the AK as the last of burning brakes and rubber smoked from the wheels.

She crouched low and took aim at the pickup's tires. Two short bursts flattened them, ensuring the terrorists wouldn't be going anywhere once she got underway again. Boots landed on the street, and she emptied the rifle at them, cutting the gunmen off below the knees. Agonized screams rewarded her shooting, and she returned to the cab, heaved herself behind the wheel, and floored the gas as answering fire dimpled the passenger door and the side of the cab.

The big truck lumbered forward, dragging the pickup for several meters before it dislodged and ground to a stop, and Jet ignored the thumping of one of the two rear tires on the passenger side that had been flattened by gunfire. She knew she couldn't motor around Tripoli all night, and was painfully aware that the truck made her an easy target, especially given the dearth of traffic on the streets.

Another turn, and the steering was markedly more sluggish and pulled to the right, telling her that the right front tire was now flat as well, curtailing much more driving and leaving her stranded with a vehicle full of nerve gas and refugees. Her eyes scanned the road and narrowed at the sight of a filling station two blocks up on the left.

A pair of attendants watched in shock as the big truck shuddered to a stop by the pumps and Jet stepped from the cab wielding two AKs. They put up their hands, and she shook her head. "I'm not going to hurt or rob you. Get out of here. Now."

The men didn't need to be told twice, and took off at an unsteady run down the deserted street. Jet moved to the back of the cargo bay and pounded on the tailgate. "Party's over. Time to get out. Hurry. This thing's going to blow any second."

She unfastened the latches and dropped the gate, and a hundred pairs of eyes stared at her from the dark interior. Jet stepped back and pointed the rifles inside. "I said *move*. Anyone still in there when I get back gets shot, understand?"

Jet walked away and approached the nearest pump. She set one of the AKs down beside it, removed the nozzle from the slot, and moved to the cab, where she squeezed the pump handle and fired a stream of gasoline into the cabin. She continued until there was a foot of gas on the floorboards, and then soaked the hood and roof before walking with the nozzle toward the rear, sending a golden fountain of fuel skyward and onto the tarp.

The truck was empty when she reached the back, the refugees alarmed enough after the ride and the shooting and the sight of a madwoman with assault rifles to elect prudence over curiosity and scatter down the street. She set the nozzle on the gate and climbed into the bed, and made her way to the nearest crate. The barrel of the AK served as a reasonable lever, and she pried the top off and eyed the green metal canisters inside, their Chinese script unmistakable even in the dim light.

When she returned to the nozzle, she hosed down the interior of the bay until all of the crates were soaked and the wooden floor was slick with fuel, and then ejected the AK magazine and wedged it into the nozzle so it continued pumping fuel, and left it in the bed. A lake of gasoline slowly spread beneath the truck, and Jet walked unhurriedly to the gas station office, where she found a disposable lighter beside a package of cheap local cigarettes.

A wadded-up newspaper and part of a cardboard fuel conditioner display served as reasonable kindling, and within a minute the office was glowing with flames. Jet noted the spreading pool of fuel seeping from the truck and calculated that it would reach the doorway of the office within a couple of minutes, and smiled in satisfaction when she saw a bicycle leaning against the exterior wall.

Jet was a block and a half away when the station exploded in an orange fireball that lit the surroundings like a flare, and cringed at the deafening blast that accompanied it. When she'd made it another four blocks, she paused and extracted the sat phone and placed a call to the director to let him know how his "routine extraction" had gone, and to tell him what she needed if she was going to make it out alive.

He listened until she was finished, agreed to her terms, and she signed off, the sound of approaching vehicles commanding her attention. Jet pedaled hard down an alley, heading in the rough direction of the harbor, where if she was lucky, Tariq was waiting for his shipment but was instead going to receive the ugliest surprise of his life.

CHAPTER 47

Jet pushed the bicycle the final block to the harbor and leaned it against a lamppost in the parking lot where Leo had parked his scooter. The Vespa was still there, and she tried Leo's keys until she found the right one and confirmed that it turned. The engine caught on the first try, and she steered it across the boulevard and stopped in the gloom to peer through her binoculars at the middle section of the waterfront where the commercial boats were moored.

She could hardly miss the activity at one of the warehouses, where the smaller truck with the refugees was parked alongside a dozen pickups and SUVs inside a fenced area. A few lights on the building illuminated the grounds, where at least a hundred gunmen ringed the compound. She scanned the scene and froze when she spotted a man in a white robe gesticulating at the truck, the men he was speaking to clearly deferential by their body language. Jet wasn't close enough to confirm it was Tariq, so she dropped the binoculars back into the satchel and eased the scooter forward to close the distance between herself and the commercial dock.

Jet kept to back streets until she estimated that she was close enough, and parked the scooter in an alley behind a wrecked car, where it wouldn't be easily seen from the street. She made her way to the waterfront and, when she was two blocks from the commercial port, stopped in a doorway and scanned the dock again.

This time she was more than close enough to see the man in the white robe, and she could make out Tariq's features in the high magnification like he was standing across the room. He was engrossed in a conversation with another man, and both were clearly agitated. After a few moments, Tariq snatched a handheld radio from the man's hand and raised it to his lips, his face twisted in fury.

Jet lowered the glasses and headed toward the warehouse, the AK in one hand, the MP7A1 in the other. When she reached the empty boulevard, she took cover behind a half-height wall that ringed a government building and peered over the top. She was too far for a guaranteed kill – she estimated the distance to the gate at about a hundred and fifty meters – so she ran along the wall to a particularly dark area and cut across the boulevard to an overpass almost directly across from the warehouse.

When she was no more than a hundred meters away, which was well within the accurate range of both the small submachine gun and the larger assault rifle, she stopped. She was switching the AK firing selector to full auto when Tariq made an abrupt gesture, pushed past the larger man with the radio, and stalked to one of the SUVs.

Jet watched the others run toward their vehicles, and readied the AK when Tariq's SUV surged forward to the gate. A gunman unchained the lock and rolled the barrier aside, and when the SUV was passing through the gate, she fired a twenty-round burst at the SUV's windshield.

The vehicle coasted to a stop, the glass a spiderweb of white, and six gunmen ran to it, four of them firing indiscriminately in her direction. Ricochets pinged around her and she ducked behind a concrete support column, but not before she saw two of the gunmen drag the driver from the SUV.

The gunfire intensified, and Jet didn't dare peer around the column for fear of a stray taking her head off. She waited for the inevitable lull in the shooting and, when it came, opted for survival over vengeance and sprinted back across the boulevard, keeping the column between her and the gunmen to the extent possible. The marine layer that had cloaked the harbor in gloom worked to her advantage, as did her black outfit, but only for a few critical moments, after which she could hear shouting from behind her as the gunmen gave chase.

The shooting stopped while they crossed the boulevard behind her, and then started again, but the rounds went wide, which told her that the shooters were firing blindly in her general direction rather than at her. She dashed into the alley where she'd stashed the scooter, and rolled it from behind the car, and then started the engine and ducked low over the handlebars as she tore along the narrow passage, the motor revving far too loudly for her liking.

The gunmen reached the alley mouth and began shooting at Jet, but she was moving too fast and had successfully put enough distance between them so that they had no chance of hitting her. She weaved and stayed low and, when she reached the next street, skidded around the corner and juiced the throttle. The scooter responded agilely, and within two minutes she was coasting slowly toward the harbor again, to take stock of the effect of her efforts.

Tariq's SUV was gone, as were half the trucks, but there was still a substantial contingent of gunmen on the wharf. Jet settled in three blocks away to wait for the terrorists to call it a night, and when they did, to follow them to wherever they were holed up. If Tariq had managed to survive her attack, he would no doubt be surrounded by his most loyal entourage, but once she figured out where he'd gone to ground, she could relay the location to headquarters so they could deal with him.

She removed the sat phone from her satchel and powered it on. When the director answered, she gave him a quick report.

"You're positive all of the nerve gas was destroyed?" he asked.

"All that was in the truck. It's possible there's more at the hotel." She described the building and told him the cross streets. "You'll probably want to organize something just in case."

"We're already on it. You have no idea whether Tariq's still alive?"

"Negative. Assume the worst – that he escaped unscathed." She told him that she was lying in wait so she could follow the gunmen, and it earned her another grunt.

"Very well. Let us know when you find his headquarters."

"Will do." She paused. "Did Leo make it out alive?"

"Yes. He's in stable condition, and he'll pull through."

"Great. Which brings me to my final question: how do I get out of here?"

"We'll arrange for an evacuation. Don't worry about it."

"If you say so."

Jet hung up and powered the phone off. She had no idea how the director would evacuate her, but she was confident he would find a way. He might be a conniving old man, but he'd never lied to her, and his word was typically gold. If he said he would do it, he would.

She slid the phone back in the satchel and patted her spare magazine for the MP7A1, glasses glued to her eyes, watching the gunmen from a safe distance and counting the minutes until they realized there was no chance of the nerve gas making it, and decided to pack it in.

CHAPTER 48

Jet had snatched five hours of sleep after her stakeout, but her revving mind wouldn't allow her any more, and she was running scenarios as she paced around Leo's apartment. She'd eventually followed three of the trucks from the waterfront to a mansion in the embassy district, and judging by the number of gunmen sitting in trucks around the grounds, she intuited that it was Tariq's Tripoli headquarters. Lights had been blazing in the windows, even at two in the morning, and she'd stayed in place to surveil the guard schedule until there was a change at dawn.

Most of the men had seemed undisciplined and overly apprehensive, but a few had appeared more serious and methodical and probably had military experience, judging by how they carried themselves and their weapons. Jet guessed that they were operating on six-hour shifts, and there were easily a hundred men on the grounds during the time she spent watching it.

Jet was listening to a small transistor radio as she showered when the music was interrupted by the deep voice of an announcer.

"We have a special broadcast from an honored guest here in Tripoli. Tariq Qaddafi called in, and the station feels it is in the best interests of our listeners to put him on the air. Mr. Qaddafi? You're live."

"Thank you." A pause. "I've traveled a great distance to return to my homeland. For some time I've felt a calling to change its direction after seeing how foreign meddling nearly destroyed it. So I am here, in Tripoli, and have agreed to become the new head of state now that the puppet government imposed by the West has turned tail and fled. As my first act, I will impose Sharia law, so that we may return to being a moral nation rather than the whore of foreigners who care little for our well-being."

Tariq spoke for ten minutes without interruption, and by the time he finished, Jet was seething with rage. He'd not only managed to survive, but seemed certain that his power grab would be celebrated by most of his countrymen. He'd stated that he was now the de facto ruler of Libya and would be negotiating on its behalf in all matters – a convicted felon and known terrorist of the lowest order.

The image of Salma being shot sprang to Jet's mind, and her teeth ground at the memory.

She toweled herself dry and thought through her possible actions. First, she'd call the director and give him the bad news. That call would determine how she proceeded.

Jet pulled on her pants and shirt, which were stiff from being hand-washed and dried by the open window, and moved to the table where the satchel with the sat phone rested beside the MP7A1, her expression as grim as it was determined.

Tariq blinked away sleep and sat up. The room was pitch black, and he couldn't make out his hand in front of him. Something had awakened him, but he wasn't sure what. Perhaps gunfire or an explosion from somewhere in the city? There was still sporadic shooting as his men took over districts, sometimes having to fight criminal gangs or pockets of resistance block by block. He figured it would be a week before the entire city was contained, and he wasn't worried – Akmal's men had drummed up sufficient support for him as the new ruler of Libya that a return to normalcy was all but assured once the last of the resisting factions threw in the towel.

His radio address had gone well, and it had been replayed every hour on all local stations throughout the afternoon, lending legitimacy to his claim of having assumed command of the country. He'd studied successful coups while imprisoned, and they'd all had the same thing in common: assumption of control by a strong leader with a clear vision and a promise to bring order to the land. Tariq's vision was as clear as they came, and he was a powerful speaker, he knew, and burned with the passion of the righteous, which was evident to anyone who listened.

A rustle from nearby drew his attention, and he was reaching for the pistol on the nightstand by his head when a female voice spoke from only inches away, and the cold, sharp bite of steel against his throat stopped him.

"You almost pulled it off," Jet said. "But almost doesn't count, does it?"

She drove the razor point of the survival knife up through the base of Tariq's chin, into his mouth, and finally into his brain with the heel of her hand. He jerked like a beached fish and stiffened as the point gouged through his cerebrum, and then Jet was retracing her steps on catlike feet to the window through which she'd entered, as Tariq expired on the bed.

The curtain rustled as she slipped through it, and she rappelled down to the ground floor and darted for the wall over which she'd come, the guards so focused on threats from an armed force that they'd left the grounds vulnerable to a lone assassin, being positioned to fend off a large attack rather than stop a single threat. A mistake that she'd exploited, and which had just altered the country's history.

The director had okayed her suggestion that she perform the sanction rather than targeting the building with a cruise missile, and she'd accepted the job willingly, eager to have Salma's murderer subjected to the same brutal justice he'd employed on her.

Jet reached the wall and checked the surroundings. The nearest gunmen were in the back of a gray pickup fifteen meters away, talking in low voices, their rifles pointed into the air, their attention on the approaches rather than on the compound itself. Jet withdrew a grenade that had been in Leo's safe, pulled the pin, and tossed it at the truck.

When it exploded a few meters from the vehicle, the blast was deafening. Screams of alarm shattered the night, and then she was over the wall and running across the street, a figure in head-to-toe black who moved like smoke through the darkness and had vanished before the guards knew what had hit them.

CHAPTER 49

Tel Aviv, Israel

The driver who'd met Jet at the airport pulled away, leaving Jet standing in front of a simple row house in a downscale community four kilometers outside town. Jet walked to the front and slid the key the driver had given her into the lock. The bolt opened, and she stepped inside to find a spartan two-bedroom home with cheap finishes and cheaper furniture.

"Matt? Hannah?" she called, setting the keys on a long, narrow table in the foyer.

"Mama!" Hannah's voice cried from down the hall, and tiny footsteps drummed their approach and the little girl appeared from around a corner. She threw her arms around Jet's legs and hugged her tight, and then looked up at Jet's face with a sunny smile.

"Hello, angel! You look happy," Jet said, smoothing her hair.

"Matt and I were playing catch in the backyard."

"You were, were you? That sounds like fun."

Matt entered the hall and walked over to Jet, who embraced him and gave him a long kiss before disengaging. He looked her up and down with concern and then took her hand and led her into a small living area with a worn couch and a pair of dilapidated easy chairs.

"Welcome home," Matt whispered in her ear as they sat on the couch. Hannah ran to the sliding glass door and pointed at a small strip of artificial grass.

"Look, Mama! It's way better than the other house."

Jet smiled in agreement. "It is indeed."

Hannah slid the door open and skipped outside. Matt's expression was etched with concern. "You know what happened, obviously."

"Yes. They've identified the man. Or they think they have. A freelance hit man. Russian."

Matt looked away. "Who do you think he's working for?"

Jet shrugged. "The list's too long to be useful. The main thing is that the director said he's confident he can keep us safe."

"Confident?" Matt repeated, skepticism clear in his tone. "This bastard was sitting outside Hannah's school. How did they find her? Or you and me, for that matter?"

Jet frowned. "There might be a leak in the organization."

"In which case we're never going to be safe."

"Israel is a small country. As long as we stay out of sight, we should be fine. The borders are tightly controlled – more so than anywhere else in the world."

"Which is all good. But we still had a Russian hit man at Hannah's school. So whoever hired him knows about her, and me. The question is how."

"And who. But one issue at a time. I'll talk to the director tomorrow about how exactly he intends to keep us safe." She leaned into Matt and kissed him again. "The mission was a disaster."

"David's sister?"

"Didn't make it."

Matt shook his head. "Then what was the point?"

Jet watched Hannah playing in the yard, hopscotching to an imaginary pattern, her smile beaming in the afternoon sun. She looked back at Matt and sighed heavily.

"The point was to try." She told him what had happened, and how the mission had finished up.

Matt's eyebrows rose. "So they hit the hotel with a cruise missile?"

"That's right. And the Americans are forming a new coalition government."

"Which will probably be about as effective as the ones in Iraq and Afghanistan. Or the last one in Libya."

"Not my problem. I did what I had to do." She took Matt's hand and snuggled against him. "Just like we'll do whatever we have to in order to stay together and keep Hannah safe."

He shifted on the sofa. "Yes, we will."

She yawned. "I haven't gotten that much sleep this week. You feel like taking a nap?"

Matt offered a crooked grin. "What about Hannah?"

"She's a good napper too. Let's see if she's interested." Jet made to rise and then paused. "Does our bedroom have a lock on it?"

He nodded. "First thing I checked."

"Then let's tell her Mama's tired."

"Good idea."

It was her turn to smile. "I'm full of them lately."

About the Author

Featured in *The Wall Street Journal*, *The Times*, and *The Chicago Tribune*, Russell Blake is *The NY Times* and *USA Today* bestselling author of over fifty novels.

Blake is co-author of *The Eye of Heaven* and *The Solomon Curse*, with legendary author Clive Cussler. Blake's novel *King of Swords* has been translated into German, *The Voynich Cypher* into Bulgarian, and his JET novels into Spanish, German, and Czech.

Blake writes under the moniker R.E. Blake in the NA/YA/Contemporary Romance genres. Novels include *Less Than Nothing*, *More Than Anything*, and *Best Of Everything*.

Having resided in Mexico for a dozen years, Blake enjoys his dogs, fishing, boating, tequila and writing, while battling world domination by clowns. His thoughts, such as they are, can be found at his blog:

RussellBlake.com

Visit RussellBlake.com for updates

or subscribe to: RussellBlake.com/contact/mailing-list

Books by Russell Blake

Co-authored with Clive Cussler
THE EYE OF HEAVEN
THE SOLOMON CURSE

Thrillers
FATAL EXCHANGE
FATAL DECEPTION
THE GERONIMO BREACH
ZERO SUM
THE DELPHI CHRONICLE TRILOGY
THE VOYNICH CYPHER
SILVER JUSTICE
UPON A PALE HORSE
DEADLY CALM
RAMSEY'S GOLD
EMERALD BUDDHA
THE GODDESS LEGACY
A GIRL APART
A GIRL BETRAYED
QUANTUM SYNAPSE

The Assassin Series
KING OF SWORDS
NIGHT OF THE ASSASSIN
RETURN OF THE ASSASSIN
REVENGE OF THE ASSASSIN
BLOOD OF THE ASSASSIN
REQUIEM FOR THE ASSASSIN
RAGE OF THE ASSASSIN

The Day After Never Series
THE DAY AFTER NEVER – BLOOD HONOR
THE DAY AFTER NEVER – PURGATORY ROAD
THE DAY AFTER NEVER – COVENANT
THE DAY AFTER NEVER – RETRIBUTION
THE DAY AFTER NEVER – INSURRECTION
THE DAY AFTER NEVER – PERDITION
THE DAY AFTER NEVER – HAVOC
THE DAY AFTER NEVER – LEGION
THE DAY AFTER NEVER – NEMESIS

Made in the USA
San Bernardino, CA
09 May 2020